Rachel struggled over a mound of boulders, several minutes into her hike, and spotted the movie group. They all stood near the edge of the precipice which jutted out sixty feet above the old landing strip. Rachel stopped to catch her breath.

She viewed the scene in front of her. It played out in a kind of time warp, almost in a series of slides instead of real time, as Rachel watched Richard Markman move toward the ledge. He appeared to have everyone's complete attention as he waved his arm and pointed to the outcropping. He flung his arm back in a motion as if he were throwing something behind him. He repeated the action a few times and then Dixie moved toward him.

Mesmerized by the sight of the group perched near the edge of the cliff, all Rachel could think of was Ekberg's warning about "high places." She stood, paralyzed with horror and unbelief as she saw Dixie approach the ledge and step on the outcropping.

"Get back! Get back!" Rachel screamed and waved her arms frantically.

A man with a halo of black curls burst from the group and grabbed Dixie's arm. He yanked her forward, causing her to tumble on top of him. Then Rachel heard the unmistakable sound of the crack and felt the shudder of the earth even from where she stood. *This can't be real,* Rachel thought, as she watched the rock ledge brake free and hurl itself through space.

Just when JT Carpenter and Buddy McCain finally begin to show a profit from the old hotel on Blood Mountain, they run into trouble. Sales Director, Rachel Ryan, has over-booked the hotel with two groups that mix like gasoline and matches. Richard Markman arrives to film part of his new movie on Blood Mountain, but his secret plan is to kill his movie star wife, Dixie. Then the Church of Inner Light checks in along with their leader and self-styled prophet, Lars Ekberg, whose spirit guide warns Dixie of her possible, but eminent, demise, igniting the already explosive relationship between Richard and Dixie.

When she befriends the frightened Dixie, who is accused of murder, Rachel gets drawn into the twisted world of Hollywood scandals. But as she investigates to help her friend, Rachel puts her own life in jeopardy by uncovering a series of poisonous secrets and unveiling the true motives of the hotel's guests.

KUDOS for *Blood Mountain Prophecy*

In *Blood Mountain Prophecy*, the sequel to *Blood Mountain*, Rachel Ryan is at it again. This time she is convinced that her new friend, movie star Dixie Markman, is going to be murdered by her husband. Of course, Rachel has good reason to be concerned. Not only does she witness a series of near accidents in which Dixie escapes death by the skin of her teeth, but there are rumors that Dixie's husband is having an affair and wants to be rid of her. To top it off, a medium who heads the Church of Inner Light warns that Dixie will die. He even seems to predict the near accidents that she seems suddenly prone to. Like its predecessor, *Blood Mountain Prophecy*'s characters are well developed and three dimensional, and its plot will keep you turning pages from beginning to end. – *Taylor Jones, Reviewer*.

Blood Mountain Prophecy is another feather in Joanne Taylor Moore's cap. As well written and entertaining as Moore's first book, the sequel reunites us with our old friends from *Blood Mountain* and introduces us to some delightful new characters like the movie stars, Richard and Dixie Markman, and the head of the Church of Inner Light, prophet and medium, Lars Ekberg. As before, Moore's characters are very believable, human, flawed, and motivated by mundane, everyday things, like greed, love, sex, and the need for constant attention. Just like real people...The plot was strong, and even though it brings in a touch of the paranormal, it was totally believable. Like the first book, *Blood Mountain Prophecy* is one you will want to keep on your shelf and read again and again. – *Regan Murphy, Reviewer*.

ACKNOWLEDGEMENTS

Blood Mountain Prophecy would never have been published without the help of my friends and family, so I want to thank the usual suspects in my library writers' group: Debbie Lee, Robin Christiansen, Pinkie Paranya, and, in particular, John Coultas, who made me rescue PROPHECY from the trash bin. I also want to thank my mentor, Don G. Porter, and Valarie Donnelly, Gail Thompson, and Joan Stanhope for their work and unwavering support.

A special thank you goes out to all the amazing talent at Black Opal Books with an extra nod to gifted editor Lauri Wellington, and to Jack Jackson, who created the beautiful cover.

I greatly appreciate our grandson, Evan Boardman, who assisted me with technical advice, and most of all my husband and biggest supporter, Larry Moore, who labored with me from beginning to end.

BLOOD MOUNTAIN PROPHECY

Joanne Taylor Moore

A BLACK OPAL BOOKS PUBLICATION

GENRE: MYSTERY/SUSPENSE/ROMANTIC ELEMENTS

BLOOD MOUNTAIN PROPHECY
Copyright © 2013 by Joanne Taylor Moore
Cover Design by Jackson Cover Designs
All cover art copyright © 2013
All Rights Reserved
Print ISBN: 978-1-626940-77-2

First Publication: NOVEMBER 2013

Published by Black Opal Books **http://www.blackopalbooks.com**

DEDICATION

This book is dedicated with much love to our children:
John Taylor, Kent Taylor, Lynn Boardman,
and Kevin Moore.

Thank you so much for your great love and support.

Prologue

It was a stinking-hot day in August when Richard Markman figured out how he could kill his wife and get away with it.

He stood near the top of Blood Mountain, drenched with sweat, and stared at the rocky ledge. He envisioned his wife tumbling over it, wide-eyed and shrieking, her arms and legs flailing, her skirt flying up as she plunged through the air.

A shudder of excitement flowed through him as the vision replayed itself like a scene from one of his movies. His eyes glowed in anticipation. He saw his life, his perfectly wonderful future, without his wife.

Montana de la Sangre—or Blood Mountain, as the gringos called it—was located in the middle of a mountain range that bordered the north end of Mesquite, Arizona. It was named for the shade of red it became when the setting sun painted the rocks on its surface, although some said it was named for the blood that had been spilled on it over the centuries.

Regardless of the name's origin, the massive peak had long been an object of curiosity, even worship. It was a focal point that helped identify the non-descript farming town of Mesquite, which lay next to the Mexican border. Good thing, too. Other than the huge monolith and a river snaking through the valley, Mesquite had little else to distinguish it from the long stretch of desert it inhabited.

Richard Markman had toyed with the idea of killing his wife for quite a while. He had fantasized about Dixie's death and the extravagant funeral he would arrange for her. He envisioned all the important people in Hollywood attending and extending their sympathy to him, the poor, grieving widower.

To their fans, the Markman's marriage looked ideal, but the reality was quite different.

In their last few years together, Dixie had become a tiresome burden in so many ways, like a bag of rocks Richard constantly carried around on his back. He was always propping her up, acquiescing to her stupid, incessant demands, and he was continually being pushed into the background.

Regrettably, divorce was not an option. It came down to a matter of simple finance: most of the wealth he now enjoyed belonged to his wife. Pity. Richard so desperately craved the power, the prestige, and the physical pleasures money bought. He couldn't bear to lose any of it. Not one blasted cent.

He also had a problem with the tabloids. The paparazzi would swarm like roaches at the first sniff of a divorce between a Hollywood producer-director and his movie star wife. They'd park in front of his home, take unflattering pictures, and twist him into a caricature uglier than the devil himself. Even worse, people would stop going to his movies.

That was the real problem. Everyone loved Dixie Markman. She was America's sweetheart. She was charming and cute with her red pixie hair and big chocolate eyes—and she was never rude to fans or the press.

Richard was another story, though. He hated the press, and the press hated him. Even worse, Markman's latest flick was a dud. He couldn't risk the public turning against him and his next film by divorcing one of America's most-loved stars.

He picked up a rock, tossed it over the edge, and watched it plunge down to a wide ledge below. He pondered his decision. Blood Mountain seemed like the perfect solution. Dixie's death would appear accidental, and it would take place in front of credible witnesses. Most importantly, her "accident" would take place away from the eyes of LA County detectives who were far too experienced in alimony murders for his comfort.

"Mr. Markman? Mr. Markman?" Stanley Belinski called, rousing Richard out of his trance-like state.

"What did you say?" Richard asked, not bothering to turn around. He continued to gaze over the edge of the precipice, oblivious to the sun boring down on his head. He estimated the drop to the ledge below. It was at least sixty feet. No one could survive a plunge like that.

"I said we really should get going," the real estate agent prodded and wiped the sweat off his face with a soggy handkerchief. The extra seventy pounds he carried added to the problem of his over-active sweat glands. So did the pressure of trying to make the deal. "It was a hundred and two when we left and I'm sure it's hotter now." Belinski gazed up at the vultures circling above them. He mopped the sweat pooling around his neck and took a couple steps toward Markman. But that was as close to the edge as he dared to go.

"Yes, I suppose we should leave." Richard was unmindful of the fat man's pain. "I think I've seen enough, but I have one more question." He still faced the north overlook and his mind raced through the details of his plan. "What about the security situation? Do they have municipal police here?"

Belinski had to stop and think. He managed to reply with some truth, yet put the best spin on it. "Well, actually, Mr. Markman, we have so little crime here, so few problems, all we've ever needed is the local Deputy Sheriff." He pictured old Deputy Tucker with his bow-legged walk, watermelon belly, and walrus mustache. "But if you have any concerns at all, we can arrange to hire extra security."

"Oh, no, that won't be necessary," Richard said, brushing a damp curl away from his forehead. His hair was dyed black, naturally wavy, and he was so engrossed in his own thoughts he didn't notice the moist ringlets that were forming all over his head. He suppressed a smile, happy to hear only one officer would be around to investigate any accidents, and suspected any deputy assigned to the boondocks would be old and dull. "We have our own security guards. I was just wondering, that's all."

He turned away from the ledge, finally looking at the realtor, giving the portly man his attention. Belinski's face was flushed with heat and his shirt stuck to his chest with sweat.

"I think we're done here," Richard said. "I'm happy with what I see. This is the perfect location for my next film." He stepped through the rocks, giving a wide berth to a cholla cactus with medusa-like arms. When he reached Belinski, he was smiling. "If you're sure the old hotel will be renovated by March, we're in business. That will give you seven months."

Belinski tried to contain his elation. "I don't see any problems with that. The property is listed on the county's tax sale for next week. My buyer is ready to purchase, and my brother is slated to be the contractor on the re-modeling of the hotel. As you saw, the basic structure is sound, so it won't take much to whip it into shape."

"Good. Then we have a deal," Richard said, turning his head for one last gaze at the overlook. "I'll contact the hotel later with a list of my requirements. We should be ready to film here by the first of March."

He followed the heat-flushed, sweat-soaked agent back down the mountain, savoring the pleasure of his find. But at that time, there was no way Richard could foresee that the realtor's plans were doomed. There was no way he could know that just three days before the tax sale, ownership of Blood Mountain would pass into entirely different hands.

As it was, while he trekked down Blood Mountain in the white-hot heat, plotting the death of his wife, certain strange, irreversible events had already been put into motion. Richard Markman had no idea that a prophecy from the dead would forever alter the path of his destiny.

Chapter 1

Seven-and-a-half months later:

Rachel Ryan sat in her office and stared at the March calendar with pale green eyes, her blonde hair streaming over her shoulders like corn silk. It had just dawned on her it had been six months to the day, since she started working at the Mesquite Mountain Inn. Her probation period was over.

She glanced at the lobby through the open french doors. Hotel guests were checking in, and hotel staff were busily crisscrossing the lobby, heading to their assignments. Her boss, JT Carpenter, was nowhere to be seen. Good news. Since JT hadn't shown up to fire her, she figured she was still employed as the hotel's Director of Sales.

Rachel was also the hotel's concierge, tour guide, catering manager, and "whatever-else- comes-up" person, something she pondered as she mentally checked off a list of her past contributions. Perhaps it was time to ask for a raise. Heaven knows, she needed one. She hadn't bought a new outfit the entire six months of her employ.

She mulled over the possible ways that she could present her request. Granted, JT already had enough ammunition from her history with him to fire her, so she needed to use utmost caution. She didn't want her approach to color his decision, especially since she didn't have another job lined up.

She tapped her foot nervously and considered the way JT's personality irritated her—like tiny cactus prickers that stuck to her skin—and wondered if a more indirect route to a raise would be smarter.

Rachel was sure that JT wouldn't have hired her to begin with, except for the fact that her sister, Heather, was JT's wife. *Of course! Heather—the obvious solution.* Rachel blew out a breath of air and her brain began spinning out a plan. It might be sneaky, and definitely manipulative, but her sister was the perfect conduit to her objective.

That decided, she turned away from the calendar. Assuming she was still gainfully employed, Rachel went back to work and considered the logistical problem she was currently facing: two big groups were due to check in at the same time and they didn't have enough rooms to put them in.

That's when the phone rang.

"Rachel Ryan speaking," she announced with a smile in her voice, something she learned early on in hotel school. "How may I help you?"

The voice on the other end of the line was Heather, warning her that JT was heading her way. *Uh-oh.* A private visit with His Highness rarely meant good news for her. *Maybe I'm going to get fired after all.*

She turned her eyes to the files that lay on her desk, flipped through her papers in a quick attempt at organizing the mess, and JT walked in. Big boned and six-feet-six, he dominated the room. He lowered his bulk down in the chair in front of Rachel's desk, folded his arms across his chest, and squirmed. The chair he was sitting in was one of those stiff-backed, elegant, skinny-legged, upholstered-in-silk antiques that Heather had recently purchased.

"Rachel, I want to talk to you about your little problem."

That was typical JT. Never a preamble. Always straight to the bottom line.

"What problem?" Rachel looked up at him with her most innocent expression.

"Don't bother giving me that dumb-blonde act." His deep brown eyes never left her face and they seemed to bore right through her. "You know perfectly well I mean the overbooking problem you created." JT never bought the innocent-look ploy, but it didn't stop Rachel from an occasional try.

"Oh, *that* problem," she acknowledged with a nod of her head. "You see what happened is that last October I booked the Circle of Inner Light Church group, for the two weeks starting with the March Equinox, on the twenty-first. Then, if you'll remember, just before Thanksgiving, I signed Richard Markman—"

"Yeah, yeah, skip it," JT said, waving his hand. "Just tell me why you overbooked."

Rachel shot him an annoying look, disappointed she couldn't divulge the full drama of the event, especially the part about how she was *not* really responsible.

"Richard Markman had to reschedule because one of his major stars had to go to rehab for a couple weeks. I figured you didn't want me to tell Markman and all his money to take a hike, so I rescheduled him, which caused the current overbooking. So, since we're out of rooms, and you don't like to hear about a problem without a solution, I suggest management give up their suites and sleep in trailers on the old tennis courts."

She pulled out a paper from her file, held it up between her thumb and forefinger, and let it dangle in the air. "Here's the info on the trailers, if you want it. I've arranged to have delivery of two units, after a call from you, and they'll have us set up within three hours."

JT shifted in his chair, still trying to get comfortable, and focused his eyes on the paper. "Okay," he finally said, rubbing his hand nervously over his hairline. "Since there's not another decent hotel for sixty miles, I don't think we have much choice." He squirmed again in the chair. "And having a couple trailers available on stand-by is a good idea, maybe even on a permanent basis. We've been full several times already this winter." He snatched the paper from her hand. "I'll get it handled."

Rachel watched JT walk away with a stunned look on her face. *What just happened? A miracle.* She didn't get fired. She didn't even get scolded. Something had to be up. JT popped back into the office, and Rachel jumped.

"Do me a favor, will you?" he asked. "Get rid of that stupid chair." He walked out, disappeared behind the front desk, and turned the corner to his office.

Rachel was dazed and rested her chin on her hand. It was only a quirk of fate that she had booked the Hollywood group to begin with. When Richard Markman first came to look at the hotel, JT had never heard of the Mesquite Mountain Inn, and Buddy McCain, his partner, had only childhood memories of visits there. It was only after a series of interesting—and some deadly—events that they all had come to be where they were.

Rachel preferred to think of it as destiny.

She was still working at her desk an hour later when Becky Beeman poked her mousey brown head through the doorway. Becky was the new housekeeping manager Heather gratefully acquired from a Los Angeles hotel. Although Becky was intelligent and experienced, her most endearing trait was that she had been willing to pack up and move to Mesquite.

"I got your memo about the two groups coming in," Becky said. Her bronzed face was lined with the effect of a lifetime of California sun, but she still maintained classic features and good bones.

"Yes, isn't it exciting?" Rachel said, waving her in. "Tara Linley and Dixie Markman will be here, staying at our very own hotel. Imagine that."

"I know, our first Hollywood celebrities." Becky's face wrinkled with a look of concern. She took small, tentative steps into the office. "Do you think the paparazzi will come?"

"Good luck if they do. They'll have to sleep in their cars."

Becky winced. "Yeah, I noticed we're going to be a little overbooked."

"Not to worry, Miss Beeman. Things will work out. Management may have to move out of the suites and into trailers, but, somehow, we'll make room."

Vertical creases formed above Becky's nose and her glasses slipped down. "Those trailers aren't so bad, you know. I'm very comfortable in mine and it's real quiet back there." She pushed her old tortoise-shell frames up with a finger. "I'm more worried about the demands of the divas."

Rachel nodded in agreement. "I can understand that. You used to work in Hollywood, didn't you?"

"Yes, but thankfully, that was in another lifetime." Becky finally smiled, turned, and was out the door.

ϾↃϾↃ

Lars Ekberg stood next to the window and gazed down at the city of London. Early morning light was beginning to filter in through the tall buildings—a dim light that radiated from a sun hidden behind a ceiling of low-hanging clouds. City lights were beginning to blink off one at a time, but the thick wall of glass protected Ekberg from the sounds of life that began to filter into the city.

Anthony Pander appeared at his side and looked at him warily. "You've been up a while. You didn't sleep well."

Ekberg turned toward his partner, studied his tousled hair and morning beard. "No. Too many things on my mind. I couldn't turn it off."

"What is it this time?" Pander held his breath. "It can't be the money. We took in over four thousand for the seminar. Nearly five hundred people from our British congregations showed up."

"No. No, it's not that." Ekberg turned his face back to the window.

"The readings? I know it's exhausting..." Pander made an effort to sound sympathetic.

"No. I don't mind them, really. We helped a lot of people. We also made a lot of money off them."

"Then *what*?" Pander's voice sharpened.

"It's Arizona. I just have a lot of anxiety about going there."

"Arizona?" Pander appeared puzzled and he scratched at the stubble on his chin. "But it was your idea."

"No." Ekberg shook his head. "No it wasn't. It was White Eagle's idea. He's the one that said we needed to go. I'm the one with the bad feeling about it."

"A bad feeling," Pander repeated. "Is it because of that stupid dream?"

"Hey. The dream was not stupid." Ekberg kept his voice low and his eyes turned to the window. "It was prophetic. It just happened to be *nebulous*."

"A nebulous, prophetic dream about some woman in Arizona is giving you anxiety?" Pander tried to keep his voice level, tried to keep the skepticism out of it. "Lars, I think you're just nervous about the trip. Once we get there, you'll be okay. You'll see."

Ekberg turned and glared at his partner. "Don't treat me like a child, Anthony. I know what I dreamed. Some-one wants to kill this woman."

Pander took a step back. "Okay, okay, I'm sorry. I didn't mean to sound condescending. It's just that I don't understand why something like that would put you into such a tailspin. A dream shouldn't affect you or our trip. Look at this way: White Eagle wouldn't have come up with the plan to go to Arizona if there was going to be problem. He would protect us. Nothing bad is going to happen."

Ekberg turned back to the window with a look of disbelief. "That's the trouble with you Americans. Cock-eyed optimists even in the face of disaster."

Pander started to make a sharp retort, but bit his lip when he noticed his watch. "We'll have a *real* disaster if I don't get in the shower now. We leave for Heathrow in a half-hour. We can talk about this later."

"Fine with me. I'm ready to go whenever you are." Ekberg's eyes never drifted from the view through the window. The fog still hung in the air like a gauze curtain and the sun never broke through.

e∕ɔe∕ɔ

When Rachel arrived at her desk the next morning, she considered praying for a miracle. *Okay, maybe not a real miracle,* she mused, sending her thoughts upward, *but how about a big dose of good luck?* She had spent the prior week waiting and hoping for a cancellation that would keep her from having to move. The thought of packing up those fourteen boxes sitting in her suite was not at all appealing. Even with help, it would be a major job. Even worse, it would be a job that would have to be done that very night—down to her last tube of lipstick—

so that housekeeping could move her out and clean her room first thing in the morning, at the ungodly hour of six o'clock.

Well, at least she was over her compulsion to buy shoes and wouldn't be adding to the stacks in her closet. But even if she wasn't over it, with her pittance of a salary, it would take her a year to save up for a single pair of designer footwear. In that regard, her job at the Mesquite Mountain Inn had certain built-in benefits.

She stood up behind her desk and stretched her head from side to side, trying to get rid of the pain at the base of her skull. She had more immediate problems to deal with now.

At that moment, the intercom buzzed. Rachel grabbed for it, caught the message, and snapped her eyes open. She punched the air. It finally happened. It was the cancellation she'd been waiting for.

She quickly called JT and told him they would need only one of the rental trailers. The french doors to her office were open, so she stifled the urge to do a little dance. She sat down, scrunched her eyes closed, pumped her fists in victory, and felt an ocean of relief wash over her.

"Rachel?"

Rachel yelped, nearly jumping out of her chair. She immediately recognized the pencil-thin man who stepped into her office: Lars Ekberg.

Rachel felt the skin on her face turn hot, and she wanted to melt right through the floor. "Oh, Mr. Ekberg, I'm so sorry. I was decompressing."

"I can understand that, believe me," Ekberg said, holding up a pale hand, his voice tender and sympathetic.

"I go through the very same thing every time I have to speak before a large group."

"Well, that's a relief." Rachel came around the side of her desk. "I'd hate to have you think I was an idiot right off the bat." She flashed him her most winning smile. "I was hoping for a least a day or two of grace."

Ekberg returned her smile. "You're forgetting I'm already well acquainted with your skills in salesmanship," he said, coming toward her, "and so far, you've scored a ten out of ten with the accommodations. We checked in late last night and Anthony and I were very pleased with our suites.

"Oh, I'm so glad." Rachel wanted to collapse in her chair with relief.

Ekberg's white-blonde hair was tied back in a ponytail and, when he came closer, his head caught the overhead lighting which streaked his hair with silver. "I especially appreciate the stocked refrigerator and fruit bowl you sent to the room. The restaurants were closed, but being a vegetarian, I found the fruit and crackers to be just perfect."

"Thank you," Rachel said, grateful she had done her homework. She wanted to punch the air again, but instead, picked up a hardcover book with a black and white photograph of Ekberg on the back cover and held it up. It was a flattering composition, but Ekberg was taller in person than he appeared in the photo and his complexion was even paler than Rachel's.

"Oh, you bought my book." He laughed, recognizing the tome. "I wondered who purchased the other copy."

"Don't be so modest, Lars. The sign in the bookstore said *Life of Inner Light* was number twenty-two on the best-seller list. I'm really thrilled for you." Rachel shyly handed the book to him. "Would you sign it for me, please?"

"I'd be delighted." He took the book and pulled a gold pen from his jacket pocket and wrote "To Rachel Ryan," with a long, thin hand. He cocked his head and looked at her. "You know, your name fooled me. You have Scandinavian heritage, probably Swedish. I pictured you as a pale blonde every time we spoke on the phone, but I couldn't square it with the Irish name."

"Well, you guessed right. It's my Swedish half that shows. My sister, Heather, got the Irish part."

"So—" Ekberg nodded. "—just like my sister, Cee-Cee, and me. She got the dark hair, I got the light." He went back to the book and scribbled a message.

"I'm quite impressed with your book," Rachel said, feeling a little awkward. "It's opened my mind to a whole set of new ideas. I've never read anything like it. Ever."

Ekberg handed back the book. "Thank you. I hope you find something meaningful in it."

"Oh, I already have. Your story is amazing." Rachel stopped short of gushing, opened the cover, and read aloud the note he'd inscribed: "Best regards to a special lady, at a special time and a special place, Lars Ekberg."

She looked up. "A special time and a special place?"

"Very special," he replied, gray eyes glittering. "If you'd like to learn why, you're welcome to attend my lectures, which you so graciously set up for me. Bring your sister if you'd like."

"Why, I'd love that." She gave him a grateful smile and picked up the folder with the title "Church of Inner Light" on the tab. "I have everything already set up for the seminar. Would you like me to walk you through the rooms now, and afterward, we could have lunch and make any changes or additions?"

"Yes, that would be perfect." Ekberg stood erect and turned, clicked his heels, and theatrically extended his arm toward the door. "Shall we?"

When Rachel walked past him her skin prickled, like static electricity. Something felt weird about him. Something strange, almost mystical emanated from him. *But of course*, Rachel thought. *That's exactly what Lars presents himself to be—a mystic and a medium.*

Chapter 2

After lunch, Rachel rushed back to her office, slipped out of her pointy Ferragamo shoes, checked her messages, and returned two calls. She was double-checking her current files when Heather bounced in, redefining the word "perky."

"Hey sis, anything new?" Heather asked, her blue eyes twinkling.

"My six months are up," Rachel said, waving her in.

Heather stopped dead and gaped at her sister. "You're not thinking of leaving, are you?"

"Relax. His majesty has come and gone and never fired me."

Heather plopped down into the old, overstuffed chair in front of Rachel's desk. Her hair was cut in medium-length layers, the color of iced tea, and it bounced when she sat. "Gee, it's hard to believe you've been here six months. It seems like you just arrived."

"Not for me. Too much has happened. You know— the murders, the fires, everything—it seems like two years."

"You have a point there." Heather grimaced. "Six months ago, I barely knew this town existed. Nor did anyone else for that matter."

"Ah, just for the sake of accuracy, I could name two men that did."

Heather blinked and thought a moment. "Oh. You mean Richard Markman and Stanley Belinski." She cocked her head quizzically. "I'm curious. Did Markman ever ask about him? I mean why Belinski wasn't around or running the hotel or anything?"

"As a matter of fact, he did. Last fall, when he came to sign the contract. I tried to sidestep the issue, but Markman really wanted to know what happened to the man. Normally I would have made something up, but since he was in the fantasy business to begin with, I decided to tell him the whole story, blow by blow. He was actually quite intrigued. Thought it would make for a good movie plot."

"Oh, I think it would, too." Heather gazed off dreamily, sighed, and finally looked back at her sister. "But back to your job, Rachel. I'll bet JT doesn't even realize what day it is. I mean, that your six months are up. You know how crazy things have been with the overbooking and all."

"True, but at least one problem has been resolved. Another cancellation was called in, so I won't have to move all my stuff. Chef Henri is the only one who gets trailer duty."

"Good deal." Heather waved a hand. "Chef doesn't care. I've already talked to him. He's actually looking forward to having his own stove and a real refrigerator for a few days. He said he doesn't need that much space," she said, and then teased, "Unlike some people I know with tons of designer clothes and shoes."

"What?" Rachel protested indignantly, knowing in her heart every word was true.

Heather pretended not to hear, looked down, and studied the chair that now occupied the space that used to hold the spindly-legged antique. "What happened to my—"

"Don't ask."

"You mean JT sat in it?" Heather didn't wait for an answer. "I was afraid of that," she said, petting the worn fabric. "The chair was beautiful, but I knew if JT tried it, he'd want it changed." She traced her finger along a seam that was unraveling. "I'll replace this old thing with something a little nicer, maybe stick this in Becky's office. She could use another chair, and vendors don't really care what they sit in as long as they sell something."

"Sounds good to me. I did like the little silk number, though. It was classy." Rachel pictured the elegant chair and JT squirming in it. "But then I'm not six-six and weigh two-fifty, either."

"JT weighs two-sixty-five now, and I'm putting him on a diet." Heather pointed a finger at her sister. "But don't you dare say a word about it, Rachel. You know how vain he is. If he knew I told you—"

"Don't worry. I can keep a secret." She squinted at her sister. "If I'm not mistaken, you're the one with the diarrhea of the mouth."

Heather dropped her eyes, guessing Rachel figured out who blabbed to JT about the overbooking. When she looked up, she noticed her sister looking past her. She turned and took stock of the woman at the front desk Rachel was watching.

The woman was at least fifty and had big bones and the fattest thighs she'd ever seen on a human being. She sported huge black hair—definitely dyed—weighed more than JT, and wore shoes with six-inch heels that looked as if they'd collapse beneath her weight.

From where they sat, the two sisters heard the woman complaining to the front desk clerk in a nasally voice. She waved an arm and pointed toward the back of the property, exposing the front of a designer suit and a diamond on her finger the size of a jaw-breaker.

"Uh-oh," Rachel said, as her feet felt around for her shoes. "I bet she didn't get a suite. Maybe I should go over and smooth it out." She stood up, about to leave.

"No, wait." Heather waved her sister down. "Amalia can handle it. Give her a chance."

Sure enough, within a minute the heavy-bottomed woman appeared to relax and her voice quieted. When she turned around, she was smiling. Rachel and Heather watched her totter away on the pointy-toed heels, her necklace sparkling under the lobby lights.

A wiry man suddenly appeared in the doorway. He wore a white chef's jacket and black dreadlocks. "Oh, I see you guys are busy." Chef Henri stood at the threshold without his usual blinding-white grin.

"No, come on in," Rachel called out, waving him inside. "We were just talking."

Chef Henry stood rooted to his spot and shook his head. "No, I gotta get back. But I need to show you something in the kitchen, when you get a chance."

Rachel said she'd be there shortly, and Chef Henri left abruptly. Both women looked at each other.

"Something's wrong," Heather said. "I've almost never seen him without a smile."

"Me neither," Rachel agreed. "I better go check."

As soon as Heather left, Rachel locked the office doors and stopped at the front desk to let the clerk know she'd be back shortly. She took a quick detour to the rest room and looked down at the slim ankles in the next stall.

"I'd recognize those pretty little feet anywhere, Rosario."

"Oh, hi, Rachel," the lounge manager answered, "fancy meeting you here."

When they got together at the sinks, Rachel asked Rosario how her college classes were coming along.

"Great. I'll be getting my AA degree from AWC in May."

Rachel began washing her hands under the hot water. "That's wonderful. We're so proud of you. We'll have to throw you a graduation party."

"If I'm still here," she answered barely above a whisper, grabbing a paper towel.

Rachel frowned at her friend's image in the mirror and turned off the water. "What do you mean?"

Rosario finished wiping her hands and threw her towel in the trash. She grabbed another one, handed it to Rachel, and leaned her petite frame against the sink. "I've got a three-hundred dollar problem so far this month."

Rachel studied her face. Rosario Garcia had dark, almond-shaped eyes and raven black hair, glossy as a bird's wing. Her lips were turned down in a tense, worried look.

"Are you talking about theft?" Rachel felt sickened as the words left her mouth.

Rosario cocked her head toward the door. "Come walk with me. I have to get back."

The lobby was fairly quiet; the last few of the Inner Light group were checking in. As they crossed the floor of the cavernous room, their heels clicked against the Saltillo tile floor.

Rosario stared down, avoiding Rachel's eyes. "I'm missing two bottles of Dom, three top shelf tequilas, and two premium bourbons. I haven't finished counting the wine yet," she said, barely above a whisper.

Rachel sensed the anger in Rosario's words and couldn't blame her.

"I can understand why you're upset. This is your first loss. Any ideas who did it?"

"No." Rosario almost spit the word out. "I can't believe any of my girls would do this. They've all been with me from the beginning."

"Oh, Rosie, I'm so sorry you have to deal with this. Have you told JT yet?"

"I will, just as soon as I have an exact total. I just hope he doesn't fire me."

They arrived at the entrance to the lounge and saw that customers had already filled the booths against the far wall. Low-hanging red globes cast a rosy glow on their faces. Rachel reached over and gave Rosario's arm and affectionate squeeze.

"Don't worry, JT won't fire you. It'll be okay. We'll catch the person, trust me on that."

Rachel felt drained by the time she made it to the kitchen, but she put on a smile and tried to clear her mind. One of the kitchen crew was cleaning up after lunch, wiping down the stainless steel counters, and the other was doing prep work for dinner. After cheerfully greeting them by name, she crossed over to the little cubby hole that served as the chef's office.

"Rachel Ryan at your service," she said with a smile and a mock salute.

Chef Henri stood up to greet her but failed to smile back. "Come on, I have something to show you." He stepped out from behind his desk and led the way out of the little room.

Rachel wordlessly followed him through the kitchen to the back wall where the walk-ins stood and watched him open the man-sized door to the freezer. "After you," he said, and closed the door after them.

After a couple steps, the Chef pointed to the second shelf on the left. "There. See that?"

Rachel looked at the spot, puzzled. "Where? I don't see anything."

"Exactly."

Henri motioned for Rachel to follow him out. When they got back to his office, he shut the door behind them.

"You remember all the shrimp I ordered for the Inner Light and the Markman groups? The ten big bags?

"Yes?" Rachel spoke tentatively, waiting for the bad news she was sure to come.

"They're gone. Someone stole them."

Henri picked up a clipboard and flipped through the receipts. "Here it is. I took delivery on Wednesday."

Rachel's heart sank. "Does JT know about this?"

"He will in about five minutes."

Rachel opened the office door in time to see JT walking through the kitchen toward them with Rosario following right behind.

⸙⸙⸙

The young man stood at the back door of Charlie's Bar and Grill and turned his head away from the stench of the dumpster. He knocked loudly several times, hoping to be rewarded with a quick response. The door opened abruptly and an older man clad in a stained T-shirt, rolls of fat, and a once-white apron appeared. The older man glanced at him and the box of liquor he held in his arms. With a jerk of his head, he silently indicated the young man should follow him inside.

"Hey Charlie," the fat man called out. "Your delivery's here."

The young man set the bottles down on the kitchen counter and looked around the grimy kitchen. It smelled like old grease and spicy chicken wings.

A large woman in her late fifties with cheaply bleached hair appeared through the doorway. She walked up to them wearing an armful of jangling bracelets and a tight-fitting, low cut knit shirt that emphasized her ample breasts. "This it?" she said, looking at the bottles.

"Yeah," the kid said.

"And it's not hot?"

"Yeah, it's not hot. I told you. It's overstock. The owner needs the cash."

"Right. Whatever." She picked up a bottle of Dom Perignon and turned it around, inspecting it. "It's a little high-toned for us." She put the bottle down and put her hand on a bottle of bourbon, turning it to study the label.

The young man said nothing.

Charlie straightened up, pulled a small roll of fifties out of her jeans pocket, and handed the money to the young man. "If you have any more overstock, bring me the cheap stuff."

☙☙☙

Heather caught up with Rachel in the lobby and walked beside her to her office.

"I noticed you ate lunch with an interesting-looking man today." She hung the one-liner in the air.

Rachel had a hint of a smile on her face as she studied her sister. "He *was* very interesting, but I suspect, unavailable, so you can get any of those silly, matchmaking hopes out of your head." She decided she'd settle *that* little item, at least for the day.

"Oh," Heather said, sounding disappointed. "Was he the psychic guy? Lars somebody?"

"Lars Ekberg. And he's a spiritual medium, not a psychic-guy."

"What's the difference?"

"I have no idea, and I was too embarrassed to ask. I'm just happy one of his people cancelled so I don't have to move out of my room."

"I'll bet that's right. I've seen your closet. But on the good side, JT was thrilled the hotel is booked solid."

"Thrilled?" Rachel repeated with a quizzical look on her face, and reached for the office door. *Of course, dummy, you'd be the last one he'd tell that to.* She gave her sister an exasperated look. "I thought he was upset because we were overbooked."

"Oh, Rachel," Heather said, "don't you know by now JT just loves to give you a hard time?"

"Gee, ya had *me* fooled." Rachel scowled. "I got the distinct impression he wasn't too happy about either group."

"Well, you're partly right about that." Heather gave her sister an odd look. "But it's not what you think."

"What do you mean?"

"Oh, it's mostly that 'Church of Inner Light' stuff." Heather waved her hand as if she was shooing away a fly.

"What 'Church of Inner Light' stuff?"

Heather tried to look apologetic. "Oh, you know how JT is. He looked them up on the Internet and thinks Lars doesn't have a real church. That he's a phony. A con man."

"A con man? Huh." Rachel sat in her chair and looked up. "Now, why should that surprise me?" she mused, as if asking the heavens. She scrutinized Heather. "In that case, I suppose you won't want to go to his lecture tonight. Lars gave me two tickets and said to invite you."

Heather's eyes darted back and forth, pondering her decision. "Well...it is a little tempting. But JT would have a fit if I went. I'm afraid I'd better pass on that."

"Well, *I* plan on going."

"Good. You can fill me in on all the details later. But now tell me what else happened at lunch."

Rachel was caught off guard. "What do you mean?"

"Something happened. With Ekberg. Did he hate the suite?"

"No, no. He was very pleased." Rachel dropped her gaze.

"Then what was it?" Heather crowded her. "Rachel, I was there. I saw you and the expression on your face. He said something that distressed you, and I'm not leaving until you tell me."

Rachel huffed out a breath of air. "It was just a little weird, that's all."

"Weird in what way?" Heather waited, staring her sister down.

Rachel gave up. "Lars knew about the body I found."

Heather's mouth opened and closed a little as she thought about what her sister had just said. "He could have read it in the paper. Or looked it up on the Internet or something."

"I already thought about that. But my name was never mentioned in any of the stories."

"True, but he could have found out from one of the staff. Well, maybe not. That's beside the point, anyway. How did he happen to mention it?"

"We were just talking. I started telling him about starting up the hotel, how exciting it was, and he just burst in with 'It must have been rough when you found that woman's body.' I nearly fainted right there in the booth."

"I can understand that. It would have really creeped *me* out." She considered Rachel's revelation for a moment. "Do you think he reads minds?"

Rachel took a moment to consider her wild and reckless youth. "Man, I sure hope not."

Heather giggled, and was about to ask another question when she noticed Rachel's gaze move past her to the lobby. She turned to see a flurry of activity. A busload of people dressed in casual, trendy clothing were pulling stacks of wheeled luggage and lining up at the front desk. The movie people. They looked tired and wrinkled, as if they rode over from Hollywood on a farm tractor, but more likely, it was a chartered bus.

"That must be the first wave of Markman's group," Heather said. "It looks like the fun is already starting. I better get out of here and help at the front desk." She stood up and started to walk away. "Oh, here," she said, handing Rachel a magazine. "I thought you might be interested in this. There's an article about Richard Markman's new movie in it. Did you know he lost a ton of money on his last film? The article made him sound like he was on the brink of bankruptcy."

Rachel took the magazine and glanced at the cover photo of Dixie. "No kidding? You'd never guess it the way he spends money. It's nothing but the best for him."

"Maybe that's why he's going broke," Heather said as she left the office.

Rachel surveyed the activity in the lobby while Heather scurried over behind the marble counter. Dozens of movie people were milling around, talking, and getting in line to check in. They parted like the Red Sea when

Richard and Dixie Markman walked up, followed by a man dressed in a pilot's uniform.

The Markmans were easy to spot. Dixie wore her hair in her trademark orangey-red pixie cut and sported gobs of eyeliner and mascara. Big fake eyelashes, too. She was forty, looked twenty-five, and was adorably cute and curvy. Rachel recognized Richard from a personal meeting the previous November, and if anything, he looked younger and more energized. She looked at both of them with envy. *They say money can't buy happiness, but it can pay for a heck of a lot of plastic surgery.*

A short, moon-faced man with Albert Einstein hair walked over to Richard, with a check-in packet in his hands. He conferred with Richard a moment, handed him the packet, and pointed to the back door of the lobby where a bellman was already dragging two empty carts headed towards their piles of luggage.

Rachel was about to get up to greet them when she saw JT approach, shake hands, and give them the usual blah-blah he reserved for important guests. Standing next to JT, Dixie looked tiny, like a little doll. Actually, most women looked short to Rachel since she was five-eight in bare feet, but Dixie was even shorter than most. Markman wasn't any bean pole either, standing at least a head shorter than JT. But the good part was that both he and Dixie looked happy while JT chatted them up.

Rachel breathed a big sigh of relief. Everything worked out, after all.

She buried herself back in her work until the recorded voice of Carrie Underwood reached her ears. Happy Hour in the lounge. Rachel looked at her Gucci watch, which she set five minutes faster than the clock on the wall. She put her files away, tidied up her desk, clicked on her voice mail, and slipped on her red Ferragamo shoes. She decided she had good reason to get happy.

∽∾∽

The lounge was already filling up with noisy people and the vintage-styled jukebox was pumping out a current country song Rachel hated. After looking around and not seeing anyone she wanted to talk to, she concluded it wasn't the atmosphere she was looking for, after all. She ordered a frozen margarita—a deluxe Cuervo Gold double shot in a big mug—and carried it across the lobby towards the rear exit.

Once outside, Rachel looked around. The air smelled fresh and only a few mackerel clouds floated low on the horizon. She sauntered along the flagstone path towards the pool, occasionally stopping to sip her drink and enjoy the feel of the sun on her skin.

No one was in the pool, but at the far end of it near the waterfall, Dixie Markman was lying next to a little round table with a tall gin and tonic on it. The chair next to her was filled with two towels and a huge tote bag, probably to discourage interruptions to her privacy.

She wore a lime green bikini that didn't quite cover her ample breasts, and was stretched out on a lounge chair carefully positioned so that her pale skin was protected by the shade of a cluster of date palms.

Rachel walked over and introduced herself, offering Dixie one of her cards.

Dixie lowered the book she was reading and peeked out at Rachel over the dark glasses that covered half her face. "Wow. You should be a model," she said, taking the card.

Rachel laughed. "I tried it, but I didn't like it."

"I don't blame you. I'd much rather eat, too," Dixie said with a mischievous twinkle in her eye.

Rachel immediately felt at ease with her and noticed what she was reading. "I see we have the same taste in books," she said, eyeing the star's copy of *Life of Inner Light*. "I'm about halfway through mine. What do you think of Lars Ekberg?"

"Sit down," Dixie said, pointing to the chair next to her, leaving Rachel to place the tote bag and towels on the flagstone decking. Dixie put her hand up to her face as if she were telling a secret she didn't want anyone to overhear. "He's either a rare and brilliant man or a total screwball."

Rachel nodded and smiled. "I haven't quite made up my mind either, but all that stuff about living past lives is so fascinating."

"Indeed it is," Dixie said, with wide open, expressive eyes. "And I noticed the sign in the lobby. Lars Ekberg is actually *here*."

"Yes, he is. His church is having meetings and lectures the next few days."

"Lectures?" Dixie's eyebrows shot up and the freckles on her nose looked almost three-dimensional. "When? Can anyone attend?"

"Well, the first meeting is tonight at seven-thirty." Rachel hesitated. "But it's not open to the public."

Dixie looked at her expectantly.

"Lars did, um, invite me to attend," Rachel added, feeling a little awkward. "Actually, he invited me *and* my sister. But my sister has no interest in going…"

"Really?" Dixie's eyes brightened and she sat up. "Do you think *I* could go instead?"

Rachel blinked. *Dixie Markman wanted to go with her to a lecture*? Rachel's mouth opened but nothing came out.

Dixie looked Rachel up and down in an obvious way and gave her a devious grin. "You could tell them that *I'm* your sister." She giggled at her own little joke and Rachel immediately decided she'd like Dixie for a friend.

An hour later, Rachel and Dixie were still sitting by the pool, laughing and chatting with four empty glasses sitting on the table between them. The phone inside the tote bag began to ring and Rachel handed Dixie her bag, then stepped away to give the woman some privacy.

Just then Rachel's phone rang and she took the call.

"Do you want us to order for you?" her sister asked, a little impatiently, and Rachel remembered her dinner plans. She mumbled her choice and disconnected, noticing Dixie had finished her call, too.

Dixie giggled, slightly silly from the two gin and tonics. "I'm late for dinner."

"Me, too," Rachel said with a grin, a bit high herself. "I'll see you at seven-fifteen."

Rachel rushed back to the lobby, trying to think sober thoughts as she entered the Plantation Dining Room. Romantic piano music drifted out from the overhead speakers and the waterfall against the back wall gurgled its way to a small pool.

When she slid into the booth, JT looked pleasant enough, but he reminded her that they had agreed to meet at an earlier time because of her request.

"I was talking to Dixie Markman," Rachel said, as if that would excuse her own rudeness, and then proceeded to relate much of their conversation. "We're attending Ekberg's lecture together," she gushed, totally missing the way Heather looked down at the table and hardly spoke a word.

The food was served, and Rachel dominated the conversation with information about Dixie, barely hearing anything JT or Heather said. Finally she excused herself, leaving her plate with most of the food still on it, saying she needed to freshen up before the lecture.

Rachel slid out of the booth and Heather reached for her sister's hand. "Come by after the lecture, okay?" she asked, anxiety dulling her voice. "I'd really like to hear about it."

"You bet," Rachel said, rushing off.

JT put his hand of top of his wife's. "Don't worry, honey," he said and turned to watch Rachel leave. "This will pass. In one week they'll all be gone and Rachel will forget all about Hollywood."

"I know." Heather nodded, but her voice lacked conviction and her eyes followed after her sister. "It's okay."

၄၃၄၃

Rachel rushed along the walk, and a gust of wind blew the flap of her skirt up. She stopped abruptly and looked around. The sky was a curious shade of gray tinged with pink and she heard the brass tubes of her wind chimes clinking in the distance. That was a quick change, she thought, scanning the sky and remembering how hot the sun felt on her skin earlier. *Where did that cloud cover come from?* Weird. She shivered and checked her watch. At least she'd have time to change into something warmer.

Back in her suite, Rachel picked out a black shell with a silk jacket in a black and white print. Dressy black pants and peep-toed heels completed her ensemble, but her Kate Spade purse didn't work. Rachel dug around in the closet and found the retro purse she treasured, a white satin clutch embroidered with crystal beads and tiny white pearls.

Outside again, Rachel was glad she had changed outfits. The wind was stronger than before but she felt comfortable in her Carolyn Herrera jacket. She also felt confident Dixie wouldn't be embarrassed to be seen with her. That Dixie even wanted to go with her to the lecture was a surprise to begin with, and Rachel thought about how they had met and just "clicked." *She acts so normal and self-depreciating. Why, it's no wonder everyone loves her.*

Wind whipped through Rachel's hair and the chimes were clanging loudly now. The delicate branches of a mesquite tree danced to its tune as she rushed along.

The air smelled different, moist, she thought, like an early spring day when snow is melting off the sidewalk. Rachel laughed to herself. *It's spring, all right, but Mesquite never has snow. They hardly have sidewalks.*

A gust of wind suddenly roared through the trees, sounding like rain. Rachel stopped again and looked up, but nothing fell from the sky. *What's going on?* A little spooked, she quickened her pace until she reached the lobby door. When she touched it, everything became still. She glanced around again, shivered, and went inside.

Rachel compulsively glanced at her watch, checked it again against the clock hanging on the wall over the front desk, then perched herself on the arm of the sofa in the middle of the lobby. *What if Dixie doesn't show up?*

Several people were milling around near the front entrance. The din of their laughter blared over the soft music from the overhead speakers. Rachel recognized a few of the people as local folks who frequented the bar for happy hour and sometimes stayed for dinner.

She tapped her foot out of nervousness and occupied herself trying to guess what scent Heather was having piped into the lobby that month. Spring rain? Flowered fields? She couldn't quite place it. She scanned the room for signs of Dixie and noticed a petite woman with long black hair, wearing wire-framed glasses with rose colored lenses, approaching her. It took a few seconds before Rachel recognized Dixie in her new accessories. It was the expensive suit and the Hollywood shoes that did it.

"You look pretty as a brunette," Rachel said. "And I like the glasses. They give you that intellectual look."

"Thanks. I wore this wig hoping no one will spot me at the lecture." Dixie flipped a long strand of hair with her hand. "I don't want to end up being dissected like chopped liver in the gossip rags." Her eyes swept the lobby as if she expected the paparazzi to jump out any second from behind a sofa.

"Well, if you do, the information won't come from any of our employees."

"Yeah, JT told me he'd fire anyone who blabs to the press. It's one of the things I like about being here. No waitress secretly taking notes on what I order for dinner, no paparazzi lurking around trying to take unflattering photos of me at a bad angle."

"Geez."

"And that's just the good stuff." Dixie's eyes floated over Rachel then took on a look of resignation. She let out a sigh. "You know, I always wanted to be tall and thin like you."

"And I always wanted boobs like yours," Rachel quipped back.

"Well, you can always buy them where I bought mine." Dixie said and then burst out laughing as if she were suddenly surprised by her own joke.

I like this woman more every time I see her, Rachel thought. *She's crazier than I am.*

When the two women reached the Saguaro and Ocotillo rooms, a small-boned man, exquisitely dressed in a brown Armani suit, greeted them at the door. He introduced himself as Anthony Pander. Rachel handed over her tickets and introduced herself and Dixie, adding that she received a personal invitation from Lars Ekberg to attend.

Pander, recognizing Dixie as *the* Dixie Markman, immediately shifted his total attention to her and didn't let loose of her hand.

Pleasant looking, but nondescript, Pander was of medium height, with medium brown hair and a medium complexion. Even his receding hairline looked average. He was like the color beige and blended into everything, but Pander made a big show of fawning over Dixie, hoping to stand out and be noticed by one of Hollywood's rich and famous.

Not used to being ignored by the masculine sex, even the gay ones, Rachel was annoyed by Pander's rudeness. She looked around with a phony smile stretched on her face and resisted rolling her eyes. She pictured herself sticking her finger down her throat, but was sane enough at the moment not to do it.

When Pander finished his bowing and scraping act, the two women entered the room and found seats in the last row. Dixie acted like nothing unusual had happened. *Interesting life,* Rachel thought, deciding adoration was a common occurrence with Dixie and wondered how Richard's ego survived their marriage.

After Rachel and Dixie settled in, they looked around. "I don't see anyone I know," Dixie whispered.

"Is that good?" Rachel whispered back.

"Of course. I really don't want anyone to recognize me here."

Rachel mumbled an "Uh-huh," and nodded, but wondered if Dixie was telling the truth, considering the way she lapped up Pander's adulation. "I really like your outfit," she added, admiring the silk pant suit Dixie wore. The rose color matched her lenses, her lipstick, and her cheeks.

"Thanks, it's a Givenchy," Dixie said, then whispered, "It set me back fifty-two hundred bucks." She studied the delicate, jeweled purse in Rachel's lap. "I like your purse."

"Thanks," Rachel said. She smiled and winked at Dixie. "It's a yard sale find. Twelve dollars."

Dixie laughed. "That's funny. And that's a great bargain," she pointed out. "You need to take me to yard sales with you."

"You have to be willing to fly to Boston."

"Boston, huh? Is that where you're from?"

"Well, it was my last place of employment. I was the Sales Director at the Balmoral Suites."

"Balmoral Suites. I know the place. I stayed there once, a while back. It was lovely, right on the bay." She gave Rachel an odd look. "Um, you actually left *there* to come *here*? I mean, this is a nice little place and all, but…"

"Yeah, I know, it's no thousand-room Balmoral." Rachel leaned over to whisper in Dixie's ear. "Actually, I told off my jerk of a boss in a very big way and more-or-less had to quit. It was either that or be fired. My brother-in-law, JT, took pity on me and gave me a job here."

"JT's your brother-in-law?" Dixie's eyes lit up. "Wow. He's quite handsome."

Rachel thought about putting her finger down her throat again, but Anthony Pander distracted her by clicking the door shut behind them and walking briskly up to the front of the room.

Rachel took a quick look around while everyone's attention was focused on Pander. With the room divider open, the twin rooms contained enough space to move around, but were comfortably filled with rows of padded chairs that were formed in semi-circles around a large club chair seated on a raised platform. She counted only six empty seats.

The majority of the attendees were women, rich-looking women, Rachel decided, and the men didn't look poor, either. Heather's words echoed in Rachel's head. "JT would have a fit if I went," she remembered her sister saying. "He thinks Lars Ekberg is a phony and a con man."

Well, as far as being a con man was concerned, there was no fee to attend, and although Rachel noticed a donation basket by the door, she wasn't required to drop anything in. She decided she wouldn't, either, regardless of how great the lecture was, just to prove JT wrong. She couldn't help it. Sometimes JT was just a wee bit too righteous for her.

A hush fell over the room when Lars Ekberg walked in. Anthony Pander was right there waiting for him, made the introductions, and explained the difference between a psychic medium and spiritual medium. Ekberg was the spiritual kind, he explained, because he was also a minister. Rachel really couldn't see a whole lot of difference, herself, since they both supposedly consulted with spirits from the great beyond. It also occurred to her that a church's income might be tax free.

After Pander sat down at the side of the room, Ekberg started off his lecture with a parable, but not one Rachel recognized from *The Bible*. Not that Rachel ever spent time reading *The Bible*, but she did attend Catholic school, albeit sporadically, and by the time she finally graduated, she managed to pick up a few stories here and there.

Ekberg's parable was about his spirit guide, a Native American by the name of White Eagle who lived three hundred years ago next to the river that ran through Mesquite long before Mesquite got its name. The river was close to Blood Mountain, which wasn't even named that until the Spaniards moved in, started naming places, and massacred a lot of the natives.

But what interested Rachel the most was what Ekberg told the group after the story. He said the reason he picked the Mesquite Mountain Inn for the Inner Light conference was because of its location on Blood Mountain.

Apparently, Ekberg's spirit guide, White Eagle, decreed that the so-called astral coordinates of Blood Mountain destined it to be the location of the seminar for the members of the Inner Light Church.

Ekberg also explained that White Eagle, himself, spoke *through* him. He said that all the spirits of the "First People" who were buried in the old Indian burial ground on Blood Mountain would converge there during the Equinox. He also indicated that anyone open to being approached by the spirits, might possibly experience that opportunity.

Rachel smiled to herself. She couldn't wait to get that little tidbit of information to Heather. It just so happened, *that very night,* was the night of the Equinox. And since Rachel knew Heather would tell JT everything, she experienced the delicious thought of JT lying in bed, awake, waiting to get haunted.

She also thought about how strange the weather conditions were when she left her casita to come to the meeting. She remembered the pinkish sky, the sudden wind, the creepy feeling it gave her, and how it all suddenly stopped when she put her hand on the lobby door. Was it the spirits converging, flying through the air, stirring up the atmosphere? That certainly was a spooky thought.

Anthony Pander walked to the front of the room and waited until everyone's attention was riveted on him. He informed the group that Ekberg needed absolute quiet so he could center himself. Ekberg settled into the club chair behind Pander, leaned his head back and closed his eyes.

Pander explained that the spirit of White Eagle would find the pathway to Ekberg's body, and enter it. When that happened, White Eagle would use Ekberg's vocal cords and speak through him.

Rachel stole a quick look at Dixie, who was looking at her, wide-eyed.

In a show of drama, Pander then lit the circle of candles that surrounded Ekberg's chair. When he finished, he clicked off the overhead lights and allowed everyone to adjust to the glow of candlelight and the scent of patchouli the candles brought forth.

Everyone's eyes were now on Ekberg. It was dead quiet. The glow of the candles was mesmerizing, and the scent of patchouli drifted back to the last row of chairs. It was too dark for Rachel to see Dixie's face, but she felt Dixie's hand reach for hers. It was cold and, Rachel could swear, it was trembling. After a few moments, Ekberg's mouth dropped open. His head flopped down, rolled to the side, and sank into his chest. He looked quite dead.

Chapter 3

Richard paced in his suite, waiting for the knock on his door. He walked back to the kitchenette that separated the living room from the bedroom. The marble counter top was laden with two bottles of wine, seven bottles of spirits, and all the accoutrements that contributed to a fully loaded bar.

He refreshed his Wild Turkey 101 and sipped it, enjoying the feel of it slipping down his throat.

He set out two wine glasses and opened one of the bottles on the bar, an imported Rhine, still cold from being in the refrigerator. He sniffed it and let it air. The woman he was expecting preferred margaritas with salt on the rim. Unfortunately, salt encouraged a woman to retain water, and cameras weren't very kind to those women, so Richard hid his recent purchase of Herradura tequila under the sink.

At the first sound of a tapping fingernail, Richard rushed to the door, opened it, and pulled a stunning young woman inside.

Her face was shaped in a perfect oval, with large blue eyes and fleshy, pouty lips. A touch of pink colored her cheekbones, making them appear even more promi-nent than they were, but her lips were colorless, and the minty-fresh flavor of spearmint escaped from them. She wore a fedora and a long sweater with a tuxedo collar with a self belt that was tightly wrapped around her waist. The top of her sweater gaped open to reveal large, firm breasts. They were reinforced with silicone, but they looked perfect, and in Hollywood, that's all that really mattered.

"Hello, Richard," she said, breathlessly, the fra-grance of spearmint flowing out of her mouth and into the room. Her voice, sweet and high, registered in the range of a first soprano, but as everyone knew, she couldn't car-ry a tune. Not that it mattered—to men—anyway. She pulled off her hat, and long gold waves, smelling of musk, fell and swirled around her shoulders. The fra-grance of her shampoo drifted over to Richard and he pressed his face into her hair.

"Oh, baby, I've missed you so much," he whispered, drinking in her scent. "You smell so delicious I could just eat you up." He was trembling now, drugged by the pher-omones the young woman was emitting, and tugged on the belt around her waist until it gave way. He looked down and, with a sharp pang in his loins, saw there was absolutely nothing under the sweater.

∽∾∾

The weather front was passing through Blood Mountain at lightning speed. Not a drop of rain fell, but the wind raged with fierceness high above the mountain, forcing clouds to race across the moon in eerie strips.

JT hurried down the sidewalk toward the lobby, head down, blown-in sand scraping the bottom of his shoes. He felt the strangeness of the night and pulled his jacket close for no good reason. It wasn't cold, but it felt that way, with branches swaying, dancing on whiffs of wind. Something odd was going on, a feeling of darkness closing in on him, pressing on his chest.

He shut the lobby door behind him, and the oppressive feeling left, evaporating in the sights and sounds of human life. He shook it off, relegating it to the file of things not understood and easily forgotten.

He spotted a man coming toward him, walking with a familiar bow-legged gate, his cowboy boots tapping on the hand-made tile. Deputy Sheriff Dewey Tucker looked like an apple on a stick with a big mound of abdominal fat padding his front, skinny legs, and no butt. JT wondered how his pants stayed up.

"Hey, JT," Tucker called out.

"Where you been lately, Dewey?" JT grabbed the extended hand of the deputy and gave it a hard shake. "Got time for coffee?"

"Always got time for coffee." The smile on the older man's face balled up his fat cheeks and twitched his long mustache, causing him to resemble a big, happy walrus. "Especially if ya still got some of that homemade pie around."

They turned into the Hibiscus Cafe. It smelled like coffee and apple pie but looked like Hawaii. Ceiling fans twirled at the lowest setting, and tropical print drapes hung from the windows. The bamboo blinds were fully raised, and the overhead lamps were dimmed down for the evening. Anyone sitting at a window seat had a view of the valley below speckled with lights.

Tucker grunted as he parked his bulk in the booth. "You been outside?"

"Yeah. It was weird out there."

"Ain't that the truth? Funny thing, though," Tucker said, resting his Stetson on the seat next to him, "I just came up from town and it was quiet as a graveyard there."

"No kidding?" The discarded memory of the evening's weather popped back into JT's mind. "The barometer feels like it's jumping up and down on a trampoline. I could feel it on my chest."

"What you're prob'ly feelin' is them two double burgers with cheese and bacon you jus' ate."

JT laughed. There was some truth to that.

A chubby waitress with a long, black braid down her back came to the table and took their order for pie and coffee.

JT placed his napkin on his lap. "Haven't seen you around much, Deputy."

"Well, what d'ya expect?" Tucker pulled on his mustache, "Ya stopped comin' up with them dead bodies."

"Praise God and knock on wood." JT rapped his knuckles on the table.

"Hedgin' your bets, huh?"

JT laughed again. "I need to. We went through a pretty rough time for a while. So what brings you in tonight? Besides pie, I mean."

"Ah, nothin' much. Been pretty quiet. I thought I'd come by and see what's goin' on at the hotel. Got a couple of posters for the employee's room. Two Arizona females, two teens, missing."

JT shook his head. "Oh, man."

"Yeah, I know. Makes me sick, too. Young girls just ain't careful enough these days. I don't know what the parents are thinkin'."

The waitress arrived at their table, set down their order, and smiled brightly, revealing a small gap in her front teeth. "Anything else, gentlemen?"

Tucker looked down at his apple pie with vanilla ice cream, gazed over at JT's chocolate caramel, and pointed to it. "I need one of them, too, to go." He caught JT shaking his head and his mustache twitched. "Hey, we're not talkin' real need here, pardner, we're talking desire."

The men took swigs of coffee and attacked their pies in silence.

Finally JT said, "Didn't some other girl disappear last month?"

"Yeah, and one the month before that." Tucker's mouth was full of pie. "It's startin' to get worrisome."

"Isn't it already worrisome? I hope we're not having some kind of serial kidnapping going on."

The waitress came to the table with the pie-to-go in one hand and a coffee pot in the other. Tucker held up his mug to the waitress. She set the pie down, filled both the mugs to the brim, and left.

"There don't seem to be a problem just yet," Tucker said. "The missin' females are all from different areas, one up by Parker. But other than being females, there's no pattern."

JT pushed his empty plate aside and wiped his mouth with his napkin. "Isn't being a female pattern enough?"

"Could be. But they're different races. There ain't been any bodies, either. I think it's just girls runnin' off, leavin' home—you know—bein' stupid." The deputy popped open the plastic container and looked at the piece of caramel pie. "And that reminds me. How's your sister-in-law doin'?"

"Rachel? She's fine. Actually, she's been doing a great job of filling up the hotel. Right now we're completely booked."

"Huh. That's a surprise." Tucker almost looked disappointed.

JT understood Tucker's response. The deputy and Rachel usually took opposite sides of any issue, and each believed the other was lacking in gray matter.

"I noticed the parkin' lot's full. Is it the movie people I heard about? The one with the pervert director?" Tucker stuck his fork in the caramel pie, broke off a piece and plopped it in his mouth.

JT did a double take. Leave it to Tucker to dig up all the dirt. "Pervert director?"

"Yeah, it was a while back. I take it you didn't know."

JT swallowed some coffee. "No. No I didn't. What'd he do? The old casting-couch routine?"

"Pretty much. 'Cept this time the girl was under age. There was a pretty big scandal at the time. It was in all them gossip magazines next to the checkout at the grocery stores."

"Oh, man." JT's stomach flipped over. "Markman go to jail?"

"You kiddin'?" Tucker made a sour face. "Not in Hollywood. You know how it goes. Somebody paid somebody off. The whole thing got buried." He stuck his fork back in the pie. "Just thought you might want a heads-up. Know who you're dealin' with."

JT's hand went instinctively to his forehead and he nervously rubbed his hairline causing a wave of dark brown hair to fall over his fingers. "I do appreciate that, Deputy. I'll add it to my list of things to worry about. They'll be here a full week." JT took another swallow of his coffee. That was followed by the sound of someone dropping a stack of plates in the kitchen and some angry Spanish words. JT flinched. "On top of that, we've got a psychic here with his group."

"Humph." Tucker broke off another piece of the caramel pie. "Heard about him, too. A real wacko. Does séances. You know, like them TV things where they talk to dead people." He stuck the pie in his mouth.

"Yeah, I know. I looked him up on the Internet. He's got a book on the best seller list and is the head of some so-called church. Overall he appears to be pretty harmless, but that doesn't mean he's not loony tunes."

"Ain't that the truth? But all that business about talking to dead people—"

"Yeah, I'm not happy about that either," JT interrupted, "but at least his lectures aren't open the public. I'd be more concerned if the folks from town were going to be exposed to him."

Tucker nodded. "I know what you mean. A guy like that could be bad for business."

"That's true. I wouldn't want any of our locals to be taken in by that kind of stuff. I wouldn't have booked the group to begin with, but Rachel already had him signed up and took his check. Not much I can do about it now, even if he is a phony." JT poked around at the few crumbs left on his pie plate. "Oh well, at least his money is real. Rachel went to his seminar tonight with Dixie Markman so I'll probably get the low-down on him from Heather later on."

"Dixie Markman, huh? That's sounds about right for Rachel," Tucker said, and held up his fork. "I could tell you a few things about Dixie, too."

JT held up a hand. "How about if you save that for another time? I'm not sure I could handle any more wonderful news tonight."

Tucker dropped his head and stared down at his plate, an action that did not go unnoticed by JT.

"What is it?" JT asked, another twinge of worry prickling him in the gut.

"Ah, JT…" Tucker's voice trailed off, not wanting to share another bit of troublesome news. "It's nothin', really."

"Nothing? Well then, just spit it out, my friend. I might as well get all the bad news at once."

Tucker raised his head and eyes just a bit. "I hear you're getting' some competition."

"Competition? What kind of competition?"

"Ah…I hear Stanley Belinski's brother, the contactor, is puttin' the finishing touches to the old Henley building downtown. Gonna make a big, fancy eatin' place down there, with a bar, fancy pastries, the whole ball of wax."

There it was. The knife was now in his gut, twisting. "I haven't heard anything about it."

"Yeah, I know. Supposed to be a big secret. They passed the liquor license though the town council fast and quiet."

"Huh." JT was now looking down at his plate. How could he have not heard about this? Easy, he decided. Too much going on at the hotel. Not paying enough attention to what was going on in town. He lifted his head. "So who's the owner? Anybody I know?"

Tucker's eyes shifted away. "Some guy out of Phoenix is gonna manage the place, and they got a fancy chef from one of the hotels there—some woman who comes from New York originally. Talks French."

JT grunted. "So who's the owner? You never said."

Tucker shifted in his seat and uttered the last epitaph in a low, quiet voice. "The whole thing is being financed by Venkman. But I think the daughter, Anna, is runnin' the outfit."

JT sank back into the booth and stared up at the ceiling. Venkman. His nemesis. "Ah, man."

Tucker was quiet, letting the bad news sink in. He lifted his fork and picked at his pie, waiting for JT to come back. After the second bite, he said, "So how's your partner doin'? He gonna marry Rachel?"

"Oh, man, I sure hope not." JT looked up in a silent prayer. "But Buddy's fine. I guess I'll have a lot of news to share when he comes back. He's supposed to fly in tonight."

Tucker put his fork down. "He's away again? He ain't been here much lately."

"What'd you expect? It's March, it's tax season. He added another full-time person to his business, and a temp, but he still works twelve hours a day."

"Yeah," Tucker nodded. "I forget he's a CPA." He pushed himself back from the table.

"Yeah," JT said, his gaze falling on Tucker's empty plastic box. "And you forgot that piece of pie was to go, too."

♥๑♥๑

Rachel and Dixie left the main building and strolled along the sidewalk toward the casitas in silence. They stopped in front of Dixie's place.

"I wish I could stay and have a drink with you." Dixie said, affectionately squeezing her new friend's hand. "But after hearing what Lars Ekberg said, I think I better talk to Richard right away." She looked up, frowning at the stairs that lead to her suite.

The lights were on and the sliding glass door to the deck was partly open, but Rachel couldn't detect any sound or movement from where they stood. "Maybe some other time."

"You know, I'd like that." Dixie glanced at her suite again, then back at Rachel, and tried to smile. "I really enjoy being with you, Rachel. You're a lot of fun. Richard is gone a lot and I get lonesome sometimes. But I've always made it a practice not to get too friendly with the other actors. There's a lot of backstabbing going on in Hollywood."

"I'll bet that's true." Rachel attempted to sound cheerful in spite of her disappointment. "But you've got my card. If you need anything, call me. I put my private cell number on the back."

"Thanks. I appreciate that," Dixie said, her eyes giving way to a look of apprehension. She turned to the stairs, watching the glass door as she ascended.

Rachel stood forlorn in the shadows, her eyes following Dixie up the stairs until she entered her suite. She turned to leave and remembered the strange weather a couple hours earlier. It felt oddly quiet now. Had the spirits stopped stirring things up?

She drifted back to Heather's casita, the first in the row of twelve. As she climbed the stairs, she turned to look at the view of the valley studded with lights. She remembered JT had chosen that unit because of the panorama below and the town of Mesquite beyond that. She smiled at the thought: a billion dollar view out here, in the middle of nowhere.

She smelled something exquisite and followed her nose. The natal plum plants below her were blooming. Under the lights, the white blossoms were gleaming against dark, waxy leaves.

Heather answered the door quickly, already dressed for bed, her face scrubbed clean, and her hair damp from a shower.

"Come in, come in." Heather was excited and pulled her sister into the room. "Did Dixie show up?"

"Yes, she did, and the whole evening was just..." Rachel stopped and searched for the right word. "Amazing."

"Really?" Heather's eyes lit up in anticipation of a juicy story. "Come sit down. I want to hear every last, lurid detail." She sat down on the sofa and tucked her legs beneath her.

Rachel sniffed the air and looked around for one of the scented candles Heather was hooked on. "Let me guess," she said. "Cherry blossoms?"

Heather nodded. "Cherry-vanilla cola. Close enough."

Rachel spied the scandal sheets lying on the coffee table. "Are you still buying those trashy magazines?"

"Hey, a girl has to have *some* vice to keep her interesting," Heather teased. "Actually, I picked them up to see if I could find any stories about any of our guest celebrities. I figure it's better to be informed than to make some major faux pas."

"True." Rachel nodded thoughtfully. "That's really a good idea. I should have picked up a few myself. Maybe I better borrow them for a quick read before I make some major blunder. Except for the movies they've made and the awards, I really don't know that much about the Markmans...or any of the other actors, for that matter."

"So, tell me about the lecture," Heather said, practically bouncing on the sofa with eagerness. "Was it interesting?"

"It was incredible," Rachel answered with awe in her voice. She then related the events of the evening starting with Dixie's black wig, meeting Anthony Pander, and ending with a brief summary of Ekberg's little talk. She made sure she mentioned the part about White Eagle and the spirits of the dead "First People," and noted with particular emphasis the news that the spirits were converging on Blood Mountain that very night, and would be skulking around, available for meetings.

Heather's eyes widened. Rachel guessed she was already thinking about how to relay that information to JT.

"There's even more," she said, and then hesitated.

"What? Tell me," Heather prodded, bouncing again on the sofa.

"Well, this part is *really* weird. I hope you're up for it."

"Oh, for Pete's sake, Rachel, I've raised twin teenage boys. I know weird."

"Okay, you're forewarned," she began, and told Heather about the candles and how Ekberg went into his trance.

"He didn't die, did he?" Heather asked.

"Of course not. He just looked like he did. At least for a little while." Rachel lowered her voice almost to a whisper. "After a while, he raised his head up and began to speak in a different voice, a lower voice, and the voice identified itself as White Eagle. He talked to us in a kind of halting English, one word at a time. Dixie and I just stared at him goo-goo-eyed."

"Wow," Heather breathed.

A cool breeze blew in from the patio and the drapes fluttered. The women shivered and looked at each other. Rachel jumped up to close the door and looked out. Narrow strands of clouds slipped in front of the moon. It looked eerie—and it felt that way, too.

When Rachel came back, Heather was hunched forward, her arms wrapped around herself. "You're right. It *is* weird." Her eyes were wide open. "So what did this White Eagle say?"

Rachel stared off and mentally transported herself back to the meeting room. "He talked a lot about what people are doing to the environment, how they are destroying the land, and about how the spirits of the "First People" as he called them, are not happy." She paused.

"And?"

"Well, when he finished with that part, he suddenly started announcing things to the audience about themselves. You know, like, 'there's a man here, his first name starts with an M and he has undiagnosed heart trouble.'"

"Okay," Heather said, leaning back, letting out a breath. "I'm afraid that last part sounds a little phony. Like your typical stage show where they have ear phones and all that."

"Yeah, it sounded phony to me, too, at first. Except Lars went on to say there was a woman with the initial R who has seen too much of death and still needed therapy. He added that she was still drinking too much and needed to take extra vitamin B to counteract the alcohol."

Heather tilted her head a bit. "Do you think he meant you?"

"What do *you* think? I certainly didn't tell him anything like that."

"Hmm," was all Heather would commit to. They had walked down that road before and she had no intention of making a judgment on her sister's alcohol consumption.

"Heather? Have you ever seen me drunk since I've been here?"

Heather looked down and examined her fingers. "No, I've never seen you drunk. But you are the only one that can judge if you are drinking a *lot*." She looked up. "Are you?"

"No more than usual. I mean, I *have* been cutting back."

"Well, the vitamin B can't hurt, and I suppose that vague kind of information could apply to more than one person in the room." Heather hesitated a moment. "What about the therapy? Another session or two probably wouldn't hurt you. When was the last time you talked to Dr. Kent?"

"It's been a while. But I've been fine," Rachel insisted. "We had a phone conference after the end of the—you know—the murders."

"Humm." Heather allowed the comment to hang in the air, realizing more and more that White Eagle's words seemed to fit. "Okay, what about Dixie?" she asked, deciding to move on.

"Well, Lars did say a woman with the initial D had an unfaithful husband who was seeing a much younger woman. He said the wife needed to protect herself. That kind of freaked her out. She was half-way convinced it was true."

Heather grimaced. "This morning I read in one of those magazines that Richard Markman was seen around with Tara Linley. He's more than *twice* her age." She glanced at her stack of scandal sheets, but decided to forgo looking through them to find the story. "Did Lars mean the wife needed to protect herself as in physically protect? Or financially?"

"I have no idea. But it sure got Dixie's attention."

"That's pretty scary. I mean the whole thing is pretty scary." Heather thought about that a moment and scrunched up her face in a puzzled look. "You know, if Ekberg is accurate, I wonder where he's getting his information."

"What do you mean?"

"I mean he could be getting his information from the dark side."

Rachel blinked at her. "The dark side?"

"Yeah. The *dark* side," Heather repeated in an ominous voice. "I once read that people like Lars are getting their information from *evil* spirits, like demons," she said, whispering, as if they could overhear. "Demons know things, too, you know. Not everything…but some things. They often pretend to be dead people."

"Demons?"

The puzzlement cleared from Heather's face. "Yes, I'll bet that's it." She nodded with finality. "Rachel, I think it would be a good idea if you stayed away from our Mr. Ekberg."

"Too late."

"Too late? What do you mean?"

"I mean that after White Eagle flew off and Lars came back into his own body, Anthony Pander announced that if anybody wanted a personal reading with Lars, they could sign up at the door on the way out. Dixie did. She made me promise to go with her for support."

Heather gave her sister a piercing look. "*You* didn't sign up for a reading, did you?"

"Are you kidding? At three hundred dollars a pop? I don't think so."

"Three hundred dollars?" Heather sighed with audible relief. "I guess that's one benefit of making you work for slave wages."

"Don't worry. I don't think I'd go for it even if I were rich. I might be gullible in some areas, but when money enters the picture, I guess I'd rather buy shoes." She looked down at the pair of Jimmy Choo's on her feet. "In fact, I usually find myself taking after my skeptical brother-in-law and start thinking con man."

"Uh-oh. You're not really thinking that."

"I'm not sure *what* I'm thinking right now. I was really sold on Lars at first. I mean, the lecture was totally free. There was a donation basket by the door, but no pressure to drop anything in. It was all love and peace and pick-up-your-trash green stuff." Rachel stopped and thought about Pander's sales pitch. "Anthony Pander talked about the readings as a way to help people with their problems, but only casually mentioned the three hundred dollar charge—ahem—donation, later. I guess time will tell if he's legit or not." She looked at Heather. "But please don't mention that part to JT."

Heather's eyes dropped to her hands which were now twisting in lap, but she murmured a promise not to tell. She looked up at her sister with searching eyes. "So you really like Dixie Markman, huh?"

Rachel noticed her sister's expression and, with a pang, realized a few things at once and wanted to kick herself. It was now painfully obvious that Heather was jealous of the time and attention she had given Dixie and maybe even felt threatened about their relationship. Why hadn't she seen it before? Stupid, stupid, stupid. Even worse, as Rachel recalled their dinner earlier, she had to admit she behaved like a self-absorbed jerk. True, Heather was too "motherly" at times, but she loved Rachel. Perhaps she was the only person in her life who truly did.

"Oh, she's okay," Rachel replied, downplaying the friendship as a pain sliced through her insides. "It's kind of fun hanging around with a movie star for a couple days, but that's all it is. I'm sure once she leaves, she'll never think of me again. Besides, it's not like having a *real* friend, not like someone who really cares about you and that you can share everything with."

She squeezed Heather's hand and gave her a loving smile, hoping her sister was reassured by her comments. She rose to leave. "I really wish *you* could have come with me tonight instead of Dixie."

"Me, too." Heather took hold of her sister's hand as they walked to the door and hugged good night.

As Rachel dawdled along to her suite next door, she realized she was still feeling a little guilty for making Heather insecure about their relationship. *You are such a jerk,* her inner voice scolded. She dragged her feet up the steps and promised herself she'd pay more attention to her sister, and her behavior, in the future.

As Rachel undressed for bed, she heard loud voices—like people shouting at each other—coming from outside. Curious, she threw on a robe, opened the sliding glass door, and listened as an argument next door escalated. A man and a woman were really going at it and, with a shock, Rachel remembered the people next door were the Markmans.

She crept to the end of the covered patio, leaned over the side railing, and stuck her ear out. She could definitely hear Dixie's higher-pitched voice and what sounded like Richard's deeper voice through the sliding glass door, but their words were muffled. She couldn't understand what the argument was about.

Suddenly, a high-pitched scream sailed through the night. It was followed by a crash and the sound of smashing glass.

Chapter 4

JT decided he needed to walk off the chocolate caramel pie. That was one of the hazards of owning a hotel with two mouth-watering restaurants. Delicious desserts were always available to him. When they lived in LA, Heather made sure the fridge was always stocked with fruit and cheese and those horrid cut-up little vegetables. The hotel's walk-in was stocked that way, too, but now he needed to make a choice. Raw vegetables or Addie's delectable homemade pie. Gee, tough decision.

At least he wasn't chained to a desk all day, he considered. If he wanted to move rocks and work it off, it was always an option, and one he liked. He circled around the pool and noticed the light was on in the maintenance barn. That gave him an idea. Perhaps he could turn the maintenance barn into a real exercise room instead of the little cubbyhole off the lobby that housed the treadmill and exercise bikes. He'd check it out.

When JT stuck the key in the door, he noticed the door wasn't locked. When he opened it, he smelled the fragrant odor of fresh wood chips and noticed the huge, dark, Native American with massive arms and upper body standing behind the work bench.

"Hey, Mr. Carpenter," Toro said, holding a small saw in his hand.

"Toro, what are you doing here? I thought you were off at three."

"I was," Toro answered. "One of the men called in sick. I decided to cover for him since I couldn't get nobody else. Then I noticed one of the trees blew over in that wind. Broke the supports."

"Yeah, that was a pretty weird front that came in. Real fast, too."

"More than weird." Toro answered in a murky tone and made a face that wrinkled the scar running vertically down his face.

"What do you mean?"

"Bad spirits, Mr. Carpenter. Bad spirits." Toro shook his head and picked up two long one-by-two poles with chiseled ends. "I think this will work."

JT walked out with him. "Are you going to be okay, working a double?"

"No problem. I'm off tomorrow."

"Good. Sleep in." Then JT decided to ask, "Hey, Toro, what do you think about turning the maintenance barn into a real exercise studio? You know, with weights, an upper arm machine? Some of that fancy stuff?"

A smile curled the corners of Toro's lips. He studied JT. "The missus been on your case about the fifteen pounds, huh?"

e∕ɔe∕ɔ

Heather was asleep when JT climbed into bed. "Hi, sweetie," she mumbled, awakening, and rolled over to him. She snuggled up against him and pressed her face into the hair on his chest. Fresh out of the shower, he smelled like Irish Spring soap. "Rachel came by to tell me about the Church of Inner Light meeting."

"Oh, yeah? What'd she say?" JT kissed her forehead. He guessed it was a set-up. He suspected Rachel told Heather exactly what she wanted Heather to relay to him but he wanted to hear about it anyway.

Heather repeated the conversation with her sister with her eyes closed and her arm draped over JT. When she finished, she dropped back off to sleep like she'd never awakened.

JT lay there for a few minutes thinking about the information Rachel passed on about the ghosts of Blood Mountain and the discussion he had with Tucker about the weather. He quickly pushed those thoughts out of his mind, but another one wedged its way in: Toro's remark about bad spirits causing the weird weather. Just ancient mumbo-jumbo, he decided, but then he recalled the strange feeling he experienced when the cold front blew through. It felt weird, all right—and dark, malevolent. But that was just a coincidence, he told himself, and turned over. *Then what about that thing about the pervert director?* He pictured the little man and his wife. *Was that going to be a problem now? Here? Thank goodness both groups would be gone in a just a few days. But what about the new restaurant down town? Could Mesquite really support another upscale restaurant? How would it affect the Plantation Room? They really couldn't hold out over the summer with a strong competitor.*

JT squinted at his watch in the soft glow of the hotel lights coming in around the edges of the drapes. It was after midnight. Maybe things would look better in the morning. He flipped his pillow over to the cool side and finally went to sleep.

꧁꧂

The next morning was the time of the weekly staff meeting. Because all the smaller meeting rooms were already set up for meetings or parties later in the day, JT called everyone to meet in the cavernous ballroom. He was the last to arrive and sat at the head of the table to the left of his wife.

All chattering ceased. JT surveyed the group, making sure everyone was present. The attendees, dwarfed by the size of the room, consisted of all the department managers, his secretary, plus Heather and Buddy.

Byron Edward "Buddy" McCain, JT's partner, was more like a younger brother to him than a business partner. The perfect counterbalance to JT, Buddy didn't have a serious bone in his body, but he did have a broken bone once, in his nose, courtesy of an irate husband that Buddy didn't know existed. Unlike JT, Buddy wasn't endowed with a lineman's body, but received as compensation a movie-star smile and a thick bush of sandy hair, usually sun-bleached, that fell below his ears and usually needed a cut.

Loaded with charm, and money, Buddy earned the reputation of being one of LA's premier bachelors (except during the brief times he'd been married.) Heather considered it her solemn, sisterly duty to try to remedy the "bachelor" part.

Rachel was sitting next to Buddy, reeking of Eternity toilet water, which she accidently spilled on herself earlier that morning, and began rearranging the stack of folders neatly placed in front of her. The rest of the chairs were filled by the other members of the management team.

A waitress brought in a large tray of glasses filled with iced tea and, while she passed them out, Rachel studied JT, looking for signs of fatigue. She couldn't find any and finally asked. "Did you sleep well, JT?" She couldn't help herself.

JT smiled at her, refusing to take the bait. "Like a rock. How 'bout you?"

Disappointed that the spirits didn't haunt JT, Rachel wanted to say she also enjoyed a wonderful night's sleep but felt duty bound to recount the incident next door.

"I had a problem with my neighbors," she admitted. "They appeared to be contending for the lightweight title and battled it out for a while. I heard a scream, immediately followed by a loud crash, and ran back inside to call nine-one-one. But then they settled down. They sounded like they were both still alive, so I guess the damage was limited to whatever it was they smashed."

JT evidenced concern. "Becky?" He looked down the table at the housekeeping manager. "Do you know anything about this?"

"Yes, sir," she answered. "One of the maids called me this morning and I went over to check it out. One of those mica and copper lamps was smashed beyond repair, and the glass out of one of the prints was destroyed. I requested maintenance replace the lamp with one from supply, along with a new print, and told the front desk to add it to the Markman's bill.

"The fight was at Richard Markman's?"

"Yes, sir. It's not that unusual for celebrities to get into spats and even trash places. Where I've worked before, we took photos, kept the broken articles, and added the expense to their tab." A worried look crossed her face. "I—I guess I just assumed that was your policy, too."

JT nodded. "It is now. This is the first time we've encountered a problem like that, and I hope we don't have many more. And Becky?"

"Yes, sir?"

"Don't call me sir."

"Yes, sir. I mean, JT, sir."

Irene, JT's secretary, tried not to smile while she took careful notes. She was a pretty girl, full-figured, with a long, dark braid that hung half-way down her back. She looked up at JT, hands on the laptop in front of her, waiting for his next pronouncement.

JT shifted his attention across the table. "Rachel? What's happening with the western party for the Markman's group?"

"All taken care of, JT." Rachel flipped open a file in front of her. "The hay bales will be delivered Friday afternoon and Toro and the men will have the pool area set up by three. Chef Henri expects delivery on the extra food this afternoon. We're having steaks with a potato bar and a salad bar with shrimp bowls. Buddy flew in a load of western décor and costume accessories from LA this morning. He and I will be hosting the party." She looked up from her papers and smiled at the group. "Yeah, I know it's a dirty job, but somebody's got to do—"

"Right." JT cut in on the old joke and resisted rolling his eyes. "What about the service, the bar and entertainment?"

"Carmen hired a couple temps to help rather than make the regular staff do more overtime. Rosario is setting up the portable bar outside, next to the pool, and I've hired Handy Randy, out of LA, as entertainment. He's a one-man band, a little more "randy" than he is handy, but I think the Hollywood gang will appreciate that."

JT stared at her as a few snickers went through the group, but he didn't comment. He asked Chef Henri for his report.

After a brief update about his department, Henri paused. "We had three people turn in resignations this week." He looked crushed. "Three good people. They've all given us two weeks' notice, so we won't have a problem while the two groups are here. But still…"

JT nodded solemnly. "The new restaurant?"

There were a few soft gasps from the group, and JT related the gossip he had heard from the deputy sheriff.

"What can we do?" Rachel asked. "We can't afford to lose that income."

"I just found out about the place yesterday evening, and all I've heard, with the exception of Henri's report, has been gossip. With a little time, we'll put a good plan into place." He looked at Chef Henri. "We'll hire a couple temps if we need them, or we can promote a couple bus people to wait staff if they're capable, at least until the crunch is over. Worse comes to worse, we'll author-ize some overtime. Meet with me later about this."

"Okay," Chef Henri said, nodding. "Do you think we should go over and spy a bit?"

For the first time during the meeting, JT cracked a smile. "Not yet."

He looked around the table and asked the remaining department managers for their reports. After a few well-thought-out questions and comments, he finally turned to his partner.

Buddy flashed his million-dollar smile. He once joked that he kept his dentist on a retainer and his teeth looked it. Perfect pearly whites gleamed from his tanned face and tuffs of thick sandy hair stuck out from his head in waves and odd angles. While he wasn't handsome in the classic sense, he was certainly attractive and was well-known for his irresistible charm.

"I am extremely happy to report to all of you that for the first time since the opening of the Mesquite Mountain Inn, we are operating in the black," he said.

Everyone applauded and cheered. Buddy nodded, still smiling, and waited for the room to become quiet again. He gave a little speech thanking the staff, compli-menting them on their professionalism, hard work, and exceptional dedication. He looked around, making eye contact with the all the department managers seated at the table. "After some thought, JT and I have decided, in ap-preciation of all your efforts, to give each of you a bonus in next month's first paycheck, dependent upon the length of time of your employment." That bit of news was met with even more cheers and clapping.

Rachel was overjoyed at hearing the report, realizing her efforts contributed to the bottom line. *So that's why JT didn't care about the overbooking. Huh. I guess that means I can start thinking about that raise again.*

JT, not one to let things lag, dismissed everyone on that high note. He was the first to leave and Buddy followed him out of the ballroom.

"So what do you think, JT?"

"I think it went great."

"I mean about the movie people. Heather told me what Tucker said about the pervert director."

"Ah, between them and the psycho preacher, I've got a few more gray hairs."

Buddy laughed. "You worry too much."

"Really? They'll be here nearly a week. Add Rachel to the mix and anything could happen."

"Hey, forget the gossip Tucker passed on. It's history. I'm telling you, JT, you've got to relax. All those problems we had earlier, they're history, too. It's been three months of steady increases in revenue, and you know Rachel is mostly the reason for that. That's the reality."

JT stopped and turned to his partner. "Yeah, you're right, Buddy. We've had three months of quiet and Rachel hasn't caused us a single problem. That's exactly why I'm worried."

Some of the department managers back in the ballroom still milled about, sharing gossip and the excitement of getting unexpected bonuses. Rachel and Heather walked out ahead, trailing a little behind Becky Beeman.

"Hey, Becky, wait up," Rachel called. In a moment, she and Heather caught up with her. "I was wondering about the Markman's suite. Was it badly trashed?"

Becky shrugged her shoulders. "I've seen worse. At least there wasn't any blood."

"Oh, I'm so relieved," Rachel said, letting out a breath. "It sounded to me like he was killing her."

"I really wouldn't worry about it. I heard they've fought like that for years." She raised her eyebrows. "And I suspect this time Richard was the one who was getting clobbered."

"Really?" Heather asked, wide-eyed. "Why would you say that? Dixie is so tiny."

"Yeah, but she's a spitfire and she's jealous. So it's possible," Becky said, raising her eyebrows again and pushing up her glasses with her index finger, "Dixie might have become upset if she found out her husband entertained a young, female visitor around seven-thirty last night."

Rachel gasped and did a quick calculation. She met Dixie in the lobby at seven-fifteen. "You saw this?"

"I was going back to my trailer after eating dinner. I saw her sneak up to the door and then Richard pull her inside real quick. It wasn't like you'd normally walk up to a door and knock and wait."

"How awful," Heather cried, indignant. "And you said she was young?"

"Eighteen. Barely legal."

Rachel frowned. "How would you know how old she is?"

"*Everybody* knows how old she is. Two months ago, all the tabloids published photos of her birthday party."

"Oh, my goodness," Heather gasped, her hand over her heart. "She was Tara Linley."

෴

Anthony Pander sat at the oak table in his suite, fingering his electronic calculator. Checks and cash of several denominations were lined up in front of him.

Lars Ekberg paced the floor for several minutes. He stopped when the click of the calculator did and towered over Pander. "Well, how much did we take in last night?"

Pander held up his hand for quiet and continued fingering the machine in front of him. "Twenty-six hundred and fifty dollars," he said, finally looking up.

"That's all? Only twenty-six hundred and fifty dollars?" Ekberg looked as if he could hardly believe it and grasped his hands in front of him, twisting his long, elegant fingers.

"That's not too bad, considering we have eighty-three appointments lined up for the next five days. That's almost another twenty-five K."

Ekberg shook his head. "That's not enough." He began to pace. "Where are we on book sales?"

Pander sighed. "I'll check." He was beginning to tire of this anxiety about money. After walking into his bedroom, he picked up a navy binder off the desk and brought it back into the living room. He flipped the pages and found the one he wanted. "Okay," he said, not bothering to mention they had just discussed finances the day before. "We're at forty-seven hundred plus for the month."

"Forty-seven hundred?" Ekberg continued pacing and wrung his hands. "What about Stockholm? Tell me again how we did there."

Pander huffed and gritted his teeth then flipped back a few more pages. "Thirty-eight seven."

Ekberg frowned. "Not even forty thousand? Not even forty thousand for Stockholm?"

By now Pander could see Ekberg was headed for a full blown panic attack. "Lars, settle down. Sit down!" he said, raising his voice.

Ekberg looked at him, startled. He obediently walked to the opposite end of the room and sat down stiffly on the edge of the sofa, both feet firmly planted on the floor. After taking a deep breath, he exhaled slowly. He did this three or four times before Pander came over and sat down next to him.

"You know, Lars," Pander began softly, his hand resting gently on Ekberg's knee. "Maybe it's time for us to do what White Eagle has suggested."

"White Eagle, White Eagle. I'm sick and tired of While Eagle!" Ekberg exclaimed and clutched his head.

Pander was startled by the outburst and wasn't sure how to respond. He sat mute, hoping Ekberg wouldn't go into a meltdown while he figured out what to do.

"Everything is White Eagle," Ekberg groaned, rocking back and forth on the sofa, still holding his head. "What about me? What about Lars? I can hardly find my way back to my body anymore. Everything is White Eagle, White Eagle, White Eagle."

Pander leaned over and rubbed Ekberg's back like he would a baby's and combed his fingers through Ekberg's hair. "Hey, it's okay, it's okay. I know it's hard for you. I

know what you go through is difficult." He patted Ekberg's back again reassuringly. "You're just exhausted.
How about if we go back to the condo after the conference and you rest for a couple weeks? Miami is beautiful
this time of year. You can lie around on the beach all day
if you want. We can cancel our seminar in Palm Beach
and you won't even have to contact White Eagle."

Ekberg stiffened and slowly turned his head toward
Pander. "Don't you understand? White Eagle contacts *me*
now. He wakes me up at night. He talks to me in the
shower." Ekberg squeezed his head in his hands. "And
that's not the only problem we have. We need to do
something about the *Island of Light* development. Joe
Diamond is constantly on my back. Between him and
White Eagle, I don't have a moment's peace."

Without answering directly, Pander stood up, took
off his jacket, and walked back into the bedroom again
wondering how long it was going to take to get Ekberg to
settle down. He was back shortly with a folder made of
glossy cover stock. On the face of it, the words *Island of
Light* were imprinted in raised script and overlaid with a
muted rainbow. The background of the cover was a photograph of a tropical island: a white sand beach, coconut
palm trees, and a breathtakingly beautiful, turquoise sea.

"Here, open it," Pander said.

Ekberg looked up at Pander and cautiously reached
for the folder. He opened it to the first page, a thin
parchment sheet watermarked with the words *Island of
Light.* What followed was a well-designed presentation of
a village which appeared to be built on a small, private
island off Jamaica. The artist's conception detailed con-
dominiums, shops, and recreation areas dotted with draw-

ings of thin, beautiful people swimming in huge, crystal pools, or simply relaxing, or laughing happily among lovely gardens and fountains. The print described, in glowing terms, all the benefits of living on the Island of Light, which was tantamount to spending one's days in paradise.

"I was saving this for when we were finished here, but I'm thinking it might make you feel better to see it now, to see how beautiful it's going to be." Pander kept his voice calm and reassuring.

Ekberg slowly turned the pages. When he got to the last page, he noticed that instead of drawings, photographs of a completed luxury condominium graced the front and back sides of a pullout sheet. "What's this?" he asked.

"That, my dear Lars, is the first condo built on the Island of Light."

"What? What do you mean? They built it?" An alarmed look crossed Ekberg's face. "It's actually finished?"

"Yes, it's actually finished."

"But—but—we haven't decided to go through with the plans."

"You're right. We haven't. Nor do we ever have to go through with the plans. It's only one condo, and it's not even ours. We don't have one penny invested in it. Nothing else has been built."

"But why? Why would they do that?" Ekberg appeared to be thoroughly confused.

"Diamond Industries decided to build one unit on spec, that's all. We don't have to take it. We don't have to go through with the deal at all. There's no pressure one way or the other."

"One unit on spec? And you're saying we're not obligated?"

Pander just smiled and slowly shook his head.

Ekberg looked down at the folder in his hands and pondered that. He seemed to relax a bit and flipped through the folder a few more times. "You know, we don't have to do everything White Eagle tells us."

Pander was startled. That was not the reply he had expected. Nor wanted. He placed his hand gently on Ekberg's arm and lowered his voice another notch. "Lars, has White Eagle ever steered us wrong?"

Ekberg stared at the folder, slightly embarrassed. "No."

Pander waited in the silence of the room. "Here's what I'd like to do," he began gently. "At our meeting tonight, I'd like to present the program to the group just to see what they think."

Pander pulled out a flyer and a letter from the back of the navy binder, put it in Ekberg's hands, and looked at his partner earnestly. "I'd like to mail this out to all the members of our congregation and see what kind of reaction we get. Maybe not enough people will go for it. Then we're done." Pander gestured with open hands. "But if enough people decide to sign up, we call Joe Diamond and tell him it's a go. If that happens, you won't be under such pressure to do readings."

"I don't know." Ekberg looked up from the letter he was reading. He shook his head back and forth. "It worries me. If we purchase the Island of Light, I'll have to take on even more financial responsibility. You're talking about a huge investment. There's no way I'll be able to back off doing more readings." He looked at Pander, anguish clearly showing on his face. "The strain of White Eagle is really wearing on me. I don't think you understand how exhausting it is to have your spirit actually leave your body and wander around while another spirit takes over. Most days, I have been able to handle it, but it's getting harder, and White Eagle is coming even more frequently. I don't seem to have any control over it."

Pander put a hand back on Ekberg's shoulder and looked into his eyes. "Lars, I do understand. I see you. I feel everything you go through," he said, his voice soothing and sympathetic. "But that's the beauty of this whole plan. You won't ever have to worry about money any more. That's why White Eagle steered us on to this. He knows how you worry and wants you to be secure. You've helped a lot of people. Now it's your turn to be helped."

Pander took the pullout sheet from the folder and held it up. "Look at this condo. It's a steal at a million. But even if we only built studios for five hundred members of our entire congregation, we're talking two hundred and fifty million dollars. You'll never have to deal with White Eagle, or any other spirit again, for the rest of your life."

Ekberg looked away, stared out at nothing. "But I still have a problem with Joe Diamond. Something about him really bothers me. I don't like dealing with him."

"You don't have to deal with him, Lars. You don't have to do a thing but minister to our congregation like you did in the beginning. I'll deal with Joe Diamond from now on. I'll take care of all the business with Diamond

Industries." Pander cupped his hand around Ekberg's chin and turned his face towards him. "Please. Allow me to do that much. After all, that's what you're paying me for."

ↇↄↇↄ

The next morning Rachel glanced up from her desk and frowned at the figure in the doorway. "Are you okay?"

Dixie Markman slunk into the office wearing rumpled pants and a sleeveless sweater. She wore no makeup, except for her black-rimmed eyes, and slouched down in the chair in front of Rachel's desk. "Yes and no."

"Would the *no* part be what I couldn't help overhearing last night?"

Dixie raised her sad, raccoon eyes at Rachel. "We were that loud, huh?" she answered in a low monotone that sounded more like a statement than a question.

Rachel stepped out from behind her desk. "I—I heard the crash. I have to confess I almost called nine-one-one. I was really worried about you."

Dixie fixed her gaze on her hands, clearly embarrassed. "I missed Richard's head. I tried to hit him with the lamp but smashed the print instead." Her voice was matter-of-fact, but when she looked up at Rachel tears were forming in her eyes. "Next time, I'll aim better."

"Oh, Dixie, I'm so sorry." Rachel went to her friend and hugged her. She looked around, proceeded to the french doors and pulled them shut for privacy, then tugged over a side chair.

Dixie gritted her teeth. "You know that stinking rat, dirty scumbag, worthless piece of crap, cheated on me."

Rachel was speechless.

"Tara Linley came over, *alone,* and spent time with Richard right after I left to go to the meeting with you." Dixie began to tear up again. "He denied it at first, but then I found two empty bottles of wine in the trash. Rhine wine. They were in the refrigerator when I left. Tara drinks Rhine wine. Richard drinks Wild Turkey."

Rachel grabbed her hand, held it in both of hers. "That doesn't mean Richard had sex with her. Maybe they were discussing the movie or something."

"Yeah, right." Sarcasm dripped from Dixie's lips. "Same thing he said. But I know better. He's always had a thing for the young ones. Besides, I could *smell* her on him. She wears this musky scent—perfume, shampoo, everything."

Rachel grimaced, wishing she could think of something to say that wouldn't sound stupid.

Dixie stared off. "I guess Ekberg was right after all, about the woman with the initial D. At least about the cheating part. But he didn't get the other part right. It was Richard that needed the protection." She looked at Rachel. Then she started to giggle.

Rachel giggled, too, and then Dixie laughed harder, and Rachel laughed harder until they both were dripping tears. When they stopped, the tension was gone.

Rachel let out a deep breath. "You look like you're feeling better."

"I think I am. There's nothing like a good cry or a good laugh.

Rachel nodded in agreement and sneaked a look at her watch. "Dixie?"

"Yeah?"

"It's almost time for your reading. But are you sure you want to go through with this? You can cancel, you know."

"I'm not canceling. What time is it anyway?" She looked up at the large antique clock on the wall. "Well, it looks like we've got enough time to change clothes and repair our make-up before we walk over to the Ocotillo Room. Let's go."

Rachel stood up and grabbed her purse. "You're sure?"

Dixie looked determined. "I get to ask three questions with my reading for my three hundred bucks—and baby, wait 'til you hear what I'm gonna ask."

e/ɔe/ɔ

Richard trolled along the east side parking lot of the Mesquite Mountain Inn in his red Ferrari. He silently congratulated himself on his foresight to have his first assistant drive the car over ahead of time so it would be available whenever he wanted it, for whatever he wanted.

When he reached the rear of the main building, Tara Linley darted out of the back door of the lobby, jumped into the front seat, and buckled up. Richard stomped on the gas and drove out of the parking lot and down the curvy, dirt road that led to the valley, spinning a trail of dust behind him. Reaching the bottom, he turned left and drove along the dirt road until he reached an isolated area behind Blood Mountain.

"How's your face?" Tara asked when he parked. She reached up and tenderly touched the scratch marks on his cheek.

In answer to that, Richard grabbed her and devoured her with kisses.

Eventually, Tara pulled away, brushing back her hair. "How long will she be gone?"

"Not long, maybe an hour, or less. I just needed to see you."

"Richard?" Tara's voice was soft, hesitant. A worried look flashed across her face.

He moaned, already fumbling with the buttons on her blouse.

She pushed his hand away. "Richard. Did you ask Dixie about the divorce?"

He stopped with the buttons and looked at her. "Baby," he whined.

Tara pulled back. "Answer my question, Richard."

"That was definitely not a good time," he admitted, trying to smooth things over.

"So, *when* is it going to be a good time?" She spoke gently, soft, like an inquisitive child.

Richard stroked her cheek. "Please don't worry, baby. In six months, all this will be history. You'll be Tara Linley Markman." He reached for her again.

Tara still held herself back. "But you didn't have to put her in the film."

"Yes, I did," he insisted, his voice raising a notch. "For several reasons. We already talked about this, Tara. She needs to get over suspecting us, for starters."

"And last night was a big help."

"That was my own stupid fault. I didn't think she'd notice the missing wine bottles and go looking in the trash. I'll go into town later and I'll buy some more wine for you and you can keep it in your room." He looked away from her. "I'm sorry about this, baby, but we'll have to cool it for a while. I need to spend some time with Dixie and let her settle down, convince her that you are out of the picture. Just give me a week."

"Then what?" Tara looked at Markman out of the corner of her eye, her mouth set in a pout.

"Then I'll get rid of her."

"Get rid of her?" Tara asked. "What do you mean?"

"Look, baby, forget about this. Please. Just trust me."

Tara pouted. "But I want to be with you."

"I want to be with you, too. Just hang on a little while longer, and you will be. All the time." He grabbed Tara's hair and pressed her to his lips.

Knock, knock.

Richard jumped back, his heart skipping a beat. He turned to the window and could see the silver star though the darkened glass. "Be cool," he whispered to Tara before he rolled the window down.

A round face with a double chin and a gray walrus mustache looked into the car. "You folks okay?"

"Yes, we're fine, deputy," Richard answered with a big smile. "We were just out for a drive."

Deputy Sheriff Dewey Tucker scanned the interior of the car with his eyes and could smell the fancy perfume the girl was wearing. He could feel the tension; he could have scooped it up with his hand. The girl was flushed and she was discretely trying to button her blouse. She also looked too young to be with the man. "You okay, Miss?"

"I'm fine," Tara answered calmly and confidently, another role to play.

Dewey felt uneasy. "Maybe I ought to see some ID."

"Certainly," Richard said, pulling out his wallet.

Tara reached for her little purse.

"I've got my license and registration," Richard said, digging out his cards. He suspected the deputy's request wasn't legal, but the last thing he wanted was a confrontation with the sheriff's department, so he cheerfully handed over his documents along with Tara's ID.

Deputy Tucker studied the first card carefully, the girl's driver's license, and calculated her birthday. She had just turned eighteen in January. He recognized the name on the second driver's license, saw it was current, and handed back the IDs.

"Thank you," he said politely, his eyes making one last sweep of the car, his nose sniffing the air inside. He couldn't smell anything but the perfume, had no reason to search for anything else. "Ya'll be careful now and have a nice day." He tipped his hat and lumbered back to his truck with a bad taste in his mouth.

Tucker pulled past the Ferrari but glanced back in his rear view mirror. They definitely looked guilty of something, Dewey decided. He shook his head, guessing what it was. *Them movie people ain't got no more sense than cornbread.*

Chapter 5

Rachel squeezed Dixie's hand when they arrived in the hallway. "Well, we're here. But you can still back out."

"Nope." Dixie looked determined. "Just stay close, okay? I may need you, especially if I get more bad news like I did yesterday."

Rachel tried one more time. "Dixie, have you considered that the initial D might have been for some Dora or Denise or Debbie that was in the audience? There were a hundred people there."

"I know." Dixie nodded. "But Richard is successful, handsome, and rich. He's a babe magnet. Not to mention he's got a terrible track record."

A terrible track record? Yes, Rachel could believe that, but before she could think about it further, she caught sight of Anthony Pander. He had just stepped out of the Ocotillo room impeccably dressed, this time in a blue wool and silk jacket that looked like it cost three thousand dollars.

"Ms. Markman?" Anthony called, motioning to Dixie.

The woman Rachel had noticed earlier, the one with heavy thighs and expensive jewelry, minced out of the Ocotillo Room on another pair of tall, rickety heels. She wore a broad smile on her face.

"Good luck," Rachel said, and squeezed Dixie's hand again before she let go.

She drifted into the kitchen. It smelled like an Italian villa, heavy on the fresh garlic and rosemary from the hotel's kitchen garden. Chef Henri greeted her and she watched him and his staff for few seconds while they made lasagna. But her mind was on Dixie—she just couldn't stop worrying about her. Even though she'd known the actress for only a short time, she felt a bond with her, like they'd connected on a deep level. It was as if they'd been friends for years.

Rachel opened the pantry door and wandered in. It was a small room about eight by eight with fully stocked shelves lining the walls. It also served as a pass through from the kitchen to the Ocotillo and Saguaro rooms. She turned around and shut the kitchen door behind her. She could hear the muffled voice of Lars Ekberg coming through the swinging door and carefully peeked through the window that filled the top half, catching a glimpse of him and Dixie.

She crouched down low. It was very tempting. *After all, Dixie did say she wanted me to stay close.* Rachel struggled with her conscience, but not rigorously enough.

She pushed on the swinging door just a bit and allowed more of the sound to come through.

She heard Dixie's voice clearly. "I need to know if the movie I am currently making—*No Return*—will be successful at the box office."

The door from the kitchen opened and light flooded into the pantry. Rachel spun around to see Heather backlit against the kitchen light.

"What are you doing?" Heather asked.

Rachel held her finger to her lips, waved her sister in, and turned back to her spy mission.

"That's illegal," Heather whispered, closing the door behind her.

Rachel shook her head.

"It's immoral," Heather whispered again, this time close to her ear.

"Then don't watch," Rachel finally whispered back. "I want to make sure Dixie is going to be safe. She's in there with Lars Ekberg." Again, Rachel turned back to her mission with her ear by the door.

"What!" Dixie's voice suddenly boomed from inside the Ocotillo room. "How can that be? Wait. Don't answer that. I don't want to use up my last question."

Rachel waited. Heather couldn't resist. She knelt down on the floor and put her ear near the door, too. Neither one of them could see Dixie, but they heard the anguish in her voice.

"Okay," Dixie said, getting herself under control. "There is stuff going on around here that I don't understand. Now you tell me that the movie will never get finished. I need to know what's happening, what's going to happen."

There was a long silence. Finally Ekberg spoke. "White Eagle says, 'The hand of evil is reaching for your heart. Danger is all around you. Beware of high places and the tree of death. And remember, a gift can be your poison.'"

Dixie sat frozen. "Wait! What do you mean? Will I die?"

Ekberg's eyes rolled back until the whites showed. "White Eagle says 'Only you can determine your destiny.' That is all." His head dropped down to his chest as if he lapsed into a coma.

Heather gasped and stared at Rachel wide-eyed. Frowning, Rachel let the door close and motioned to Heather to turn. "Let's get out of here," she whispered.

Anthony Pander gently called Dixie's name and motioned to her to exit the room. Dixie rose from the chair in a daze and then slowly made her way to the door.

Rachel dashed from the panty, wove her way through the kitchen, and arrived in the hallway before Dixie spotted her.

Dixie's mouth hung part-way open and the dazed look was still frozen on her face. Rachel ran to her and put her arms around her. "Let's go to my suite," she said. "You look like you could use a drink."

Neither woman spoke a word on the way to Rachel's casita. After Dixie was settled on the sofa, Rachel walked over to her with a shot glass in her hand. "Here," she said, handing Dixie the shot of tequila, "drink this." After Dixie swallowed it in one gulp, she reached for the glass of beer Rachel held out for her. Rachel uncapped a bottle of Corona for herself and poured it into a frosted glass, already salted, with a slice of lime on the rim.

"Are you going to be okay?" she asked, sitting next to Dixie on the sofa.

Dixie crumbled into the pillows. "Well, the jury's out on that one. But Lars did say Richard and I will not divorce. That's the first thing I asked."

"So maybe Richard is not having an affair with Tara, after all."

Dixie mulled that over. "I suppose there's a tiny chance you're right." She looked at Rachel out of the corner of her eye. "But it wouldn't hurt to pitch a fit about it regardless."

Rachel smiled. "I like your attitude."

"You develop a thick skin in order to survive in Hollywood." Dixie guzzled half the beer. "Ah...that tastes good."

"So, anything else you learned of any importance?" Rachel tried to appear nonchalant, glancing down at her watch. Ekberg's lecture was scheduled to start at seven-thirty.

"Oh, yeah. This was a doozey. White Eagle said we'd never finish *No Return.*

"No way!" Rachel realized that's where she came in when she started eavesdropping. "Did he say why?"

"Nope, and I didn't ask. By that time, I was so upset and confused I barely could think. I didn't want to waste my last question."

"So then what happened?" Rachel asked, pretending she hadn't overhead what White Eagle had told her.

"Well, Lars kind of cocked his head like he was listening to someone and then announced that White Eagle said something like the dark hand of death—no, the hand of evil—was after my heart and I need to beware of heights and poison trees. And a gift could be my poison, as if any of that makes any sense."

Rachel's forehead twisted into a frown. "That doesn't sound too good."

"No kidding. I'm not sure I really understand it, but it definitely wasn't happy news." Dixie gulped down the rest of the beer and wiped the back of her hand across her mouth. "I'll take another shot, if you got one."

Rachel went to the bar and poured another drink for Dixie and one for herself. When she sat back down Dixie said, "You know, Rachel, my Jewish grandmother once told me it was dangerous to contact spirits from the dead. She also said that the reason God told us not to go to fortune tellers was because he didn't *want* us to know the future."

"That's funny. My sister told me the same thing and she's not even Jewish."

"Yeah, well, now I understand why." Dixie slumped in the sofa and gazed at the glass in her hand. "I wish I'd never asked. I wish I could turn the clock back to when I first met you." She swallowed the shot.

"Oh, Dixie, maybe Lars is wrong. Heather says psychics are accurate only about fifty percent of the time."

"Humph," Dixie grunted. "Even fifty percent would be bad enough." She slapped her hand against her forehead. "I can't believe I did this to myself. I am a total idiot."

"Don't be so hard on yourself, Dixie." Rachel reached for her hand. "Did White Eagle say he was positive that everything would come to be?"

"Let me think a minute." Dixie lifted her head and gazed off. "Humm. I believe his exact words were 'Only you can determine your destiny. That is all.'"

"Well, see? That makes more sense. Even if someone is out to harm you, you don't have to be a victim. Be aware of your surroundings. Pay attention. White Eagle said that basically your future is entirely up to you."

A light clicked on in Dixie's mind. "Of course!" she exclaimed, straightening up. "We *can* control our own destinies! That's what the Church of Inner Light is all about." She turned to Rachel, excited now. "And you can help me."

"What?"

"You can help me! I need you to watch my back. Just a little bit. Just kind of be around."

Rachel felt herself pulling back. "Dixie, I—I have a job."

"You work twenty-four hours a day?"

"Well—no." Rachel had to admit to herself she was free to come and go pretty much as she pleased. She shared JT's secretary now and Heather was always willing to pinch hit for her.

"Please, please, please! Come with me tomorrow!" Dixie begged. I have to go up Blood Mountain for my part of the filming. It's a very high place and I need you to be there. Please?" Dixie turned her big, pleading eyes, heavily gooed-up with mascara, on Rachel.

Rachel's mind jumped around like popcorn. She'd never witnessed a filming of a Hollywood movie and wanted to go. But it would mean taking the morning off from work. Dixie was begging her. But she'd have to ask Heather to cover for her at work. And if JT found out she was getting involved in a mess like this, he would not be happy. What if he fired her? But what if Dixie's life was really in danger? What if something bad happened because she *didn't* go?

Rachel finally spoke, making a decision. "I'll be there."

℅℅℅

Puffy yellow blossoms from a sweet acacia tree fell on Rachel's shoulder. She brushed them off absentmindedly, looked up, and inhaled the tree's heady fragrance. She climbed the steps to her sister's suite, thinking of the Church of Inner Light meeting she and Dixie had just attended. *Dixie's getting sucked in deeper and deeper*, her inner voice scolded. *And it's your fault.*

When Heather opened the door, Rachel noticed JT right away, sitting in one of the living room chairs, and Buddy stretched out on the sofa. Buddy jerked himself up and patted the seat next to him for Rachel to sit down.

Uh-oh. Rachel's eyes roamed the room, suspecting something was up. She sat down cautiously, aware of tension, a feeling of apprehension, around her. "What happened?"

"Nothing happened," JT said. "Heather said you would be coming by and we wanted to meet with you. We just want to talk."

"I see." Rachel nodded, not at all convinced. "Is this about the thefts? I wondered why you never brought it up at the managers' meeting."

"No, it's not about the thefts," JT replied, looking troubled. "I didn't bring it up because of one thing: we have no idea who's stealing. It could even be one of the managers for all we know, although it kills me to think that. Other than us, Chef and Rosario, no one else knows. Word may leak out eventually, but I'd like to have a little time to try to flush out the guilty party."

"You think that will happen?"

"Maybe. Maybe not. But we can try. I've tightened up a few procedures, so that in itself may stop the bleeding. I'll bring you a memo outlining some of the changes we've implemented."

"Okay," Rachel said, still uneasy. "So what it is then? The new restaurant?" She looked around. Everyone's eyes were still on her. "Yes, I admit it," she added guiltily. "I did go downtown one day when Anna Venkman wasn't there. One of the workers let me in. But I made him promise not to tell."

JT looked amused, but Buddy looked surprised.

"Really?" Buddy asked. "They let you in? How was it?"

"French."

"What?"

"French. It's going to be a French restaurant. A *fancy* French restaurant. They were stapling a velvet fabric on the top half of the walls and I spotted a large rococo mirror still in the box."

"Oh, man." JT was looking down at the carpet shaking his head.

"Am I in trouble?"

Buddy smiled and shook his head. "No, Rachel, you are not in trouble." He squeezed her hand affectionately. "And that's not want we wanted to talk about."

"All right then, spit it out." She sat up straight. "I'm all ears."

"Actually, It's no big deal," Buddy said. "We just wanted to find out what was going on with Dixie Markman and the Inner Light group."

"Oh, so that's it." Rachel nodded warily and her eyes darted around at the others. "Any particular reason?"

JT and Buddy exchanged glances and JT cleared his throat. "Dewey Tucker stopped by today and he shared some information we thought you might want to know."

Rachel rolled her eyes. She suspected the deputy of being behind all the rumors that reached their ears. "So exactly what did our local gossip king have to say?"

"It appears that Dixie's husband and Tara Linley were necking out behind Blood Mountain when you and Dixie were at the Inner Light meeting."

Rachel's eyes widened. "Oh, boy. Not again." She wondered if there were any more mica lamps in storage.

"Heather told me about Ekberg's prophecy," JT said quietly.

Rachel shot Heather a look. "Do you have to tell him *everything*?"

"Look, Rachel," JT continued, ignoring the remark. "We're a little concerned things could get out of hand, that's all. Richard does have a history with young women. Very young women."

"What? Who told you that?" Rachel demanded.

"That's not important. What's important is that we want to avoid trouble. We're barely getting back to normal after last fall."

Rachel shuddered unconsciously, remembering the murders on their property.

"That's true," Buddy said, gently. "And you know we just got ourselves out of the red."

"What we're concerned with here," JT said, moving on, "is that it appears Dixie is getting her head filled with more than she needs of Ekberg's prophecies."

"Well, that's for sure. But there's nothing I can do about that." Rachel leaned back and tucked her legs under her, finally getting comfortable on the oversize sofa. "I tried to discourage her from going to tonight's meeting, but that didn't work."

Heather handed her a cold bottle of root beer.

Rachel took a thirsty gulp. "So what do you want me to do?" She glanced around at everyone. "If you guys have any ideas, let me know."

JT frowned and rubbed his hairline. "You and Dixie seem pretty tight."

"So? Okay. We hit off. She's a lot of fun, but I don't imagine I'll be running off after her when she heads back to Hollywood," Rachel drolled.

JT raised an eyebrow at her.

"Hey, give me more credit than that."

"Heather said you asked for the morning off tomorrow to go with the movie group."

"Oh, *that*..." Rachel said and related her conversation with Dixie, ending with her agreement to go up the mountain and watch the shoot. "If anything did happen to her, I'd never forgive myself if I didn't go," she added.

"You know, you going up there may be a good idea after all," Buddy said, pushing a clump of his hair back from his face, "when you consider the prophesy Ekberg made—"

"Oh, for Pete's sake, Buddy," JT said, jumping in, "you don't honestly believe all that stupid mumbo-jumbo, do you?"

"I don't know," Buddy conceded. "I never met Ekberg." He turned to Rachel, the mica lamp casting a golden glow on his face. "What do you honestly think of the guy?"

"Well, he's different," Rachel admitted, "but I like him. He's actually quite nice. He seems to be kind, sensitive, and intelligent to me. I can't really decide if he's a fake or not, if that's what you're asking." She took a quick sip of her root beer. "It's Anthony Pander that gives me the creeps."

"Who's Anthony Pander?" Buddy asked.

"He's like Ekberg's handler, I think, maybe his business manager. I also think he's, um, Ekberg's *partner*. I'm not really sure what he actually does, but I do have the feeling he's the one that's pushing this spiritual development they're starting up. And I definitely have a bad feeling about that."

"Spiritual development?" Heather asked. "What do you mean?"

Rachel waited a moment before she answered, making sure she had JT's full attention. "It actually came up for the first time tonight. It's something they're promoting called the *Island of Light*." Rachel reached down and pulled out a couple of packets from her bag. She handed them to Buddy and JT. "I picked these up off the table, thinking you might want to review them."

The two men began flipping through the *Island of Light* brochures and Heather stood behind JT to get a glimpse of his. Rachel caught a whiff of something flowery and glanced around the room for the scented candle that was probably burning. She spotted it next to the sink. *Carnations. Definitely carnations.*

Buddy looked up from the brochure and sought Rachel's eyes. "Pretty fancy place."

"Yeah, no kidding. You should have seen the actual presentation. A very glitzy video, professionally done, followed by a sales pitch from the soothing voice of Mr. Charm, himself, Anthony Pander."

"So they're selling condo units on a Caribbean Island?" Heather asked.

"Legally, maybe not. They are supposedly selling a lifetime membership in an all-encompassing spiritual village where you get a free place to live for the rest of your life. Kind of like those old hippy communes, remember? But in actuality, I suspect the answer to your question is, yes, because the price of the membership depends on the size of the condo. Regardless of the semantics, it's an interesting sideline for a so-called church, don't you think?"

"Hmm. Let me guess," JT said, frowning. "A half a million for a lifetime membership with a free condo?"

"That's only the studio. It's seven-fifty for a one bedroom. A cool million for a two-bedroom, which does not include the association fees." Rachel shook her head. "And you know what's worse? Dixie wants to buy one."

"You're kidding!" Heather exclaimed. "Not Dixie."

"Oh, yeah. She was ready to write out a check tonight for a deposit."

Buddy stared at JT. "This doesn't look good."

"Man, that's an understatement," JT said. He looked around at the others. "There could be a lot of money switching hands around here."

"Well, I did see a few people line up in front of Anthony Pander with checkbooks out," Rachel said, "but I have no idea if they were buying into the program. I can't believe people would fork over that kind of money without seeing what they're getting."

Buddy nodded. "That would be pretty stupid. But I've seen people throw away big money before. Too bad we don't have a copy of the contract." He flipped through the packet again. "There's no application form in here, either."

"I noticed that," JT concurred. "I doubt that anyone gets to see anything until they have a check in their hand."

"Oh, they take credit cards, too," Rachel added. "All kinds." She noticed the expressions on Buddy and JT's faces and her face fell. "I'm kind of getting a sick feeling here, guys."

"You're not the only one." Buddy looked at her and then turned his gaze to JT. "Man, I sure hope you're not thinking what I'm thinking."

"What?" JT asked. "That we're housing a couple of scam artists?"

Chapter 6

The next morning the air was cool, clean, and smelled like fresh laundry drying in the sun. "Come on people, it's just a bit farther," Richard urged, leading his troop up Boulder Trail.

"What's the big rush?" Dixie scowled. "You woke me up an hour early as it is. I'd just be getting out of bed right now." She eyed the nearest flat boulder and perched on it. She turned to the young man next to her and softened her eyes along with her voice. "Ferdie? I could really use an iced latte."

Ferdinand Lamont, a thin young man with a halo of black curls, responded instantly. "Of course, Ms. Markman. You must be exhausted." He set a cooler down next to her, produced a tall cup of pale-colored liquid, and hovered over her while she drank it.

Richard tried to hide his annoyance. "We're not making much progress, people. We need to suck it up and keep moving."

"Hey, we're way ahead of schedule," Dixie snapped. "Give the guys a break." She looked at the crew and motioned for them to sit. Six men, all toting gear or cameras, happily sat down on whatever rock looked most comfortable.

Richard's eyes blazed. Dixie was usurping his authority yet again. He opened his mouth to make a sharp retort, but nothing came out. He bit down on his lip, turned his head, and swallowed his anger. *It will all be over soon,* he thought to himself.

The sun was up two fingers over the mountains and he squinted at the view behind dark glasses. Visibility was at least twenty miles. He could see a ring of mountains on the horizon, and another ridge beyond that in a more faded shade of purple. It was a perfect day. He pictured the scene over in his mind again, the one where Dixie was tumbling backward over the cliff, her arms waving frantically. He felt a calm flow around him like a cool breath from the gods.

When he turned back to the group his emotions were under control and he was smiling. He told Ferdie to start working on Dixie while they rested. The young man grabbed his make-up case, mumbling something unintelligible under his breath.

"I'll have to touch her up after we get up there," Ferdie complained. "It could take even longer. I might have to completely re-do everything."

Richard seethed. Even the make-up man did not respect his position. Still, Richard kept his temper in check. He was going to need everyone's cooperation soon enough. "Okay, forget it," he said to the man, hoisting up the bag he carried. "Let's just go. Come on, people." He started up the trail and didn't look back.

ↄ✺ↄ

JT and Heather were digging into their stacks of blueberry pancakes when Rachel arrived at the corner booth for breakfast. She slid in beside them, poured herself some coffee, and sleepily stirred in some flavored cream.

The hostess walked over and handed Rachel a note. Rachel glanced at the signature. It was from Dixie.

"What is it?" Heather asked, crooking her neck, trying to see.

Rachel read the note and sat upright. She turned to her sister with a worried look. "Dixie says Richard is taking them up the mountain an hour early. She doesn't know why." She gulped some coffee, almost burning her mouth. "Sorry guys, I've got to go," she said, jumping out of the booth, now wide awake.

Rachel grabbed a couple bottles of water from the kitchen and ran to the Hummer. She drove the SUV as far up the trail as it would go and spotted the truck the movie group had rented. It was parked where the trail narrowed and the climb became difficult. Truck traffic was impossible.

She surveyed the area and thought a moment. She knew the group was headed to the overlook above the old landing strip and had a good lead on her. Rather than follow the trail on foot and lag behind, she decided to drive the Hummer north for a while, below the boulder field. With any luck she'd be able to turn west on the diagonal before she reached the old airfield and could climb the remaining part on foot. *It's worth a try,* she decided, and put the vehicle back in Drive.

She gripped the steering wheel tightly when the shiny black nose of the Hummer dipped down to the right. It immediately jumped up when the wheels clawed the gravel on the ridge. Then the left front wheel dropped into a wash. She proceeded at an angle up the steep terrain, with an incline too great to stop, until fifteen minutes later when she arrived at a hogback. From there the ground seemed to flatten out a bit.

It was slow-going and difficult, but Rachel eventually found herself adjacent to the old air strip before she finally abandoned her vehicle. It would be a hard trek up to the overlook, but at least it would be in her line of sight.

She struggled over a mound of boulders several minutes into her hike and she spotted the movie group. They all stood near the edge of the precipice which jutted out sixty feet above the old landing strip. Rachel stopped to catch her breath.

She viewed the scene in front of her. It played out in a kind of time warp, almost in a series of slides instead of real time, as Rachel watched Richard Markman move toward the ledge. He appeared to have everyone's complete attention as he waved his arm and pointed to the outcropping. He flung his arm back in a motion as if he were throwing something behind him. He repeated the action a few times and then Dixie moved toward him.

Mesmerized by the sight of the group perched near the edge of the cliff, all Rachel could think of was Ekberg's warning about "high places." She stood, paralyzed

with horror and unbelief as she saw Dixie approach the
ledge and step on the outcropping.

"Get back! Get back!" Rachel screamed and waved
her arms frantically.

A man with a halo of black curls burst from the
group and grabbed Dixie's arm. He yanked her forward,
causing her to tumble on top of him. Then Rachel heard
the unmistakable sound of the crack and felt the shudder
of the earth even from where she stood. *This can't be real,* Rachel thought, as she watched the rock ledge brake
free and hurl itself through space.

ↄ⌀ↄ

Rachel, Buddy, and Heather sat on the sofa in JT's
office. The door was closed and an aura of distress per-
meated the room.

Heather shook her head and looked down at her
hands nervously twisting in her lap. "This is terrible."

"I saw it with my own eyes and I still can't believe it
happened," Rachel said, reaching out to hold Heather's
hands. "It was like a dream."

Before Buddy could speak, JT stepped into the office. Everyone looked up at him.

"So what did Markman say?" Buddy asked.

JT pulled his chair out from behind his desk and
moved it over to the group. "Markman didn't seem to
think it was any big deal." He frowned. "That was actually more distressing than the chunk of rock breaking off
the cliff. Had I known where he was planning to film, I
would have—"

"I can't believe this! He could have killed his wife," Heather interrupted, outraged. "The man is totally stupid."

"Or not," Rachel added calmly.

Heather turned to her. "What do you mean?"

"I was just thinking about what Ekberg predicted. Maybe Markman is trying to *kill* Dixie. Maybe she does need to protect herself from him."

"You can't mean that."

"Just think about it. There would have been five witnesses to her "accidental" death. No jury would have ever convicted him of murder.

"Well, I don't think we'll have to worry about that now," JT interjected.

"What do you mean?" Rachel asked.

"I simply informed Markman I was reporting the incident to Deputy Tucker. I also warned him about how all the rocks and cliffs on Blood Mountain are unstable and could easily shift—and that he better *not* try a stunt like that again. I also gave him a letter saying exactly that and noted that I had faxed a copy of the letter to our liability insurance company.

Heather looked up at her husband. "Thank you, honey," she said, with relief in her voice. "That was pretty smart telling Deputy Tucker and faxing the insurance company. At least now Markman will be a lot more careful, if he continues with the production, that is."

"Oh, they'll definitely continue on with the production," Rachel said. "You know the old Hollywood saying, 'the show must go on.' Just because someone nearly got killed is no excuse to stop filming."

"That's true," Buddy said, gently placing his arm on Rachel's shoulder. "But in this case, I don't think Markman has any choice in the matter."

"What do you mean?"

"Money, Rachel. The guy's broke. He lost a bundle on his last film. Several million dollars. He needs to recoup on this one or he's bankrupt."

Rachel's eyes narrowed as she debated whether to believe him. "How would you know all that?"

"Sweetie pie, I know a lot of things about people in LA." Buddy gave her a teasing smile. "I'm in the money business."

〆〇〆〇

The evening was mild and windless, perfect for a party. Strings of tiny twinkling lights hung from the trees in the courtyard, mimicking lightning bugs on the prowl. Maintenance had placed hay bales around the fire pit and pool, with an occasional wagon wheel or hay fork propped up here and there. It was a decent attempt at an old west scene.

The custom-made grill was eight feet long and filled with mesquite wood burned down to glowing coals. Fragrant smoke drifted upward and a little toward the east. Mesquite logs that had been cut and dried from the grove behind the casitas sat stacked in a tall pile next to the grill, awaiting their turn in the fire.

Chef Henri held his hand over the grate to test the temperature. After counting the number of seconds before he needed to take his hand away, he packed the surface of the grill with as many T-Bones as it would hold.

"Everything going okay?" Rachel asked. She looked refreshed from sneaking in a quick nap that afternoon and wore skinny jeans, cowboy boots, and a satin western shirt the color of red apples.

"Everything's looking good, Miss Rachel, looking good, just like you." Henri smiled wide, flashing white teeth against skin the color of roasted coffee beans.

"Now, Henri," she teased, gently yanking one of his dreadlocks. "I'm going to give you an hour to stop that." After a quick glance around her to make sure no one was near enough to hear, she stepped in closer. "Any more news on Venkman's restaurant?"

"Only that they are going to call it "Domino's" and that they've installed huge crystal chandeliers and ornate woodwork. The windows are covered, but if you look close, you can see the black and white tile floor set on the diagonal."

"That doesn't sound good."

"Don't worry about it, Rachel. It's the food and service that sells the place. 'Commandant' Venkman can spend a fortune decorating, but if the food is lousy, no one will come back for a second taste."

"That's true," she agreed, and moved on. *But what if the food is good?* She walked past the salad and potato buffet, picked up a margarita from Rosario's bar, and took a large sip. "Everything, okay?" she asked the petite beauty.

"It's going great guns so far." Rosario cheerfully pointed her thumb at the tip jar.

Rachel stepped in closer and checked to make sure no one was within hearing distance. "How are you doing with the other problem?"

"Actually, I've made some progress," Rosario answered softly. "I think whoever stole the liquor did it on the same night every week."

"Really? That's interesting. Did they stop?"

"I don't know yet."

Rachel perked up and her eyes brightened. "So…what night was it?"

"Oh, no you don't, Rachel. I know better than that. My lips are sealed."

"What do you mean, Rosie? That's not fair."

"Sure it is. The minute I tell you, you'd be staking out the place," Rosario said, adding a grin. "But the truth is, I'm just not sure yet."

Rachel tilted her head and studied her friend. "Okay. But promise you'll tell me when you are sure."

"Only if you promise me you won't go poking around."

"Ah, you're too smart for me," Rachel teased and headed towards the sound of western music.

Handy Randy, the one man western band, was off to the right of the fire pit where several of the movie people were gathering. He was dressed in a long-sleeved western shirt, singing an oldie, and plunking out the tune on his banjo while recorded accompaniments spilled out of speakers on each side of him. Rachel gave him a wink and a wave.

She walked over to one of the empty hay bales and stood quietly, checking the crowd to make sure the guests were enjoying themselves while keeping an eye out for the Markmans.

Buddy, as usual, was standing in the center of a crowd, telling jokes with his Irish brogue. Rachel was amazed at his gift of charming people, and she envied him. She talked to a few guests who came near, then she slipped away from a couple of guys who tried to hit on her. Later she looked away, pretending she hadn't noticed when she saw a man offer the powder contents of a small green bottle to a woman he was leaning toward. No one appeared to remember Dixie was nearly killed that morning. Or if they did, they were celebrating her survival.

She finally noticed Richard Markman strolling over with Dixie hanging on his arm. Not only was she hanging on his arm, she was gazing up at him with big goo-goo eyes and a chirpy smile like a baby bird. Rachel felt sickened and turned her face away. When she looked back, she could see the Markmans heading toward the grill, no doubt lured by the smell of sizzling beefsteaks.

Richard and Dixie walked to the head of the line and a blonde woman, now in first place, gestured for them to go ahead of her. They did, as was their custom, but at least Dixie appeared to give the woman a polite smile and a thank you. Chef Henri offered them their choice of steaks and served them up on thick, white china plates. Following the Markman's lead, the rest of the party-goers filled their plates with steaks and the many choices from the salad and potato bar and sat at the tables around the pool. Flatware wrapped in red and blue bandannas decorated the checkered tablecloths. Old fashioned lanterns fitted with candles sat in the center of the tables and contributed a bit of homey nostalgia. *So far, so good*, Rachel thought.

After dinner, some of the guests filtered back over to the portable bar or headed for the Jacuzzi. Tara Linley, who was wearing cowboy boots, low-cut jeans, and a bikini top, stripped off the jeans and boots and jumped in the pool with the tiniest bikini bottom Rachel had ever seen. She was immediately followed by a few others and lots of laughing and splashing.

Markman steered Dixie over to the fire pit where a waitress was setting out bowls of marshmallows, graham crackers, and chocolate, and where mesquite logs were burning in a perfect combination of flame and glowing coals.

Now out of Tara's range of vision, Markman started making an obvious effort to shower Dixie with attention and affection. At least, Rachel thought so and wondered if anyone else noticed the charade. She looked around. Apparently not.

Rachel had purchased a supply of long toasting forks with wooden handles and had set them out earlier in tall buckets by the fire. But instead of pulling one of them out the bucket, Markman lowered himself onto a hay bale and picked up a long stick lying on the ground behind him. He placed it on his lap and carefully threaded two puffy marshmallows onto it. Dixie came to share the hay bale with him and he gave her a quick kiss while Rachel casually slipped in unnoticed behind them.

Markman toasted the marshmallows over some red coals near the edge of the fire. He lifted up the stick to show his wife. "See, precious? Barely toasted, exactly the way you like them."

Rachel stared at the stick and the words "poison tree" from White Eagle's warning suddenly popped into her head. Without thinking, she lunged for the hot marshmallows, grabbed them off the stick, threw them into the fire and then yelled a colorful epithet as she waved her hands furiously in the air to cool her fingers.

Richard stared at her in disbelief. "Security!" he shouted. "Get this woman away from me."

Toro rushed over and screeched to a stop. Rachel snatched the stick from Richard's hand and thrust it at Toro. "Toro, what kind of twig is this?" she asked.

The attention of everyone nearby turned to the huge man with dark, weathered skin and lengthy scar running down one side of his face. He brought the stick to his nose, smelled it, and examined closely it with his eyes. "It's a fresh oleander twig, Miss Rachel. There's still enough poison in it to kill everyone at this party."

Some of the guests gasped. Rachel stared at Markman expectantly, hoping for an explanation, or at the very least, vindication. But Richard simply glared at Rachel with such hatred, she shuddered.

"Come on, sweetheart," he finally said to Dixie, venom dripping from his lips, and grabbed her hand. "Let's get out of here." Dixie allowed herself to be tugged along, looking back at Rachel with an apologetic expression.

Rachel stood rooted to the ground, staring at Dixie in disbelief while she disappeared into the crowd. Partygoers awkwardly slithered away one by one. *What just happened? Did I somehow step into an alternate universe?*

"You all right, Rachel?"

Rachel turned to see Buddy approaching her. Her face contorted like she was trying desperately to say something, but she couldn't speak.

"Hey," he said, smiling and patting her shoulder reassuringly. "No good deed goes unpunished."

Rachel was in no mood to be consoled. "I'd like to kill him," she said in a poisonous calm. "I'd like to make that rotten scumbag suffer in such a way he'd wish for an eternity in Hell instead."

A couple, one of the last to drift away, jerked their heads and stared at her. She looked back at them, her eyes glaring like poison arrows.

"And her," Rachel continued, raising her voice, "the psycho-psychotic from hell. I'm done with her. I'm done, done, done!"

She stamped her foot, swung her arms, and continued ranting. Buddy waited calmly, watching the crowd dissipate until she was spent. Finally, Rachel heaved a sigh, let her shoulders droop and turned to him. "Okay. It's over. So what do you think?"

Buddy's eyes teased. "Me thinks, me love, rumors of your Irish temper are grossly understated."

Rachel tried to suppress a smile. "That's not what I meant."

"I know, but it was such a great show, I couldn't help but comment. It made me realize it was a good idea that we made all the employees sign privacy agreements 'cause you'd make one heck of an enemy. Of course, you could probably make some big bucks selling your inside scoop of the stars to one of those trashy magazines Heather—"

"Oh, shut up, Buddy," she said, linking her arm through his, "and take me home."

"On the other hand," he continued on as if he hadn't heard her, grinning widely as he walked her out, "if you'd give me a little advance notice of your next eruption, I could sell tickets and we could probably make as much money as—"

"I mean it, Buddy," she snapped, but ended up laughing at the expression on his face. "I give up," she finally said, shaking her head. "I may be a little crazy, but you're incorrigible.

☾☽

The next morning JT answered the early knock on his door. "Uh-oh," he said at the sight of his visitor.

"Uh-oh? That's a fine way to greet an old friend." Buddy walked past JT who was still holding the door. "Why is it uh-oh, and not top o' the mornin' to ya?"

"Why?" JT asked, an exaggerated look of bewilderment on his face. He walked over to the coffee pot, ignoring Buddy. "Let me think a minute…It's five-thirty in the morning and you never get up until nine. That's one reason. Two is that I've got ESP like our fine friend in 311." He grabbed two mugs from the cupboard and set them down.

Heather called from the bedroom: "JT, who is it?"

"It's your ugly friend with bad news."

"I'll be right out."

Buddy, Heather, and JT sat around the table sipping coffee. No one was saying a whole lot, although Buddy's rendition of the western party had brought a mask of worry to Heather's face.

JT's elbow was propped up on the table. Head in hand, he nervously rubbed his hairline while watching his coffee turn cold.

"You *will* lose that hair, you know, if you keep rubbing on it," Buddy cautioned.

"Ha! You'll be bald before this baby recedes an inch. Ever take a look at my Dad?" JT smirked. "Seventy-five years old and still has every hair on his head."

Heather broke in: "Okay, macho men, this isn't fixing our problem."

"Yeah. Now tell me again what our problem is," Buddy said.

"Rachel had a meltdown at the party?" Heather asked.

"No, that would be too simple," JT said. "Not that it makes us look good by having our director of sales stomp around and scream near-obscenities about our famous guests. I think our real problem is that Rachel is much too involved in the lives of Richard and Dixie Markman and we need to get her to back off."

Heather rested her hand on JT's arm. "But don't forget, sweetie, Dixie would be dead right now if Rachel hadn't thrown those marshmallows in the fire. How would *that* make our hotel look?"

"True," JT agreed, "but you have to consider the possibility that it was an accident."

"Make that *two* accidents," Buddy added. "Remember the tumbling rock? Not to mention the fact that dead is dead, regardless of why it happens."

"Exactly my point," Heather said. "And what about Ekberg's prophecy that someone is out to kill Dixie? It's beginning to look that way, doesn't it?"

JT grunted. "From what I've been hearing, I say let him have at it."

"Don't say that," Heather scolded.

"Yeah, JT," Buddy said, lightly punching him on the shoulder. "We've already had two murders here. How will one more look? Even if she *does* deserve it?"

"Okay, okay." JT raised his eyes to the ceiling. "I guess we've verbally abused the poor woman enough. We need to figure out what to do about Rachel."

Buddy and Heather looked at him expectantly.

"What choice do we have? We either wait three more days until they all leave, or we can tie Rachel up in her room and gag her."

"Well, Rachel did say she was totally done with Dixie." Buddy looked hopeful. "So maybe the whole thing will fizzle out by itself."

JT looked up again. "I don't think we could be that lucky."

෬ඨ෬

Later that morning, a burly man in flashy western clothes walked into Rachel's office.

"Oh no," Rachel cried. She looked up at the entertainer who had worked the western party. "I forgot to pay you, Randy."

"Hey, no problem. I know where you work." Randy grinned at her and plunked himself down in the chair in front of her desk. "And considering what happened last night, I'm not at all surprised you overlooked the check."

Rachel grimaced in embarrassment. "That was quite a display of temper, wasn't it?"

"Can't say I blame you. I saw the whole thing. I wanted to slam my fist in Markman's face myself. But I kind of felt the need to cover for you and keep on playing."

"And I thank you for that. I don't think my little tantrum had that big of an audience, anyway.

"Nah. Only about forty, fifty people." Randy grinned again, displaying a beautifully matched set of whitened teeth.

"Gee, thanks." Rachel slumped in her chair. "Well, I hope the audience remembers Richard Markman almost killed his wife, accidentally or not." She looked down at her desk and moved some papers around. "I know I've got your check around here, somewhere...ah, here." She handed it to him. "You really did a nice job, Randy. Thank you."

"Thank *you,* Rachel. Actually, I was surprised to see they were still together." He leaned in to take the check, folded it, and put in his shirt pocket.

"Who? You mean the Markmans?

"Yeah. I thought they split up a long time ago."

"Really? What makes you say that?"

Randy stood up. "Oh, nothing."

"Don't say 'Oh, nothing.' It was obviously something or you wouldn't have said anything to begin with."

Randy scratched the close-cropped beard on his cheek. "I just knew them, way back when."

"Way back when, *when*?"

"Back before Miss Dixie was a big star."

Rachel looked at him intently.

He shrugged and looked away. "We—you know—partied together."

Rachel was surprised. "You partied together? Weren't you a little young to hang out with them?"

"Yeah. But don't you know? They both like them young. Always did."

"What?" Rachel half way rose up from her chair. "Are you serious? Are you talking about Dixie?"

"Aw, Rachel, where you been?" Randy shook his head. "Everybody knows about Dixie.

"I don't." Rachel felt stung. "Tell me you're joking."

"I'm not joking, Rachel." Randy shook his head. "I know one of the special effects people real well. He and I shared an apartment about five, six years ago. He told me Dixie still has quite the appetite, and not just for marshmallows."

Rachel sat stunned as Randy flashed his big white smile at her. "Later," he said with a wave, as he drifted out the door. "Call me anytime."

Rachel watched him leave but could only stare at the open door. How could this be true? She really liked Dixie; she had felt that *bond* with her. Now this? *Could I really be that naive?* She needed some coffee. A lot of it. She needed to think.

Wanting to rid herself of the bad feeling Randy left her with, she hurried out of the office and over to the Hibiscus Café. After chatting briefly with a few of the patrons, she poured herself a mug of the house blend, grabbed a muffin, and headed back to work in a little better mood.

Crossing the lobby, caffeine in hand, she looked ahead and noticed Dixie standing in front of her office with a hang-dog look about her. After a less than enthusiastic greeting, Rachel unlocked her door. Dixie skulked into the office behind her and sank into the overstuffed chair.

"Oh, Rachel, I'm so sorry about last night," she whined, the soft chair nearly swallowing her up. "And yesterday morning, too. Richard can be such a jerk at times."

"Ya think?" Rachel said, angrily turning her face away. "But what I can't figure out is why you put up with him." A thought flashed into her mind about how Dixie might manage, but she set that aside.

Dixie hung her head, looking guilty. "I know, I know," she muttered. "Sometimes I think I must be totally stupid. But in spite of everything, I'm still madly in love with Richard. And I know he loves me. He needs me."

"Oh, that's just great. He needs you. But what about him needing to drop you off the cliff?"

Dixie looked shocked. "Richard had no idea that rock was loose. You saw how horrible he felt when the rock fell over."

Rachel's mouth dropped open and she stared at the woman in disbelief. "Okay, but what about the oleander twig? He sure didn't feel horrible about trying to poison you."

"Richard told me he found it by the hay bale," Dixie entreated. "He said he thought someone left it there to toast marshmallows with. He had no idea it was an oleander twig."

"Oh, boy." Rachel pressed her thumb against her lips to keep herself from speaking. *Was Dixie blind to her husband's flaws? No, no. Co-dependency was the better choice of words.* Rachel kept thinking. *Or maybe Dixie is just nuts, plain and simple.* Perhaps it was time for her to end her friendship with Dixie, especially in view of what

Randy had told her. Even if just a *little* of what Randy had said was true.

"Rachel?" Dixie was watching her intently, looking lost.

Rachel blinked and came back. "So what about White Eagle's Prophecies?" she asked, deciding to change subjects.

"Oh, I just don't know," Dixie said, shrugging her shoulders. "Richard said it was a bunch of bunk. But he still thinks I ought to buy the membership."

Rachel squinted at Dixie. "You mean *I* as in *your* money?"

"Well, yes—" Dixie hesitated. "You see, right now most of Richard's money is tied up in this new movie we're making. But as soon as it's released and starts paying off, we'll pay off the condo. In the meantime, we'll both buy additional life insurance to cover the purchase price in case something hap—"

"Stop." Rachel held up her hand, wondering if any human being could possibly be that stupid. "Dixie, do you have any proof this place even exists? Anybody can make up a brochure and take photographs. These guys aren't even real estate agents. This could be a total scam."

Dixie's eyes popped open.

"Yeah, Dixie. People get sucked into stuff like this every day. Don't do this. At least let me check it out first." Yes, Rachel thought. This island of light thing really needed looking into—and right now. "What if it really *is* a scam?"

Dixie's eyes darted around the office, rested on the antique clock on the wall, darted around some more, and finally stopped on Rachel. "So how are you planning on doing that?"

Rachel propped her elbows up on the desk, rested her face on her hands, and thought a few moments. When she lifted her head, her eyes sparkled. "I just figured it out. Come knock on my door at eight o' clock tonight."

Chapter 7

Buddy angled his BMW into a parking place in front of the old Henley building and peered out at the short, wrought-iron fence that enclosed part of the sidewalk. "What do you think, JT?" he said, "It looks like Miss Venkman is planning to have an outside café."

JT had been staring at the large black and white sign centered over the tall double doors that said "Domino's." His eyes dropped to the embellished fence. "You're right. Unfortunately, it's a great idea. I would have done it myself."

"Shall we take a look?" Buddy popped open the car door and stepped out.

The two men sauntered across the sidewalk, unlatched the gate, and stepped into the wide entry. "Pretty nice, so far," JT muttered. He walked up to door where the sunset had turned the glass inserts to gold. Part of the brown construction paper had fallen away from the window and JT pressed his nose up to the glass.

The evening light was fading behind JT, and a couple of bare bulbs illuminated the interior enough so that he could see most of the layout.

"I heard they put in some really fancy crystal chandeliers," Buddy said, waiting for his turn.

JT finally pulled away with a frown on his face. "Take a look."

Buddy whistled when his eyes scanned the interior of the two-story room, first noticing the dazzling chandeliers that hung on long chains from the ceiling. "Man, they dumped some big bucks into this joint." His eyes rested on a larger-than-life figure of a court jester positioned near the entry. The jester wore a diamond-patterned, black and white costume with pointed cap to match. "I wonder if the dude is going to double as a body-guard," he joked, and then pulled away from the glass.

"Did you notice the antiques?" he asked, turning back to JT.

"Yeah, I noticed. They're reproductions, but they look pretty good. I noticed the tile floors, too. From what I could see, they looked like marble." He started to walk towards the car and turned back. "You coming?"

Buddy had taken another peek. "I was checking to see if there were any meeting rooms."

"I couldn't see any, but I'm willing to bet they have two or three."

"It doesn't bode well for us, does it," Buddy remarked, coming along side of him.

"No, it doesn't. If their food and service are good and they don't gouge the customers, they could really hurt us."

"But why? Why would they dump that kind of money into a restaurant? They could do it a whole lot cheaper and still make a really nice place out of it."

JT opened the car door and slid inside. "I've been thinking about that."

"And?" Buddy asked, turning the key in the ignition.

"Well, it's obvious the Venkman's—what's left of them, anyway—hate our guts. I can't help but wonder if it isn't like a personal vendetta—you know, like deliberately trying to show us up. In addition to taking our customers away, that is."

"Do you think they could do that? Take some of our loyal customers?"

"Not only *could* they, but unless the place is overrun with cockroaches the opening day, they *will.*"

Buddy grinned at him. "Did I ever tell you I used to collect bugs as a kid?"

JT sternly pointed his finger at his partner. "Don't even think about it, kid. Just get us out of here. We've got work to do."

❧❧❧

"Where are you taking me?" Dixie asked. She and Rachel plodded up the hill just west of the casitas, leaving the lights of the hotel behind. Darkness enveloped them from the knees up, but solar lights illuminated their path of steppingstones and gravel.

"You'll see," Rachel answered. "But don't worry, you'll be safe."

In a matter of minutes they stood in front of a thirty-five-foot travel trailer and Rachel knocked on the door. "This is Chef Henri's temporary housing," she whispered. "We're dealing with a little overbooking problem this month."

Dixie nodded her head knowingly. The door opened and a small, wiry man grinned at them. "Good evening, ladies. Welcome to my palace."

Rachel made the introductions. Henri clasped Dixie's hand and kissed the back of it. "Ooo, Ms. Dixie, I am such a big fan of yours. You were amazing in *Forever Love.*"

"Why, thank you, Henri, I'm a fan of yours too," Dixie said coyly, her heavily mascara-coated lashes blinking rapidly. "You do the most amazing things with food. I've gained almost a half-pound since I've been here."

"May we sit down?" Rachel asked, interrupting the mutual-admiration-society meeting.

"Of course," Henri said, extending his arm towards the sofa.

"Here's the deal, Henri," Rachel said, opening up the *Island of Light* folder. "These condos are selling for a half-million and up and we don't know for sure if they even exist."

Henri took the folder and turned past the parchment paper to a full glossy map of the Greater Antilles. Bright turquoise-colored ocean surrounded the islands, and a box showing an enlarged map of Jamaica was superimposed on the bottom right-hand corner. A bright red star was planted on the east end of Jamaica with a rainbow colored arc shooting out from it. Imprinted on the rainbow were the words *Island of Light*.

Henri studied the maps and his forehead knitted itself into a frown. "Okay," he said, looking at Dixie. "This star here," he said placing his finger on it, "this is your *Island of Light*?"

"Yes, it is," Dixie nodded.

Henri's mouth drooped and he bit on his lower lip.

"Is that a problem?" Dixie asked.

"Well, here's Port Morant, where I used to live," he said, pointing to an area west of the star. "It would be your closest city. It's near the coast, three or four miles as the crow flies, but if you could see the map in more detail, you'd see there aren't many roads. You'd have to go the long way around. It would take a while."

Dixie shrugged. "Well, the whole idea is that we'd have an island all to ourselves. We wouldn't need to go off it very often."

Henri exhaled through pursed lips. "The problem is…there is no island there. It's a peninsula."

Dixie thought a minute. "Okay, I can accept that. Island, peninsula, it doesn't matter, really. It's going to be a private, luxurious, spiritual sanctuary complete with library, shops, and entertainment. I'm sure they'll simply wall off the part connected to the main island."

Henri nodded. "Okay. All this area around here," he said, pointing, "I've been there. My cousins and I used to surf there. We'd take the boat to the lighthouse and mess around. It's quite pretty."

Dixie looked at him. "But?"

"But the land's been government owned as long as I've known about it. Nobody even lives near the area any more. Hurricane Ivan and Dean saw to that."

Dixie's expression changed to one of dismay.

"I'm sorry," he said.

"But maybe they bought the land in the last—whenever—since you've been living in the states."

"Yes," Henri said. "I suppose that's possible. But what about water? Look at these drawings, Ms. Dixie. These pools, these fountains, these waterfalls. All of these apartments here. They'll require lots of water to build and maintain."

"And you're saying there is no source of fresh water there?" Rachel asked.

Henri nodded sadly. "That's what I'm saying. I've been there many times with family. We'd take whatever water we needed with us. Food, too."

Dixie dropped her head and breathed a loud moan. "So we've been scammed?"

"I don't honestly know." Henri shrugged. "Maybe someone has come up with a way to bring water over there. Give me a minute to see what I can find on the satellite map." He rose to his feet. "Would you ladies please excuse me while I check my computer?"

Rachel and Dixie waited, listening to him singing along with the reggae music coming from the other room. In a couple of minutes he was back.

"Well, ladies, I don't have good news." Henri handed Dixie a close-up map of the area. It was covered with trees. "There is no indication of any building going on in the whole area. If anyone built the condominium in the last six months, the one that's in the photograph you showed me, you'd see a large open space and a building instead of all these trees."

Rachel looked at the map. The coast was lovely, with a wide strip of beach following the curves of the peninsula, and it, too, was devoid of anything except the two government buildings and the lighthouse, which were far from recent additions.

"I e-mailed my cousin," Henri said. "I asked him if he'd check around and let me know if anyone was developing anything over there."

"Oh, Henri, you didn't have to ask your cousin go through all that trouble," Dixie said, her face drooping. "I think I've heard enough to drop the whole thing."

"But Dixie, you don't understand," Rachel said. "If Lars Ekberg and Anthony Pander are setting up some kind of scam, and we're talking millions of dollars here, lots of people could be hurt. We need to call the police and maybe the FBI."

ℰↄℰↄ

Dixie ambled up the stairs to her suite, disheartened about the *Island of Light,* hoping Richard would be there. She opened the door to a candlelit room.

"Hi, baby," Richard said. He glided over and swept her up in his arms.

Dixie, her mind still on her meeting with Chef Henri, broke away from him. "Richard, I—I think that Island of Light deal is a hoax. A scam."

Richard stood back and considered her. "So what, precious? We didn't put any money in it. Just forget about it. I only agreed to buy the condo because I thought

it would make *you* happy." He took her hand and led her
to the sofa. "Look, darling. I made us a snack. Luscious
fruit, raw nuts, and your favorite cheeses."

Dixie's face lit up as relief flooded over her. He
wasn't angry. He even seemed happy. "Why, Richard—
how sweet of you." She noted the artfully-arranged plate
looked like the work of Chef Henri, but Dixie tactfully
ignored the thought. She whirled about, finally noticing
the room. "And candlelight?" she said. "And champagne?
Dom Perignon? Wow. What's the occasion?"

"No occasion, precious," he said, bringing her fingertips to his lips for a lingering kiss. "I know things have
been a bit rough with us lately, and I thought maybe we
could enjoy a quiet evening together, just the two of us.
When I got home I found your friend sent some champagne over."

"Really? Who?" Dixie studied the tray with the
champagne and the milk glass flutes. She picked up the
little card. "Best of luck with your new production," it
read, signed by Andre Bouchard.

"Andre Bouchard?" Dixie frowned and read the card
again. "I don't recall knowing any Andre Bouchard. Isn't
he your friend?"

It was Richard's turn to be puzzled. He shook his
head. "The only Andre I know is Andre Lamoreaux and I
hardly know him. I don't know a single Bouchard."

Richard and Dixie sat on the sofa, staring at the bottle as if trying to divine the image of Andre Bouchard.
Finally, Richard spoke. "You know, precious, I don't really care who sent the bottle. I just want to celebrate with
the most beautiful woman in the world." He gave his wife
a deep, meaningful smile and pulled the bottle out of the

ice. After wiping it with the towel he popped the cork. He poured champagne into each glass, never taking his eyes off her, while Dixie sliced a piece of Brie off a wedge and coyly looked up at him. The anxiety she felt after finding out about the Island of Light had completely dissipated.

"Here's to us," Richard said raising his glass, his eyes brimming with love for her, "forever and ever."

"Here's to us," Dixie repeated, "forever—"

"Wait," Richard blurted. "I almost forgot." He put his glass down and hurried to the bedroom.

Dixie dropped the cheese in her mouth and looked down at the glass in her hand. White Eagle's words suddenly came back to her. *A gift can be your poison.* A sudden surge of panic rose from her chest. *No, no. It couldn't be. Lars is a fraud.* She stared at the glasses. *Could the wine be poisoned? What should I do?*

"I'll be right there, precious," Richard's voice, muffled, called from inside the large walk-in closet.

Dixie looked down at the tray again. She quickly switched the position of the glasses.

Markman came back into the room. "I bought this for you before we left and wanted to wait for a special moment." He held out his arm and opened his palm to her. "This is the moment."

Dixie gasped with delight and fixed her eyes on the green velvet box.

"Here, open it."

She took the box with a twinge of guilt, and flipped it open. "Oh, Richard—it's just beautiful," she said, as she gazed at the ring inside.

"I thought emeralds would look good on you. I know how beautiful you look in green."

"I—I don't know what to say. It's the most beautiful ring I've ever seen." Tears of joy and guilt overwhelmed her. She stared at the three one-carat stones set in a gold band, finally slipping the ring out of the box and onto her finger. "It must have cost a fortune." She raised her eyes to her husband in adoration.

He beamed. "So what? Money is nothing, baby. You know I could live with you in a shack and be happy." He leaned over and planted a soft, tender kiss on her lips. Satisfied with himself, he sat opposite her and raised the wineglass in front of him. "To us, forever and ever."

Dixie lifted her glass and touched it to his. "To us, forever and ever." She slowly brought the glass to her mouth. Her lips and tongue burned at the touch of it and she instantly jerked her hand back, spilling some of the drink onto her lap. She shot a look at her husband. His eyes were popping out of his head and his mouth was open in a scream like in a silent movie.

Richard ran to the kitchenette as a warbled cry came out of his mouth. He turned on the water, full blast, and stuck his mouth under the faucet.

Dixie jumped up, her lips on fire. She ran to the bathroom, flooded her mouth with water and ran back out to check on her husband. Richard was holding up his cell phone with one hand and clutching his neck with the other, screaming the muffled cries of a wounded animal.

Dixie grabbed the phone as 911 answered. Richard bent over the sink and thrust his face back under the faucet, his body contorting with pain.

"Help us! Help us! Hurry!" Dixie cried into the phone. "We've been poisoned!"

Rachel heard the sirens scream their way to the parking lot and leaped up. She was already out the door when the ambulance and fire truck pulled up in front of the Markman's and she ran ahead of the emergency crew.

Dixie screamed at her from the landing, her arms waving wildly about her. "Someone's poisoned us!"

Rachel ran into the room in time to see Markman lift his face up from the sink. His hands clutched at his throat and the lower part of his face, which were now swollen to twice their normal size. His face was contorted with pain as he struggled to breathe, but only a hissing sound escaped his lips.

The two EMTs burst into the room behind Rachel and rushed toward Markman just as the injured man crumpled to the floor.

Rachel pulled Dixie out the door, away from the scene, while Deputy Dewey Tucker climbed up the stairs towards them. "Here's the deputy," Rachel cried, hoping to distract Dixie from the activity inside.

Upon reaching the landing, the deputy hiked up his pants to cover his overhanging belly and took a moment to catch his breath while Rachel quickly introduced them. Dixie, with tears spilling down her face, sputtered out what had happened. The three of them stood on the landing while Tucker shifted his attention back and forth between Dixie and the action taking place in the living room. Finally, when Dixie was finished, the deputy cocked his head toward the room, indicating they should enter.

Markman lay on the sofa with an IV hooked up to his arm and a dose of morphine surging through his blood. An oxygen tube was attached to his nose.

The emergency technicians left to get the rest of their equipment. Dixie rushed to Markman's side and clung to him, whimpering. The techs quickly returned and pried Dixie away from Markman, who was now lying still with his eyes closed, his brain floating about in happy-land as the morphine traveled through his body. The two EMTs moved him onto the stretcher in one sure move and strapped him in.

Rachel wondered if it was a state of shock or the morphine that rendered Markman quiet, but whatever it was quickly wore off when Dixie threw herself at the gurney, sobbing hysterically. Markman's eyelids snapped open and he stared at his wife. Then his eyes flashed wildly around the room as if in a panic. Tucker pulled her away and sat her down on the sofa so the EMTs could take Richard down to the ambulance.

"You can see him in a little while," Tucker said, a little too harshly. "Right now he needs treatment and we need to get to the bottom of what's going on here."

Rachel sat down beside Dixie and gently took her hand hoping to comfort her, completely forgetting about Dixie's past and bizarre behavior. The deputy went over to the coffee table and studied the tray. He pulled a pair of latex gloves and a plastic bag out of his pocket and put the gloves on. Carefully lifting the bottle of Dom by the very bottom, he looked at it from all angles. He brought it slowly to his nose and smelled it.

Tucker went back to studying the table. "You make this cheese tray?"

"No," Dixie answered. "Richard said he did. But I kind of wondered if he didn't have the chef make it."

"I can call Chef Henri right now and find out," Rachel offered.

"Go ahead. I'll need to talk to him later, though."

The deputy toddled around the room, studying everything. He pulled a pen and a little notebook out of his pocket and turned abruptly towards a whimpering Dixie. "You touch both glasses?"

Dixie jumped at the sound of his voice. "N—no," she stammered, dabbing at her eyes, which were now ringed with raccoon makeup and staring at the big man who pointed his finger at her.

The deputy picked up one of the flutes. It was white and became translucent when Tucker held it up to the light. "Ya know we're gonna have these glasses checked for prints. Be a shame if your prints came back on both of 'em."

Dixie's mouth dropped opened a little and her eyes darted around the room like a scared puppy looking for a way to escape. "Well, actually, I think I did touch both of them."

"You think you did touch both of them," Dewey repeated. He waited. He took a few more steps around the room and spun around to face her. "Why?" his voice boomed out at her.

Dixie jumped again.

Rachel overhead the last of the deputy's dramatics as she entered the room. *I don't believe anyone could be this ignorant.* Glaring at Tucker, she sat beside Dixie and reached for her hand.

"What'd you find out?" Tucker asked Rachel, his voice modulated.

"Chef Henri made up the cheese plate," Rachel replied in a civil tone, holding her annoyance with Tucker in check. "Richard requested it earlier in the day, specifying which cheeses he wanted. Chef sent Benny Ammato out with the order. He said when Benny got back he told Chef he saw the bottle and glasses already on the table, and set the cheese plate beside them. He made a point of it because he knew the wine was super-expensive and never had seen a bottle of it before. He also mentioned seeing the milk glass flutes, knowing we use only clear ones."

"Humph," Tucker grunted. He crossed his arms over his chest, and tugged at his mustache. "You eat the cheese?" he asked Dixie.

"Yes, sir. One bite of brie."

The deputy eyed the plate of cheese and fruit. He picked up a chunk of cheese, smelled it, and plopped it in his mouth. "Well, it ain't been poisoned."

"I already knew that," Dixie said, tiring of his antics. "It was the champagne that burned my mouth."

Rachel focused on Dixie's mouth. It was swollen, and a blister was forming on her bottom lip. "Your lip looks sore. Let me get you some ice." She rose and went to the kitchenette. If nothing else, the trip made her feel useful.

"Now let's get back to the wine glasses, Ms. Markman," Tucker said. "You said you did touch both glasses. Now, why was that?"

Dixie lowered her eyes. "Well, actually, I switched them. I changed my glass for Richard's glass."

Rachel stopped mid-step. She looked at Dixie and Tucker caught the look. Rachel continued on and gave Dixie a towel containing a couple ice cubes which Dixie promptly placed on her lip.

"And why did you feel the need to switch glasses, Ms. Markman?" Tucker continued.

Dixie dropped her eyes. "I, um, I was afraid of the wine. You see, Lars Ekberg prophesied that a gift I'd get would be poison, so I switched glasses. He was right about the rock on the cliff and the poisoned wood, so I thought, well maybe, the wine was poisoned."

"Lars Ekberg, huh? We'll get back to him later. So you say you switched glasses, thinkin' you'd give your husband the poisoned wine?"

"No! No, not exactly. You see, Rachel thought Richard was trying to kill me, and so I wondered if…well, I thought maybe I should switch glasses just in case he did, even though I know he never would, uh, put poison in the wine to try to kill me."

Dewey eyed the two women sitting next to each other. He didn't know that much about Ms. Markman, but he had a history of dealing with Rachel and suspected at this point he was looking at Rachel and her intellectual clone.

"But you saw him open the bottle."

"Yes, I did. But I also saw a movie once where someone injected poison right through the cork with an insulin needle."

Tucker turned around so the women couldn't see his look of incredulity. He grabbed another chunk of cheese, this time with a cracker, and tossed the whole thing in his mouth.

"Um, Deputy?" Rachel's voice was hesitant. "I tried to call Becky Beeman to see if maybe one of her girls delivered the wine. Sometimes they do it if the bell staff isn't available. But Becky didn't answer her phone. So would it be okay if I run over and check with her in person?"

Tucker gave Rachel a look of surprise. "That's actually a good idea, Miss Ryan. And if she knows, let me know. I'll be here for a while. I think I'm gonna need to hear this story all over from the very beginning."

୧୬୧

Becky's white aluminum-clad trailer sat among five other units on the hotel's property that had been tennis courts in a former life. Rachel rushed up to the door and knocked. No answer. She knocked again. Still, no response. A door popped open at the trailer in the next space, and Chef Henri stepped out on the metal stair. "She's not there, Rachel."

"Oh, Henri. I hope I didn't disturb you. I need to talk with Becky."

"No, I'm fine," he said, stepping down. "What's going on? Does it have something to do with the cheese tray you called about?"

"Yes and no." Rachel moved toward him. "Somebody tried to poison Richard and Dixie Markman."

Henri's eyes got huge. "What? You've got to be kidding." He studied her face. "Please tell me it wasn't my cheese."

"It wasn't. It wasn't that kind of poisoning, anyway. Something burned Richard's mouth and throat pretty badly, some kind of chemical."

Henri grabbed a handful of his dreadlocks. "This is horrible. Are you *sure* it wasn't my food? The new restaurant would jump on a story like that. I'd be ruined."

"I'm sure. It had nothing to do with our food." Rachel touched Henri's arm in reassurance. "Deputy Tucker was happily chomping away at the cheese when I left. In fact, the culprit appears to be the bottle of Dom Perignon. I called the bellmen, but neither of them admitted to delivering it. That's why I need to see Becky."

Henri glanced around the area. "She'll be back, I'm sure. I've seen her go out this time of night before. She takes a flashlight and walks up the hill."

Rachel tossed back strands of hair away from her face. "She does? At night? When it's windy?"

"Same as I thought. But it's not really my business." Henri looked past her. "Here she comes now. You can ask her yourself."

Becky shut off her flashlight, strode over to her trailer. She was wearing jeans and boots and her hair was in rollers under a multi-colored scarf.

"Hi kids," she said, as she dug in her purse for her key.

"Becky, wait." Rachel answered, and turned back to her trailer. "I need to talk to you."

"Okay." She looked up, keys in hand. "What's going on?"

"We had a little problem this evening at the Markman's casita." Rachel studied Becky's face as she relayed her version of the events of the evening.

Becky wasn't wearing any make-up. She looked at least ten years younger without the piles of goop and her eyes grew wider and wider as she listened to Rachel.

Rachel heaved a big sigh when she finished her story. "So now we need to find out how the bottle of champagne got to the Markman's room."

Becky's face was ashen and her hands went to her face. "It was *me,* Rachel!" Her voice trembled. "*I* was the one who delivered the tray to the Markman's room."

℃℃℃

The following morning, a wide brown band of pollution hugged the horizon and the sky was glazed a dull blue. The sun, a pale yellow ball hanging in the sky, was partially obscured, as if in a fog. Heather and Rachel huddled together on the sidewalk, eyes nearly closed against the sand storm. They were headed to the main building for breakfast with JT following right behind.

"I can't believe how cold it is," Rachel grumbled, leading the group. "The wind blew all night long, banging the screen against my bedroom window, roaring through the mesquites. I hardly slept."

"Welcome to the desert," JT quipped, his head down.

Rachel pulled her sweater tight around her. "But just the other day, people were swimming in the pool. Now I'm freezing to death!"

"Oh, for Pete's sake, Rachel, it's sixty-one degrees," Heather said. "Hardly Alaska."

"Yeah, and if you weren't just skin and bones you'd be warmer," JT added. "Put a little meat on your bones and you'll be fine."

"Gee, thanks for all the sympathy, you guys." Rachel reached the door first and held it for the others.

JT took the door from her and motioned for Rachel to enter. "Trust me," he said. "You'll live. Eat a hot breakfast and drink some coffee."

"And I want to hear the story about the Markmans," Heather said, turning back to her. "I can't believe the one time we take a break and leave the hotel we have a crisis." She noticed several people were already milling around the lobby and didn't speak again until they were seated comfortably in their usual booth in the café. She leaned closer toward her sister so she wouldn't be overheard. "So what happened?"

Before Rachel could reply, Dolly squeaked up to their table wearing her white waitress shoes and a bright smile and held up a carafe full of fresh brew. "Coffee, anyone? You might need it after last night."

Rachel and Heather exchanged looks and held up their mugs in silence. JT pointed to his.

"Don't forget me," Buddy said, appearing right behind her. He slid into the booth next to Rachel and gave her a quick hug.

Dolly took their orders, left the carafe on the table, and sashayed herself back to the kitchen.

"So tell us what happened," Heather insisted, "since it looks like we're the last to know."

Rachel related the events of the previous evening to the group, up to the point where she talked to Becky.

"So Becky actually admitted she brought in the tray?" Heather asked.

"Yes, she did bring the tray up. She saw the champagne on the bell stand, noted the room number, and pointed it out to the front desk, suggesting the guys deliver it immediately. Julia said the guys were all tied up so Becky said she'd take it up for them since she was going by the Markman's suite anyway. She said she left the tray on the coffee table."

Rachel fell back against the booth. "I'm so exhausted I can hardly think."

"I can't imagine why," Heather said. "What time did you get to bed?"

"Well, I didn't fall asleep until three with the windstorm and all. I had taken Dixie to the emergency clinic to see how Richard was doing and by the time we got back and I got into bed, the wind was banging away at my screen and I couldn't stop thinking about weird stuff."

"Weird stuff? Like what?" JT asked.

"Like the insane relationship Dixie and Richard have. Like Benny Ammato and the creepy way he kind of slinks around. Plus the fact that he was in the Markman's room with the poisoned wine. I mean, what guy would notice the type of glasses on a room service tray? And Like Becky Beeman. She delivered the wine. That's not even her job." Rachel stirred her coffee and stared into her cup. "You know, there's something very odd about her."

"Like there's nothing odd about you?" Buddy teased.

"Maybe I do have my quirks," Rachel said. "But I don't look ten years younger when I take *off* my make-up. And I don't wear a big, fake mole near my bottom lip."

"She wears a fake mole?" Heather asked. "Why would someone do that?"

"Yes, why indeed?" Rachel said, staring off into space, her eyes barely open.

Heather noticed her sister was about to fall asleep and gave her a sympathetic look. "I have an idea, Rachel." she said, gently touching her hand. "Why don't you go home and take a nap. I don't have anything to do right now and I can take over your office for a couple hours. If something really important happens, I can always call and wake you up."

"Bless you, my child," Rachel said, her voice full of gratitude. "I would love a couple hours off to take a nap. But first I need to do a little snooping in the personnel files."

૯⁄ઝ૯⁄ઝ

A half an hour later Rachel was on her way to her casita, clutching copies of the papers she made, holding them tight against the breeze. She reached the end of the west side guest rooms when she saw Ekberg coming toward her wearing a pale summer suit. The sunlight falling through the gaps in the overhead vines made odd shadows dance on his giraffe-like frame.

"Playing hooky are you, Rachel?" he teased, coming to a stop in front of her.

"Oh Lars, I confess. You caught me sneaking off for a nap," she laughed. "And here I thought I'd get away with something."

Ekberg shook his head playfully but his eyes held on to hers. "Don't do it. You always need to play it straight, Rachel. You're the kind of person who always gets caught."

"Now you tell me," she said.

Ekberg's smile disappeared and his hands came up in front of his face, fingers touching, almost as if he were in prayer. "I can tell you something else—" he said, and hesitated.

"What?" She noticed the somber look on his face. "What is it?"

Ekberg's eyes went off focus, as if he were looking right through her. "Someone is going to hurt you, disappoint you…a…a woman. Someone is not who you think she is. Be careful."

Rachel was speechless. *What was he saying? Who was the woman he was referring to?* Before she could formulate a reply, his head suddenly jerked to the left and his mouth dropped open as if in surprise.

She turned quickly, focusing her gaze where Ekberg was looking, but there was nothing out of the ordinary going on that she could tell. Then she realized she could not see what Ekberg was seeing. He was shaking his head back and forth, saying "No, no," and began to clutch the sides of his head. He began to sway and dropped against one of the pillars that supported the trellis.

Rachel reached for him but knew instinctively not to touch him. As soon as his body touched the pillar he came back from where he was and he refocused on her.

"Are you okay?" Rachel wanted to do something to help and realized there was nothing she could do.

"I'm okay." Ekberg shook his head, and what little color he had came back to his face. Then more honestly he confessed, "No, no I'm not. Not really." He gripped his forehead with his hand. "This has been happening more and more. It's making me crazy." His voice was pained. He looked off into the distance, his eyes distressed. "I saw something, Rachel—something awful."

"What? Was it about me?"

"No—no—not you," he said, looking around at his surroundings. Then it was as if Ekberg realized he said too much. He straightened himself up and tried to regain his composure. He looked at Rachel, focusing on her face, and said softly, "I must ask you to keep this a secret." He took her hand. "You must not tell anyone about what just happened, about what I said. No one. Not even your sister, who will insist you tell her."

Rachel felt a chill at the words he spoke. Somehow he knew that Heather liked to pry information out of her, something she never mentioned to anyone. She was puzzled. "But, Lars, I don't understand. I don't *know* what just happened," she whispered. "I have no idea what you saw."

Ekberg looked confused for a moment, then he let Rachel's hand go, stood tall, and took a step back. "Of course you didn't. Of course. Good. Then we'll let it go at that." The smile came back that had been there when Rachel first walked up to him. "I'll see you later, Rachel. Have a nice nap." he said with a forced brightness and moved on, a few strands of fine hair blowing around his face.

Rachel stared at the space where Ekberg had stood, stunned by his change in mood, puzzled by everything that had just transpired—*whatever it was*. She couldn't bring herself to turn around and watch him walk away. *What if he's not there? What if he disappeared into thin air? And what the heck happened just now? Am I losing the rest of what little of my mind I have left?*

She looked down at her feet. They had no answer. She kept her eyes on the sidewalk in front of her and ran all the rest of the way to her casita.

Chapter 8

The Plantation Dining Room was nearly deserted. It was close to ten o'clock, closing time. The waiter approached the table with a lone woman seated at it, a coffee pot in his hand. "More coffee, Ms. Markman?"

"Twist my arm," Dixie said, holding up her cup. "I think I'll sit here for a few minutes longer and enjoy that lovely mural and waterfall. I can pretend I'm back in Cabo San Lucas."

The waiter nodded understandingly. "You stay as long as you want, Ms. Markman. I'll check back with you later and see if you changed your mind about dessert," he said with a wink.

Dixie watched a young couple across the room, obviously in love, sharing a pot of crème Brule. *We were like that once, so young and in love,* she reminisced and then caught herself. *We're still in love!* She looked down, almost embarrassed, and brushed imaginary crumbs off her lap.

The hostess was tidying up her station near the entrance. After she organized it for the next evening's dinner, she checked her watch, closed the door to the entrance, and wended her way over to Dixie's table. "Please feel free to stay as long as you like, Ms. Markman. I'll be back shortly if you need anything," she said and proceeded toward the kitchen.

From a speaker recessed into the ceiling, notes from a piano were playing softly against the background of ocean surf. *La Mer.* One of their favorite songs. Everything made her think of Richard—the music, the mural, the young couple...

Dixie was lingering over a slow sip of coffee when Anthony Pander came up behind her.

"May I join you?" he asked, startling her.

Dixie turned her head, annoyed to see Pander intruding on her privacy. "I was just leaving, actually," she answered, her mood destroyed. "The restaurant has closed for the night."

"Oh, this will only take a moment," Anthony said, taking the seat next to her. He was immaculately groomed and smelled of expensive cologne, something woodsy. "I noticed you weren't at the lectures yesterday or today and was a little concerned."

"Concerned? Concerned about what?"

"That perhaps you were ill or something," Pander offered.

Dixie tossed her head as if in dismissal. "You needn't have been. Some things just came up and I couldn't make it." She preferred not to be rude, but sometimes it was necessary. She reached for her purse.

"Oh, that's quite all right, Ms. Markman. We understand perfectly." Anthony was all smiles. "It's just that, well, you know, the condo you picked out at Island of Light, well, in order to hold that specific one any longer, we must have your membership deposit by tomorrow morning at ten."

Dixie looked at the man and the way the dome of his head shined under the light. She could not believe his audacity.

"And I must add, Ms. Markman, you certainly did pick out the best location on the whole site. I'm sure it was an oversight on your part to—"

"No."

Pander blinked. "I beg your pardon?"

"I said no. No, as in I've changed my mind and don't want to get involved with your Island of Light."

Pander's mouth opened and closed. He forced a smile. "May I ask why you've changed your mind, Ms. Markman?"

Dixie raised her eyebrows in disbelief and wondered if she should even bother to reply to the idiot. "Okay, first of all, you're selling property and you aren't even real estate agents."

Pander put up his hand in a gesture for her to stop. "I thought we were clear about that, Ms. Markman. The Church of Inner Light is not selling property. We are offering our congregation life-time memberships in a totally encompassing spiritual community. Our homes are—"

"Stop," Dixie said, angry now. "I really don't want to hear the whole sales pitch again. I happen to know there's no water in that area of the island, so you can cut the crap. There's no condo there, either."

Pander's eyes snapped wide open and he drew back as if he were slapped. "Where did you hear that?"

"Is it true?"

Pander drew himself up with indignation. "Of course it's not true, and whoever told you such a lie is going to be hearing from our lawyer!"

"Good luck, Anthony. You're going to need a lawyer. You might have him check the satellite map of the island while he's at it, too. That is, if the police don't get to him first." Dixie left the table with a shaken Pander staring after her.

❧❧❧

The evening air was unusually crisp. The dry front, which had blown across the desert for nearly two days, had sucked out what little moisture there was. Dixie meandered along the sidewalk towards her casita, deep in thought, her skirt billowing against her legs. She was happy to have the Island of Light business all behind her, happy about the way she had put that slime ball, Pander, in his place, but the thought of her husband lying ill, away from her, crushed her heart.

"Hey, Dixie!" a voice called out. She looked up and saw Rachel sitting on her patio with a glass in her hand.

"How about a lemon martini?" Rachel asked, holding up a stemmed glass.

Dixie headed for the stairs that led to Rachel's suite. "Start mixing!" she yelled up to her.

She walked out onto the patio and seated herself before Rachel came out with their drinks.

"How is Richard doing?" Rachel handed a sugar-rimmed glass to Dixie.

"He's gonna make it, but they tell me his voice won't be the same." She looked small, fragile, her lips turned down, like a sad china doll. "He's in a lot of pain and he's still pretty angry right now. He wants to come home."

"When will that happen?"

Dixie took a long sip of her martini. "I'm not sure." She set the glass down on the wicker table. "Richard is such a terrible patient. They'll probably beg him to leave tomorrow." She gave Rachel a guilty smile.

"Then he must be a lot better."

"Not really," Dixie said, averting her eyes. "He'd have to leave against doctors' orders or whatever they call it. But you know Richard. Whatever he wants, he's gonna get." She turned her gaze on Rachel with a look that begged for reassurance.

Rachel pretended not to notice. "Have you eaten?" she offered, wanting to change the subject. "I could call room service for you."

"Oh, no thank you, I just got back from the Plantation Room." Dixie waved her hand in the air to indicate she couldn't eat another bite. "I had the Margarita chicken with truffle fries. I'm stuffed. But you won't believe who snuck in to talk to me after the door was closed."

Rachel watched her face. Dixie's lips were pressed together in a smile and she was wearing a look of self-satisfaction.

"Not Pander."

"The very same." Dixie looked down at her drink and lifted it toward Rachel. "Make me another one of these babies and I'll tell you all about it."

By the time they were half-way through their third martinis, Dixie and Rachel had completely dissected both Pander and Ekberg. Rachel was tempted to tell Dixie about her unusual meeting with Ekberg on the sidewalk, but she remembered his request for secrecy. Besides, what if the woman he warned her about was Dixie? She didn't know yet if she could really trust her new friend.

"Well, at least it's over now," Rachel said, sympathetically. "You won't have to see either one of them again. And don't worry about Pander filing any lawsuit. Henri called me shortly before you got here."

"And?"

"Henri said his cousin checked with every agency in Jamaica that would know about any development in the works. His cousin said there is absolutely nothing happening in that area of the island."

"Wow," Dixie said, softly, with a shake of her head. "You know, I could have lost a cool million."

"Well, in that case, here's to saving a cool million," Rachel said, lifting her glass.

"A cool million," Dixie echoed, and they drank. They looked at each other. "Okay. So now what do we do?"

"We call the deputy sheriff." Rachel reached for her phone. "I've got him on my speed dial."

"Wow. This late at night? I didn't know you were close friends."

"Um, actually we're not. We barely tolerate each other."

"Really?" Dixie's eyebrows arched up. "Why?"

Rachel looked sheepish. "Well, for one thing, I'm pretty sure Dewey thinks I'm just a ditzy blonde who sticks her nose in places it doesn't belong."

"I see." Dixie nodded, mulling over Rachel's answer. "So what do you think of him?"

"Oh, he's okay." Rachel shrugged. "Other than the fact that he's a fat buffoon that must have paid someone to take his English exam at the police academy."

Dixie downed the rest of her martini, brought her fingers up to her lips, and giggled. "Maybe we ought to call the FBI instead."

※※※

It was after midnight when Rachel finally undressed for bed. She slipped into a short nightgown and went to the window to let in a little fresh air. When the glass slid open she pressed her face against the screen to inhale the coolness.

She froze. Her ears picked up a swishing, rustling noise, as if someone were moving just outside her window. "Who's there!" she cried out, slammed the window shut, and yanked the drapes together. *Someone was watching me!* She broke out in a cold sweat and began to shake, remembering she had undressed in full view of whoever was out there.

Anger overwhelmed her fear. She leaped toward the flashlight she kept by the bed and ran out the door. She skipped down the steps, raced up the hill between the two casitas, and flashed the light around wildly at the darkness. She could hear someone, or something, to the east, running through the brush. Her heart pounded as she waved the light in the direction of the sound, but the beam of light disappeared into the blackness and she could see nothing beyond it.

The sound of movement faded. Rachel caught her breath and aimed the beam of light down at her slippers. Once delicate, sexy, and trimmed with feathers and sparkling stones, her slippers were now coated with dirt and stuck with a few goat head burrs to boot. *Forget it,* they seemed to say. She was a good runner but she'd never catch up to whatever, or whoever, was out there.

The adrenaline seeped out of her as she trudged back down the hill and up the stairs to her suite. Her inner voice caught up with her. *That was a smooth move, idiot. What were you thinking? What if it was a poisonous snake? Or some rabid animal or some perverted…*She couldn't bear to finish the rest and just watched her once-fancy slippers climb the steps.

It was when she arrived at the top of the landing that she realized the door had swung shut behind her and she was locked out. She swore at the door and kicked it repeatedly with renewed anger. She jiggled and yanked at the knob. Nothing happened. Resisting the temptation to bang her head against the door, she stomped her already hurting foot and lumbered back down the stairs.

Now what? She sat at the bottom of the steps and looked around, trying to think of a way out of her dilemma. No way could she walk over to the main building dressed the way she was. Even if she could swear the desk clerk to secrecy, he'd see her—literally—in her sheer little nightie. Much too embarrassing. Besides, the lounge was getting ready to close. There'd be people floating around all over the lobby. She pictured her sister and JT sleeping soundly in their king-sized bed, their master key cards on the desk nearby. Waking them up would be the absolute last resort. She would sit by the pool and come up with a plan. At least she could hide behind one of the tables until someone came by that she knew, and her shorty-nightgown might pass for a bathing suit cover-up in the semi-darkness.

She limped across the parking lot to the courtyard, favoring her injured foot, and then drifted along the curved walkway that led to the pool. She could turn on the waterfall. At least that would help her relax and might divert any unwelcome attention away from her.

But the waterfall was already on. She could hear it its rhythmic sound spilling into the pool. That was odd. Maintenance always shut it off at ten when they went home for the night. Did someone forget? Or had someone come in later and switched the waterfall back on?

Rachel hobbled to the control panel behind the cave that supported the waterfall and opened the box. The tiny clock reported the time as 12:40. She changed her mind about sitting by the waterfall and flipped the switch to off. The water gurgled and stopped as she minced her way around the cave to the water's edge.

A man exploded out of the water. "Boo!"

Rachel shrieked and jumped back. "You moron! What are you doing here?"

The young man laughed. It was Benny Ammato in all his half-naked glory. "Come on in, Rachel. The water's great."

Rachel's heart was pounding and she pictured herself kicking him in the face. "That was a stupid, immature prank!" She glanced down at the water still churning around him. "And I hope you've got a bathing suit on."

"Maybe, maybe not," Ammato teased, patting the water. "Check it out."

"I don't think so." Her tone was venomous and she glared daggers in his direction.

"Come on, the water's warm." He swam toward her. "You can shed your little nightie over by the rocks."

"Shut up, Benny" she said, but crossed her arms over her chest to cover herself. "This happens to be a beach cover-up," she added indignantly. "And you still haven't told me what you're doing here."

He cocked his head at her, laughing. "I'm enjoying one of my perks. Taking a swim."

"After midnight?"

He reached the edge of the pool where Rachel was standing. "I didn't know we had a time limit on swims. Tomorrow's my day off so I thought I'd enjoy some time with the pool all to myself." He looked up at her slyly and grinned. "Unless, of course, you want to join me." He snapped out his hand to grab her ankle.

She was too quick for him and jumped back. "Not in your dreams."

He laughed again, but she had already turned away. *Arrogant jerk,* she thought and began limping past the pool without looking back. Suddenly she turned. "Hey Benny," she called. "You been here long?"

"Close to an hour."

"Have you seen anyone else around?"

"Nope," he said, shaking his head. "Not since I've been here. Why?"

She studied him. "No reason, just curious." She turned again, started walking away, wondering if he was lying, wondering if he was the one at her window.

"Hey, Rachel! The offer's still good!"

"No thanks, Benny." She walked away, wiggling her fingers good-by behind her. She wanted to ding him with a smart remark against his manhood, but managed to control her mouth. It was the middle of the night, and they were alone. *Might not be too smart of a move to mouth off. I've already pulled enough stupid stunts for one night.*

Rachel sighed as the last remnants of adrenaline left her body, and something ticked in her brain. Benny was a recent hire, and she knew he'd been hired on a temporary basis. He was arrogant and insulting, but he *was* handsome. He also had a body like a Greek god. Surely someone who looked like him could get a better job than that of a bellman at a small hotel in the middle of nowhere. Did he have a thing going with one of staff who had access to the liquor stock? Rachel sat down on a concrete bench at the edge of the courtyard and decided she'd check the personnel records for Benny's work history. She seemed to recall he had come from the LA area. Had he known Dixie? Had he been a past lover? A jilted lover could have a motive for murder—if Benny was a past lover and was indeed jilted. And wasn't it Benny who delivered the cheese plate? "Stop it!" Rachel cried out and grabbed her head in her hands. "Stop with the monkey brain."

It was then she remembered the reason she was out there to begin with. She was locked out of her suite. Muttering a couple of choice words, she looked up at the

Carpenter's casita and accepted the fact she was going to have to eat a little humble pie and wake her sister.

But it was JT that came to the door.

"What happened?"

"Does something have to happen for me to come by?" Rachel waltzed in past him, arms covering her breasts, and looked around for Heather.

"At one in the morning? Yes. And she's still asleep."

"No, I'm not," Heather said, strolling in from the bedroom, rubbing her eyes. "What's going on?"

"We may have a peeping tom." Rachel directed her comment to her sister.

"Aw, man," JT groaned. "What happened?"

Rachel looked down at the floor. "I'll tell you all about it if someone will bring me a robe."

It wasn't long before they were seated in the living room and Rachel was wrapped up in one of the hotel's fluffy robes. She started to recount the incident from the beginning and it wasn't long before JT angrily interrupted.

"You mean you undressed in front of the window with the drapes open? I can't believe you'd be that stupid."

"JT!" Heather scolded, giving him a sharp look.

"Hey. I never thought about it, okay?" Rachel snapped. "I mean there's nothing out there but a bunch of mesquite trees and some rocks. Besides, it was late at night. Who'd be out there anyway? A coyote? A jackrabbit?"

"Okay, okay, I'm sorry." JT held up a hand, wanting her to shut up. "I apologize. Rachel, please continue with the story."

Both JT and Heather remained quiet until Rachel finished. They exchanged glances and Heather raised a finger toward him. "Remember, JT? I *told* you that Ammato kid was a little strange. Don't you think it's a little odd for him to come back at midnight to swim?"

JT was already rubbing his hairline, looking troubled. "When I told the employees they could swim, I didn't think anyone would come back that late at night. I think I'm going to have to spell out a little more clearly what the employee perks are. I better put a lock on the control box, too, to make sure the waterfall and Jacuzzi get shut down at ten."

"That would solve one problem," Rachel said.

"Yes," Heather nodded, "but I still don't appreciate his disrespect toward you, sis."

"Oh, don't worry about that. I can handle him."

"That's not the point, Rachel," JT said. "His behavior is not acceptable. I've had to talk to him before about touching other employees and making sexual remarks."

"Um…yeah. Now that you mention it, I remember Rosario saying something about him. He cornered her in the wine cellar or something and scared her."

JT stood up from his chair and began to pace. "He practically propositioned her. I talked to him about it and he's been unpleasant to her ever since. I don't like that. He's a good worker, he's smart, but he's a cocky young man who needs to practice a lot more self-control."

"It's the way he looks at women," Heather chimed in. "He's creepy."

"In other words, he's a jerk," Rachel concluded.

"Yeah, but I can't fire him for being a jerk. Or for being creepy," JT said.

"But honey," Heather asked, "can't you fire him for sexual harassment?"

"Not if he had a bathing suit on in the pool. He was on his own free time and he never touched Rachel. It's pretty iffy."

"And I can't prove it was him out there, watching though the window," Rachel said. "If I had actually *seen* him—seen anybody—I would have called the sheriff's office right away."

JT slapped his forehead. "What am I thinking? Ammato is a temp. I can fire him anytime I want to, for any reason." He turned to at Rachel. "The problem is, I need him right now. You know we're full up, and I barely have enough staff to cover the work as it is. Some of the crew is even pulling overtime until the church group leaves."

"Then don't worry about it. I'm not worried about him, and I'll make double sure my drapes are pulled at night."

JT took his key card and insisted on walking Rachel back to her suite. Before locking her inside, he checked the place out, including Rachel's closet, which was packed to the ceiling with shoes and clothes. He shook his head. There wouldn't have been room for a mouse to hide, never mind a pervert.

Rachel's clock glowed 1:35 when she finally yawned and slipped under the covers, but questions about Benny Ammato kept her awake. Flipping over her pillow one more time, she made up her mind about one thing: she'd check the area behind her bedroom window first thing in the morning. Maybe there'd be footprints, something, anything. She'd bring along a can of bug spray, in case there were spiders back there—or larger creepy things weighing about one-fifty. Benny was short for a man, but he was muscular, with thick, strong hands. The more she thought about that, the more she wished she'd kept that can of mace that Heather had offered her.

∽∽∽

The following morning, Rachel was the first one to spot Dewey Tucker when he entered the Hibiscus Café. She waved the deputy in towards the corner booth.

Heather, JT and Buddy were all waiting with her, breakfast finished, except for Heather, who was still picking at her breakfast burrito.

"Hey, Dewey, how's the weather out there?" JT asked. "The wind start up again?"

The deputy sank into the booth. "Yep. Still blowin' and dryer than a popcorn fart." He put his Stetson on the back of the booth. "What's Lupe fixin' this mornin'?"

"Breakfast burritos," Rachel quickly answered, "but do you think you'll have time to eat? I thought maybe—"

Tucker gave her his "are-you-crazy-girl?" look while JT stuck his hand up in the air and waved Dolly over.

"Hi, sweetie-pie, how ya doin'?" Dolly said, sliding up to Tucker, flashing him a smile.

"Fine as frog's hair, and you?" Tucker said. His cheeks balled up in a happy grin.

"Just peachy. You want the breakfast special, right?" Dolly asked, setting a ceramic mug in front of Tucker.

That gave JT an idea, but he waited until Dolly left. "Dewey, have you heard anything more about Domino's?"

"Only that they been workin' twenty-four-seven. They're supposed to open in just a day or so, a soft openin', whatever that is."

"Yeah, I heard that, too. It should be a small crowd of family and friends, kind of like a dress rehearsal."

"Makes sense," Tucker said, and pulled a folded piece of paper from his pocket. "But I bet you ain't seen this. Picked it up at the Chamber of Commerce."

JT took the paper and smoothed it out on the table. He stared at it for a minute while everyone watched him. "I don't believe this."

"What?" Heather asked. "What is it?"

JT handed the paper to Rachel and turned to his wife, stunned. "They copied us, Heather. They copied our menu...even Chef Henri's specialty items."

"What? How can they do that?" Heather was appalled.

"You're right, JT." Rachel kept scanning the menu, hoping to find something original to them. "They copied everything, even the mesquite grilled steaks. Even the prices." She continued searching the list of offerings. "Look. They have a French specialty section. That's the only thing they did differently. They have six items on the menu we don't have on a regular basis, but that's all...and they're offerings we've had as a special at one time or another." She looked up in amazement. "I can't believe it. The nerve of them."

Heather looked at her husband. JT's jaw was clenched and his eyes were narrowed and cold. He wasn't drumming his fingers or even rubbing his hairline nervously. No, he wasn't worried. He was angry. In fact, Heather had only seen him this angry once before, when she and Rachel had hiked up the mountain in the one-hundred-and-two degree heat.

Buddy picked up the menu and took his turn reading it. "I guess Anna Venkman is running the place," he said. "Did you notice her picture in the top corner? All dolled up like a movie star, as compared to her usual look of Gestapo centerfold of the month."

JT looked at him but he wasn't laughing at Buddy's joke. His eyes were icy and staring straight ahead. "I always said you have to pick your battles in life. You can't waste your time fighting every little thing that comes along."

"So this?" Buddy held up the menu and waved it in the air. "Where does this fall?"

JT snatched the paper and lay it face down on the table, under the weight of his palm. "This—this means war."

The table was dead silent when Dolly came up to it with Tucker's breakfast plate in hand.

She looked around awkwardly, realizing she had come at an emotional moment, and dropped her eyes, setting the plate down in front of Tucker without a word. She started to turn away when JT said, "Dolly, when's your next free night?"

Dolly, caught off-guard, stuttered a bit before she said, "Saturday."

"Good," JT said. He turned to Tucker. "Do you have plans for Saturday, say seven p.m.?"

"No," Tucker replied with a puzzled frown.

"Good," JT said again. "You do now. I'm going to give you both a night out at Domino's for dinner, as my guest, and you can have whatever you want to eat and drink, for as long as you want to stay out."

"Ah, I get it," Dolly said. A glow spread across her face which she beamed in Tucker's direction. "You want us to be spies."

JT smiled for the first time. "Exactly."

"Sounds good to me," Tucker said, blushing a bit, and immediately dove into his breakfast burrito.

Dolly left and everything got quiet again. Rachel and Heather exchanged looks and finally Rachel asked, "So Dewey, what about Anthony Pander and Lars Ekberg? Don't you think we need to go over there and arrest them now?"

"Jus' hold your horses, Missy." He took a swig of coffee, swallowed his food, and set the mug down. "First of all, we got no proof they committed a crime. Jus' 'cause somebody's cousin says there's no development being built don't mean I can go over there and arrest them. Ms. Markman didn't give those folks any money, remember?"

"Dewey, those men are swindlers and con artists and you know it," she snapped back and looked around the table hoping for verbal reinforcements. "Surely they must have talked *somebody* into giving them some money."

"No one has complained, Rachel," JT said. "And half of those people have already checked out. The rest will be gone by noon."

"Well…well," Rachel sputtered, looking around for verbal support. "What can we do then? Just let everybody get ripped off?"

"I already called the state attorney general, and his office is gonna look into it," the deputy said, "and you all have the names and addresses of all the church people who stayed at the hotel, so don't worry about them." Tucker took another bite of burrito and a swallow of his coffee.

Rachel was crestfallen. "So that's it?"

Tucker set his cup down and turned to the group. "This Lars Ekberg character is pretty well known and not likely to disappear any time soon. He's got a book out and a web page. He owns a couple houses in the U.S."

JT nodded.

"And look at him," Tucker said, opening up a copy of the web pages he printed off the computer. "He looks like Rachel, here. He'd stand out anywhere 'cept Iceland, maybe."

Rachel bristled but kept her mouth shut.

Heather caught his eye. "Um, we have another problem, too, Deputy." She glanced over at Rachel, but Rachel gave her a quick kick under the table, realizing she was going to tell Tucker about the peeping tom.

Before Tucker could respond, Dolly sashayed up to him with a bright smile. "Y'all okay?" she asked, eyes spanning the table. "Anything else you need, Deputy?"

"Thanks, Dolly, I'm fine for right now," Tucker said. He nervously pulled on his mustache as he watched her walk away with a serious sway of her hips.

"Why, Deputy," Buddy said, mimicking Dolly's southern drawl. "Ah do believe Miss Dolly might be takin' a liken' to ya."

Tucker's face turned as red as the bandana he was patting his face with. "Now you, Mr. McCain, can be just mindin' your own beeswax."

Tucker chomped into his burrito and never said another word until he finished his breakfast and took one last sip of his coffee. He finally turned to JT. "Well, what do you think, pardner? Shall we go find our Mr. Ekberg and see what he's got to say?"

"Hey, what about me?" Rachel whined. "I'm the one who uncovered all this."

"Okay, Missy," Tucker said, with a lack of enthusiasm. "You might as well come along."

Buddy got up first and turned to JT. "I'll be at the front desk checking last night's receipts. Call me if you need me." He headed off towards the lobby.

JT slipped out of the booth. "You coming, Heather?"

Heather looked at her watch. "No, thank you. He kind of gives me the creeps."

"I thought Benny Ammato did that," Rachel said, teasing.

"Yes, he does. When Benny looks at you, it's like he's looking right through your clothes, and that's creepy all right. But when Ekberg looks at you, it's like he's looking right through your skull into your *brain,* reading your mind. That's *really* creepy." She waved her hand. "You go on ahead, Rachel. If you aren't back by nine, I'll answer the phone for you."

Rachel followed JT and the deputy across the parking lot as a blast of west wind blew sand at their legs. The doves and mockingbirds hunkered down in the trees, mostly silent.

The group spotted Ekberg heading in their direction, looking as white as an albino in the sunlight. Like Tucker said, he stood out. When they reached him, Tucker introduced himself and said he needed to ask a few questions.

Ekberg's head jerked back and forth between JT and Rachel. "What's this all about?"

"Could we go somewhere a little more private?" Tucker asked, looking uncomfortable.

Ekberg frowned, his eyes guarded. "Why? What's going on?"

"I need to talk to you about Anthony Pander."

"Anthony? Is he okay?" Panic appeared on Ekberg's face. "Did something happen?"

"We'd like to talk to both of you, if you don't mind."

Ekberg's mouth dropped open, as if he were going to say something, then he closed it. "Okay," he finally said, "but I think Anthony is sleeping in. He didn't answer his phone this morning."

"Then maybe we could wake him up. That your casita?" the deputy asked, cocking his head.

"Yes, upstairs. Anthony is on the first floor."

JT's pager went off. When he saw it was Buddy's call, he stepped away to take it, turning his back to the wind. "What do you need?"

"Nothing," Buddy said, "but you may need to know this: Anthony Pander showed up at midnight last night and removed everything from the safe belonging to the Church of Inner Light. He turned in the key."

The group was close to Ekberg's casita when JT caught up with them. "Mr. Ekberg, are you aware that Anthony Pander emptied the safe deposit box of your church last night?"

Ekberg blinked, as if he hadn't heard.

"Mr. Ekberg? The church's safe deposit box?" JT repeated. "Anthony Pander emptied it completely and turned in the key to the front desk."

"W—What?" Ekberg finally spoke, totally stunned. "That can't be possible." Ekberg appeared confused, then pulled away from the group and ran up to the casita. He pounded on the door and called out Pander's name several times.

JT and Tucker arrived at the door and looked at each other. The deputy nodded slightly and JT gently moved the trembling Ekberg aside.

"Let's find out if he's sick or passed out," JT said softly, pulling up a master key card from his belt.

When JT opened the door, Ekberg was the only one surprised by what they saw. The suite was empty, wiped down, and devoid of all traces of Anthony Pander, right down to the little hotel soaps and shampoo he used.

Chapter 9

Late that afternoon, Rachel headed out to the desert alone, relieved the winds had finally subsided. She strolled along Boulder Trail and followed it up the mountain as the sun fell toward the horizon.

After walking a while, she reached a massive group of boulders surrounded by purple verbena. She climbed to the top of the largest boulder and sat cross-legged on the flat surface. Still warm from the heat of the day, the huge rock was a dark, orangey-brown, and pitted with holes like a chunk of baby Swiss. She leaned back, letting the heat emanating from it comfort her, happy to be alone with her thoughts.

Rachel gazed out at the valley below until the sun slipped behind a cloud bank that hugged the horizon. Turning her attention to the sunset, she watched the popcorn edges of the clouds become tinged with gold. Long rays of pure white light poured through openings in the clouds, widening as they beamed their way upward.

Soon, the rest of the sky turned a bright scarlet, and as the sun dropped, it gradually faded to a pale mauve.

"Beautiful, isn't it?"

Rachel jumped. The voice belonged to JT Carpenter. "What are you doing here?" she asked, looking down from her perch.

JT stood a good six feet below her, but he still looked big. He wore well-fitting blue jeans and a blue striped shirt, a Ralph Lauren, with the sleeves rolled up once at the wrist. Even his casual clothes looked neat.

"Looking for you," he answered. "Heather was getting worried, so she sent me out to hunt you down."

"She still can't resist mothering me, can she?" Rachel turned her attention back to the sunset.

"Nope. That's just part of being Heather. But you could make it easier on all of us if you'd tell someone when you're not planning to show up for dinner, or at least leave your cell phone turned on. Since the poisoning at the Markman's, everyone's kind of on edge around here."

"True enough," Rachel said, shaking her head. "That was dumb of me. I've been walking around in a bit of a daze today and didn't even think about the time."

The sun dropped behind the mountain peak, and Rachel and JT watched the sky color to a warm plum.

"What do you say, we go back?" JT asked. "It'll be dark pretty quick."

Rachel hunched her shoulders. "I suppose. I'm not getting much figured out while I'm sitting out here." She stood up and jumped down a series of rocks until she reached the path.

"It's not in your job description to solve company problems, you know."

"I know that, JT, but I can't stop thinking about everything. Stuff keeps spinning around in my mind like a hamster on one of those treadmills." She brushed the dust off her hands and began to walk alongside him in the direction of the hotel. "We have a real mess on our hands now with Pander's disappearance. Poor Lars is having a nervous breakdown. I feel sorry for him. He told me White Eagle was after him constantly before, even interrupting his sleep, but now he seems to have disappeared. Lars keeps trying to contact him for help, but apparently our local spirit guide has flown off to the great beyond never to return."

"Well, that's pretty typical of a malevolent spirit. Lead you on and dump you."

"What?" Rachel stopped in the middle of the trail and looked at him. "You don't really believe that, do you?"

"Do you have a better explanation?"

"Uh…"

"Thought so."

"Just because I can't think of a reason doesn't mean there isn't one." Rachel walked on. "But regardless, what is poor Lars going to do? Pander took the record books *and* all the cash for the deposits on the Island of Light *plus* the three-hundred-dollars-a-pop gratuities on the readings. Now Lars has nothing and he's on the hook for those deposits. He's a total wreck."

"Oh, I wouldn't worry about his finances," JT said, kicking a stone out of the path. "He can always sell his houses. He probably has credit cards and savings accounts elsewhere, like overseas. I suspect he'll need it, too. Even if he was scammed by Pander just like his congregation, it will take a good lawyer and a lot of cash to prove it." He turned to look at a lizard that scampered past. "But you know, Rachel, that's not our problem. Ekberg will have to sort out his own mess."

"Yeah, I know you're right," Rachel admitted, "but he's really a sweet guy and I can't help feeling sorry for him. On the other hand, Ekberg *is* part of the reason the Markmans are in the trouble they're in. Ah, let me rephrase that. Lars is the reason Richard Markman hates my guts." She stopped again and looked directly at her brother-in-law. "JT, I just *know* in my heart that Richard is trying to kill Dixie. There are just too many coincidences."

"Maybe you need to detach from that, too," JT said then cocked his head toward the path and began walking on.

"Maybe. But there's something else."

"What?"

"Promise you won't tell Heather. I don't want her to worry."

He seemed reluctant. "Okay."

Rachel reached into the pocket of her jeans, pulled something out, and held it in the palm of her hand.

"What's that?" He squinted at the shiny object. "An earring?"

"Exactly. A lone earring. A small single stud diamond. A real one."

He began advancing down the path again. "So?"

"It's where I found it that makes it significant."

"Rachel, stop with the games. Just tell me."

"I found it on the ground right in front of my bedroom window and it looked like it hadn't been lying there very long."

He stopped. "Really? So, do you think a woman—"

"No. I think the earring belongs to Benny Ammato. He wears one just like this, and when I checked him out this morning, he didn't have it on."

JT groaned.

"I know, I know. Benny again. I didn't want to tell you."

"Don't ever do that, Rachel. Not tell me, I mean. Something like this is important and I need to think about it. A lot." He turned to her. "Don't say a word to anyone about this yet, until I figure out what we need to do."

"No problem. I'm not about to make myself look stupid."

They walked along in silence for a minute.

"Anything else you need to tell me?" JT asked.

"Well, how about this? Why would any woman want to make herself look older?"

"What? What are you talking about?"

They turned a corner and Rachel kicked a rock out of the path. The hotel property came into view.

"I'm talking about Becky Beeman. She's been doing that. Making herself look older. Also, she has no history prior to ten years ago. It's like she appeared out of nowhere."

"Humph," JT grunted. "Maybe she was a housewife and didn't have to work outside the home."

"No," Rachel said. "She's been alone for a long time, according to what she told Heather. And she isn't rich. She *has* to work."

"Is her social security number genuine?"

"It's in all her work history. But at her last employment, they listed her at forty-eight instead of fifty-nine."

JT reached up and rubbed his hairline. "She could be running," he said. "You know, from an abusive ex-boyfriend, or a stalker. She doesn't look too bad for someone her age."

"You mean someone close to your age, don't you?" Rachel tried to suppress a smile. "Sorry, JT, I couldn't help it. A little bird told me your birthday was coming up."

"Hey, you should look this good when you're in your forties." He brushed his fingers through his thick head of hair.

"Right. And they say women are vain?" she teased.

They stopped at the edge of the parking lot next to the employees' entrance. The outside lights around the hotel blinked on and a breeze blew some dried leaves across the blacktop.

Rachel looked up at her brother-in-law. "You know, JT, I think this is first real adult conversation we've ever had."

"I must be getting soft," he said, a crooked smile turning up the corner of his mouth.

"Or our relationship is improving." Rachel jammed her hands into her jean pockets. "Either way, things are better between us, aren't they?"

"Yeah, they're better." JT rubbed the frown on his forehead.

"What?"

"I hope I don't live to regret this," he said, pausing to look around, "but I have a suggestion for you."

Rachel looked up expectantly. "A suggestion?"

"Yeah. If you want to find out about Becky Beeman and you've hit a dead end, why don't you call someone who owes you a favor and might have access to whatever records you need?"

Rachel looked down, puzzled. When she looked up a wave of recognition washed across her face. "Alex Tucker?"

"Yes, Alex Tucker. I think he'd be happy to help you. Why don't you give him a call?"

"Humm. That's an idea," Rachel said. Her mind conjured up the image of his face, his haunting eyes. She remembered his kiss with a rush she felt down to her toes. "Maybe not a good idea," she added.

"Why not?" JT asked, hoping to encourage her. "I thought you two really hit it off."

Rachel became silent. *That's exactly the problem. We did hit it off. Lust at first sight. Then he left.*

"I mean, what's the worst that could happen?" JT continued.

Rachel looked up at him, deliberately ignoring the flashing danger sign at the back of her brain. "I guess you're right. What could it hurt to call?"

ⓔⓢⓔⓢ

The next morning, Heather walked into Rachel's office with a guilty smile on her face. "What do you think?"

Rachel immediately noticed Heather's new look. "You changed your hair," she said. Heather had always worn her hair in a simple, medium-length style and, with the barest hint of freckles, she always managed to look young, fresh, and all-American.

"Yes. Do you like it?" Heather asked, turning full circle. Her shorter bob was streaked with two shades of blonde and looked like a glass of iced tea with the sun shining on it.

"Yes, I do. It's very classy. It makes you look even younger than before."

"Thanks, I'm all for that," Heather said, with a little curtsy. She handed Rachel the papers she held in her hands. "Now you can read your fax."

Rachel looked down at the cover sheet. The fax was from the Los Angeles Police Department, Homicide Division, and Alex Tucker's signature was at the bottom. Rachel's heart leaped. Her mind spun back to the previous autumn when she'd met Alex. She remembered the fire between them as they stood, their backs against the mountain, their kiss—

"Rachel? Are you going to read it?"

"Oh, yeah," she mumbled, her mind coming back to the present. She quickly skimmed through the papers.

"So tell me what he said," Heather prompted. "Did he say he would come?"

Rachel looked up from the papers, surprised Heather had resisted the temptation to snoop. "You mean you didn't read it?"

"No." Heather blushed. "It was written to you, and I could see it was from Alex. I thought it might be—you know—private."

Rachel guessed that was the reason for Heather's guilty smile. "I'm afraid not, Miss Cupid. It's a response to a fax I sent Alex about Becky Beeman. I asked him if he could track down any information about her. But I didn't ask him to come here."

"Oh." Heather's excitement faded. "So I take it you're still suspicious about Becky's fake mole, huh?"

"It's not just the fake mole, Heather." Rachel continued reading. "Becky has changed her name, too. It used to be Reba Callahan, legally Rebecca Lee Callahan—her married name, to Becky Beeman. She also changed her hair color from golden blonde to muddy brown, changed her skin tone from fair to medium, and added ugly glasses."

"Oh."

"And look here. She also neglected to mention on her resume that she worked for several years at three different movie studios as a make-up artist, which is probably how she managed to age herself by ten years."

"Oh, wow." Heather appeared bewildered as she took it all in. "I don't know what to think."

"Yeah, neither do I." She looked up at her sister. "Why would someone leave years of work off a resume?"

"They want to hide something?"

"Could be. Ms. Beeman may be trying to hide a chunk of her past."

"That makes sense," Heather said, but continued to look puzzled. "So what do we do now?"

Rachel thought a moment. "Our best course of action may be to simply ask her." She folded the papers and put them in her desk drawer. "Are you with me, boss lady?"

"You bet. Let's go find our housekeeping manager."

The housekeeping office was across the hall from the kitchen, next door to the employee's break room. It was a windowless cubbyhole—more like a wide passage way than an office, and it led to the laundry area. The walls were painted bright white and it smelled of laundry detergent and bleach.

At this time of day, Becky was always at her desk, by the phone, always available for the maids and vendors alike. But when Rachel and Heather walked in, Becky wasn't there. The sisters looked at each other and headed toward the laundry.

Heather spotted Becky first, lying white-faced on the floor, her arms sprawled out. A small, orange prescription bottle lay an inch from her hand.

"Call 911! Call 911!" she shouted and ran to Becky. Rachel grabbed the phone.

"She's breathing. She's got a pulse." Heather exclaimed, her fingers pressed against the artery on Becky's neck.

After a brief contact with emergency services, Rachel dropped the phone on the desk, rushed into the laundry room, grabbed a clean towel, and soaked it with cool water. Heather did what she could to comfort Becky as she regained consciousness. Rachel applied the towel to Becky's head, admonishing her to lie still.

"Don't call the ambulance," Becky pleaded, trying to sit up. "I fainted that's all."

"Too late," Rachel said, "and stay down." She pressed her hand against Becky's shoulder to convince her. "Even if we call back, they still have to come."

"Please," Becky asked. "Just help me sit up, that's all."

Deputy Tucker was traveling in his SUV when he received the call from 911, already on his way to the hotel for a couple of matters, the most important of which was lunch.

When he wound his way to the housekeeping department, Becky was lying back in the club chair in the corner and Heather was hovering over her with a glass of water in her hand.

"What's going on?" Tucker asked, taking in the scene.

"I'm so sorry to bother you," Becky apologized. "I fainted, fell on my head, and knocked myself out. I feel like an idiot."

Tucker approached her. "No need to be embarrassed." He caught sight of the container of pills and squinted at her. "This ever happen before?"

Becky attempted a smile. "Well, I've fainted before, but I've never knocked myself out."

"I see," Tucker said, gently. "You on medication?"

"Yeah, I'm afraid so. You can call my doctor in LA, if you like." She nodded at the prescription bottle. "His name is on the label. You can call the pharmacy and get his phone number."

The deputy picked up the bottle and studied it. "Pretty potent stuff."

"I know," Becky nodded. "I've been having headaches for over a year. If I don't get the meds in time, the pain gets too intense and I pass out."

"I'm sorry," Dewey said, with sincerity.

Becky looked up at Heather with concern. "Am I fired?"

"No, of course not," Heather said, taking her hand.

Tucker glanced around the room. "Well, ladies, if everythin's okay, I'll be in the restaurant havin' lunch with JT, if you need me. I'll direct the EMTs back here."

Tucker left the room, and Heather pulled up the office chair and continued to hover over Becky.

"I'm really okay, guys," Becky said, embarrassed, looking from one sister to the other. "Really. The medicine has finally kicked in. I can see now, and the pain is getting under control."

Heather squeezed her hand. "I want you to go to the clinic in the ambulance, Becky. You're insured and you're covered for x-rays. We don't take chances with head injuries, and there's a good chance you've had a concussion."

She held her hand up as Becky tried to protest, then straightened up and turned to Rachel. "I'll go have lunch with JT and Dewey, if you'll take care of this."

Rachel nodded. "Go. I can get it handled."

When Heather left, Rachel took her seat. "Becky, I'm really sorry about this," Rachel began. "But I really need to ask you some questions."

Becky frowned back at her. "About what?"

"About the fact that you've changed your name and your appearance."

Becky dropped her head and looked down at the floor. "I was hoping this wouldn't come up." She looked up at Rachel. "I didn't want to go into it when I was interviewed because I was afraid I wouldn't get the job."

"Well, you got the job," Rachel said, "and if you want to keep it, you'll tell me the truth."

The whine of an ambulance interrupted the low rumble of washers and dryers in the next room.

"I'm running from an abusive ex-husband." Becky said the words with an air of resignation.

Rachel nodded. "Go on."

"Our daughter committed suicide when she was eighteen." Becky looked down to regain her composure. "I got severely depressed and my husband got even more controlling and abusive than he already was. He had an affair. I found out. By then, I'd finally had enough and filed for divorce. Only he refused to let go."

"Then what happened?"

"I ended up filing a restraining order against him. I moved, changed jobs three times to try to get away from him, but he always managed to let me know he knew where I was."

Rachel nodded sympathetically. "You worked for the studios at that time."

"That's right," she added softly. "I was always constantly looking over my shoulder. Finally, I changed careers, changed my name and tried to change my appearance. I decided to move out of state and here I am."

The ambulance's wail came to a stop signaling its arrival.

"I'm really sorry," Rachel said. "That's enough to give anyone a major headache."

"Thanks. You know, I was let go once when my employer found out about my situation and the restraining order. I guess they were afraid Mel would show up someday with a gun and shoot me and anyone else in the vicinity. I can't blame them, really. I ended up getting a good recommendation and a better job, but after that I learned to avoid the truth about my personal life."

"I can understand that," Rachel said, "and I appreciate your telling me the real story." She felt the back of Becky's head where a large lump was already forming and Becky winced. "You're going to have a real goose egg there later, and you're still very pale. Don't come back to work without the doctor's okay, even if you have to take off a couple days. I'll get Maricella to take over for you for the rest of the day and tomorrow, too, if need be."

"Okay," Becky said, reluctantly. "But I'm sure I'll be fine by tomorrow."

Rachel heard the sounds of the EMTs coming in the door. She stood up to face Evan and Frank toting in their usual equipment. "Hi guys," she said with a welcoming wave. "Long time no see."

❧❧❧

The sun hugged the horizon when Dixie Markman pulled up to her casita in the Ferrari. Opening the passenger side door, she pulled Richard out and, draping her husband's arm around her shoulder, she helped him navigate the stairs to their suite.

"Are you doing okay, honey?" she asked, watching him carefully put one foot in front of the other, and already regretting she had allowed him to badger her into taking him home.

With his neck brace on, Richard's nod was barely noticeable and he emitted a weak grunt, but his eyes were narrow with pain. He stood on the landing, waiting, his hand resting on Dixie's shoulder while she dug through her purse for her key card.

Once inside, Dixie asked him if he wanted to sit in the living room or get undressed and get in the bed. Richard focused vacant eyes at her and pointed to the bedroom. He took a step and then pointed to his stomach and his mouth.

She understood. "Okay. You're hungry. Can't blame you. How about if I order up some room service for us? Maybe some soup and a milkshake for you?"

He nodded again and took a step towards the bedroom.

"Here, let me help you," Dixie offered, taking him by the elbow. He shook her off angrily. "Okay, okay," she said, trying to placate him. She understood he was hurting and, at the same time, furious about his predicament. "I'll go call in the order."

Richard drifted toward the bedroom, discarding his shirt on the way, letting it fall to the carpet.

Dixie watched him a moment then went to the sofa. She picked up the phone and traced her finger down the face card looking for the extension for room service. "You'd think I'd know the number by now," she muttered.

Richard groped his way to the bed and sat on it, exhausted. He kicked off his shoes, flinging them against the wall. He stood up to drop his slacks and stepped out of them, letting them lay in a heap, then turned, and tore the bed cover back roughly, just far enough for him to slip in underneath. Seething, he lay back against the pillow, listening to Dixie's muffled voice discussing in great detail her order with room service, and hating her more with each passing moment.

Pain raged in his throat and fury grew in his heart. Then, as a final insult from life, from somewhere outside his body, a sharp pain pierced his foot. His right leg jerked up involuntarily, as if it had been jabbed with knife. A shriek shot through his brain and pain radiated through his leg like fire, but only a muted squawk, animal-like, erupted from his swollen throat. His body jerked again, violently, lifting him off the bed. A lightning bolt of pain hit his left thigh. He writhed with pain and confusion, unable to comprehend what was happening. Again and again a stab of pain speared his legs and he thrashed and twisted in the bed, unable to turn or get up. Adrenaline poured through his veins. His heart sped up, racing now, and his face turned scarlet. Splotches of purple popped up on his body as it swelled, and he screamed, but the sound erupting in his mind never make it out of his lips. His throat constricted, closing off the low, guttural noises he made, and he struggled desperately for a breath, flinging his arms about wildly.

Dixie stopped talking for a moment and listened to the odd din coming from the other room. "That's it for now, when can we expect you?" she said, now eager to leave the phone. She muttered her thanks, hung up quickly, and rushed to the bedroom.

She screamed when she saw her husband, red-faced and thrashing in the bed, and ran to his side, horrified. "What's wrong!" she screamed at him, waving her hands and shaking in panic.

His head jerked back, and only the whites of his eyes showed as if in answer. In a moment of clarity, Dixie grabbed the phone by the bed.

Chapter 10

Rachel locked up her office and rushed over to the Hibiscus Café for an early dinner. She noticed Heather was already seated and picking the onion rings out of her salad when she walked up to the booth. Just as she uttered a greeting, she was immediately distracted by a flash of light against the window. The sunset was reflecting off the Ferrari that was just pulling into the hotel driveway. *Must be Dixie back from the clinic,* she thought. *There wasn't another red Ferrari in the whole east end of the county.*

"You plannin' on sittin' a spell?" Deputy Tucker snapped her out of her reverie.

She looked down at the empty seat he had left for her at the edge of the booth. She had no choice but to slide in next to him as JT and Heather were already munching away at their salads.

Dolly appeared immediately, as if she located a new body by sonar. "Hi, honey. You want the ribs?"

"You bet."

"Root beer? Salad with ranch? Corn and french fries?" Dolly remembered what people usually ordered and never needed to write it down. "The rest of you guys okay?" she asked. She gave Tucker a sly wink and headed back to the kitchen, leaving a whiff of inexpensive perfume in her wake.

As soon as Dolly disappeared from hearing range, Rachel told everyone the story about Becky Beeman's past. JT, Heather and Deputy Tucker all listened with attention and murmured sympathetically.

"That's a sad story," Tucker said, "and I'm sorry to say that's not the first time I ever heard somethin' like that."

Rachel noticed some familiar-looking papers lying on the booth next to Tucker. "Are those faxes from Alex?"

"Yep. He wanted to keep me in the loop," Tucker answered with half a mouthful of salad, "since you didn't let me know what you were up to."

Rachel glared at him. "I tried to talk to you about Becky. You just blew me off, like you usually do."

"Hey, let's keep this mellow, okay?" JT said, breaking in. "The bottom line is that we now know what's been going on with Becky."

"Could we please change the subject?" Heather asked. She held her fingertips to her temples, hoping her plea would avert a war of words between her sister and the deputy.

"Sounds good to me," Rachel said. "Can anyone tell me the latest about the Inner Light church?"

"The last I looked, the remainder of the group checked out today," JT said. "Ekberg should be the only one left."

"And someone from the Attorney General's office is supposed to interview him tomorrow." Tucker added, jamming a large chunk of buttered sourdough bread into his mouth.

"Has anyone seen him this afternoon?" Rachel asked. "I talked with him early this morning and he seemed pretty depressed." She noticed some head shaking, but no one responded. "So, what about Anthony Pander? Did anyone find him or did he just blend into the background never to be noticed again?" Rachel looked from JT to Dewey and back again for an answer.

"Hey, it's outa my hands now. Nobody tells me nothin'," Dewey said with his mouth full.

"That's typical government." Rachel rolled her eyes in sarcasm almost as much as she did in silent criticism of Dewey's table manners and English grammar. "You'll never hear from the FBI. They ask for everything, never tell, and always cover their butts." Her eyes began to drift around the room aimlessly and settled on the tropical print drapes.

"You know what I wonder?" she asked, "If Lars is such a great spiritual medium and White Eagle is the great all-knowing one, how it is Lars never knew about Pander and what he was up to?"

"Exactly my point, Miss Ryan," JT said. "You may remember—"

"Maybe he's delusional," Heather said, bursting in. "You know, mentally ill? Anybody can make a prediction and be fifty-per cent correct."

"I can do better than that," JT said, and held his hand to his forehead in a solemn gesture. "I predict it won't rain in Mesquite tomorrow."

Heather laughed. "You're right. That prophecy would be more like a hundred percent."

"Hold it," Tucker interrupted. He put his cell phone to his ear and listened while concern etched itself onto his face. "Okay, I can be there in sixty seconds."

"What happened?" Rachel asked, already moving out of the booth. She nearly bumped into Dolly, who just arrived.

"Dang," Tucker said, eyeing the large tray Dolly brought. "Can ya save my ribs?"

"Dewey, for Pete's sake, tell us what happened," Heather insisted.

"Nine-one-one just got a call from Dixie Markman." Tucker reached back and took his Stetson from the top of the booth. "Her husband is having some kind of attack. She says he's dying."

Dolly stood statue-still with the tray balanced on her shoulder. Tucker tossed a few bills on the table to cover his meal and made a quick exit around her. JT, Rachel, and Heather followed him out. "Okaaay," Dolly said to the empty booth. "Let's make that four take-outs."

The group nearly ran through the lobby on the way to the casitas. The sound of sirens squealed through the air as they dashed through the parking lot.

Dixie was already out on the landing, waving her hands, waiting for help. Streaks of black eye make-up ran down her cheeks while she stood heaving giant sobs. Barely able to speak, her body shook when she tried to point towards the bedroom.

Tucker stopped to catch his breath at the top of the stairs but JT ran ahead, ignoring the deputy's cry to wait. Rachel and Heather gathered around Dixie and tried to comfort her.

"I knew it! I knew it! I shouldn't have brought him home," Dixie sobbed, choking out the words. "But he wanted out of there. He insisted on coming home and I had to sign him out ADO," she wailed. A fresh batch of tears rolled down her cheeks.

Now inside the bedroom, JT gasped at the sight of Markman's face. It was swollen and frozen in a contorted mask of red and purple. The bed linens lay in a lumpy mass around his body.

Tucker stumbled in, still breathing heavily. He scrutinized the man in the bed. "What in tarnation happened here?" he asked, almost in disbelief, and placed his fingers on Markman's neck, feeling for the jugular vein.

He slowly straightened up. "There's no pulse," he finally said, still staring at the lifeless form.

The ambulance screeched to a stop in front of the Markman's casita and Frank and Evan jumped out of the cab. Heather stood on the landing and called to them, waving excitedly, and the men galloped up the stairs two at a time.

The deputy met the EMTs in the living room and motioned for them to stop. When they read Tucker's face, they understood why. Tucker stepped up to Dixie and placed his hand gently on her shoulder. "I'm sorry, Ms. Markman," he said with a tenderness in his voice rarely heard. "Your husband is gone."

"W—What?" Dixie asked. "Gone?" She stood momentarily with an odd expression on her face. Her head fell back and she dropped to the carpet as if the bones in her legs dissolved.

The two EMTs rushed to her. Frank knelt beside her, opened his bag and retrieved a bottle of ammonia inhalant. One whiff later, Dixie jerked her head awake.

"Rachel," Tucker said quietly, speaking close to her ear. "Can you keep Dixie over at your place for a while?"

"Of course."

Tucker turned to the sandy-haired man helping Dixie sit up. "Evan, can you carry Ms. Markman next door?"

"No problem, Sir," Evan replied. Even under his shirt, the young man's muscles were obvious. He picked Dixie up in his arms with one quick swoop and followed Rachel out.

Tucker turned to Frank and then cocked his head toward the bedroom. "Go take a look."

"Yeah, I need to get an official monitor reading to make sure there's no electrical activity." Frank was a little thinner and less muscular than Evan, but wielded a little more authority.

"Okay, but I've already called the ME. We're treatin' this as a homicide. So you know the rules."

"Yeah," Frank said dryly. "Watch where you walk and don't touch anything."

Thirty seconds after Frank left the room, a bellman called through the open door. "Room service," he said, holding a tray with Dixie's order.

"They're next door, at Rachel's," JT said. The bellman took a quick look around, turned and left.

A look of pain crossed Tucker's face.

"Oh, for Pete's sake, Dewey," JT said, "pick up the phone and find out if Dolly saved your ribs. You can have them delivered."

"Nah, I better wait. It don't seem right." Tucker looked at his watch. "And Dr. Martinez won't be much longer."

The medical examiner, who had flown into Wellton earlier by helicopter, had just finished her work there. She took off immediately and landed in the center of the hotel parking lot by the east side guest rooms in only a matter of minutes. The parking lot, which had been packed until that very afternoon, had plenty of room for a safe landing. The entire Inner Light group, with the exception of Ekberg, had gone home.

Dr. Allison Martinez clutched her case and hurried up the stairs to the Markman's suite. She wore her black hair pulled straight back in an old-fashioned bun, which gave her an older, serious look, but she was young and fit enough to ascend the long flight of stairs rapidly, and unlike Dewey, didn't have to gasp for air after reaching the top.

After quick introductions, Dr. Martinez entered the bedroom and studied the interior carefully before approaching the body. She took some notes and pulled out her camera. After snapping several photos of Markman and the room from various angles, she handed the camera to JT. She motioned to Tucker to help her remove the covers so she could take Markman's temperature.

"Let's take it all the way down to his ankles," the doctor said.

They all stared at Markman's body. The only clothing he wore was a pair of blue striped boxers, and a swarm of small, translucent scorpions was crawling all over his legs.

"Whoa," Tucker said. "What have we got here?" He turned abruptly to JT. "I need some kind of container, real quick."

Dr. Martinez leaned in for a closer look. Markman's legs were covered with angry red and purple lumps.

JT came back with an empty olive jar with a screw-on lid. "I dumped it and rinsed it," he said.

With tweezers firmly in his hand, the deputy grasped one of the scorpions and held it up to the light. "White Bark Scorpions," he said. One by one, he picked up the little, eight-legged creatures and placed them in the jar. "You know this is the only kind that's deadly, don't ya?" he asked, looking up at JT.

"I know of an old man who died from the sting of one of the big black ones."

"Yeah, it happens sometimes, with babies and old folks. But this type can kill a healthy athlete on a good day."

Dr. Martinez was busy snapping photos. "How many scorpions, you think, Dewey?"

"Oh, maybe a dozen," he said, continuing to pluck away the angry little killers. "One could have done the job. I reckon whoever wanted him dead decided to finish him off this time."

"Yes, I heard about the poison." Dr. Martinez stopped to check her watch and take the dead man's temperature. "Enough to maim, but not to kill."

"Yep, that's about it. I suppose if he'd drunk the whole glass in one fell swoop it could have done him in. Not that it matters now." Tucker straightened up and grunted as he arched his back. "Man that was tough on my back."

"Let's turn him over now, and look for any injuries," Dr. Martinez said. "You can check for scorpions, too."

They carefully turned Markman over, and the ME continued snapping photos.

"One more," the deputy said, lifting the last scorpion to the light before dropping him in the jar. He screwed the lid on tightly.

JT cleared his throat. "May I ask a question?"

"Sure." Tucker said, dropping the jar into a plastic bag.

"I know drain cleaner was used in the poisoning. But how could anyone get it in the glass without either Richard or Dixie noticing it?"

"Yeah, it took me a while to figure it out."

Dr. Martinez stopped taking pictures and looked over at Tucker. "Let me guess. Whoever planned the poisoning used solid-colored wine glasses."

"Yeah, the flutes were white, like milk glass. I bought me a couple glasses, pretty similar, and tried it out. I dissolved a little cleaner in the glasses, swirled it, dumped some of it, and let it dry. I did it a couple times before it worked. Then I poured in some cheap champagne."

"Cheap champagne?" JT asked.

"Yeah, I didn't want accountin' to come down on me for buyin' that fancy stuff they were drinkin'."

"Then what happened?" the doctor asked.

"It kinda bubbled up, like champagne always does. Ya know, Markman left the room after he filled the glasses. He went in the closet to get a gift for his wife, that ring he bought her. Meanwhile the bubbles were takin' the sodium hypochlorite off the sides of the glass."

"And Dixie didn't drink while Richard was gone."

"Right. She said they always made a toast before they clinked glasses, kind of a good-luck thing before they drank. It was their little ritual. Besides," he snorted, "she was busy switching glasses."

JT nodded. "Then Richard comes back and gives Dixie the ring, and they toast."

"The wine was prob'ly a little foamy, but they don't even notice." Tucker rubbed his chin, thoughtfully. "Markman takes a swig, but Dixie barely touches the glass to her lips."

"Interesting story," the doctor said, walking away from the bed. She put the camera back in her bag.

"Anythin' on the back side I need to know about?" Tucker asked, cocking his head toward the swollen body.

"Only more bites on the legs. No other bruises or marks. It wasn't a fun way to die."

Tucker walked behind her into the living room. "It never is."

Evan and Frank returned with the stretcher and were waiting for Dr. Martinez's instructions.

"Make sure you wrap the body carefully in the sheets, and wrap the whole package in the bedspread," the ME said to them. "And be extra careful with your hands, in case we missed any scorpions. I'll meet you at the helicopter."

She turned to Tucker. "I've got two more autopsies back in Yuma," she said while peeling off her gloves and tossing them in the trash. "Gang war—one knife, one gun." Fatigue was heavy in her voice.

"When you come back, I'll buy you dinner," the deputy offered. "This hotel makes the best dang steak you ever ate."

Dr. Martinez smiled. "Sounds good to me, Dewey. Take care of yourself." She nodded her head in JT's direction. "Nice to meet you, JT."

After Evan and Frank took the body, JT and Tucker sat quietly in the room and listened to the wop-wop-wop of the helicopter blades.

"You're thinking she did it, aren't you." JT said.

"You mean the wife?" Tucker nodded. "Maybe."

"Have you considered the scorpions weren't meant for Markman? He wasn't due home from the clinic today. Dixie would have slept in the bed alone tonight."

Tucker thought a minute. "That dang Rachel's been tryin' to sell me on the idea Markman was tryin' to kill Dixie. But he wouldn't have gone in the bed if he knew the scorpions were in there."

"What if he didn't?"

"What?"

"What if he hired somebody to do the job and the scorpions were put in the bed on the wrong day or something?"

"Hmm." Tucker looked around the room and fiddled with his mustache. "So what was Rachel talkin' about?"

"It's long story, but one you may want to hear."

Tucker looked at his watch. "I got time to hear it now if you got a beer over at your place. We can even send over for them ribs."

JT locked the door to the Markman's suite and the deputy stretched police tape over it, taping it securely to the trim. They were half-way down the stairs when they spotted a young woman running from a group of movie people who were standing across the parking lot, watching the action. The woman ran towards them, her blonde hair flying out behind her.

"Sheriff! Sheriff, stop," the woman cried, waving her arms.

Tucker and JT arrived at the sidewalk when she raced up to them. She held on to her stomach trying to catch her breath.

"Sheriff," she panted.

Tucker recognized her as the young woman who was parked in the car with Markman the day he discovered them behind Blood Mountain.

"It's okay, Miss Linley," he said, gently. "Catch your breath. It's okay."

Tara lifted her head and her cheeks were smeared black and purple. "I know who did it, Sheriff," she said breathlessly. "It was Dixie Markman. Dixie killed Richard." Tara flung herself against Dewey's chest. "Get her! She did it!" Tara cried, beating her hands against him. She stopped. Her body sagged and she began to sob as if her heart was ripped apart.

୧୬୧୬୨

Tara Linley sat quietly on JT's sofa sponging her face with a wet washcloth while Tucker sat next to her holding a glass of water. The deputy had carefully talked her down from her hysterical state until she finally appeared calm enough to answer questions.

"Here, drink some more," Tucker said, handing her the water.

Tara took a sip and looked up. "Does anyone have a cigarette?"

"Sorry," Tucker said, shaking his head sadly. "That's a pretty bad habit for someone as young as you to pick up."

"Yeah, I know." Tara looked away, her energy spent.

"I need to ask you some questions," Tucker said.

"Go ahead. What do you want to know?" She collapsed back into the sofa.

"How long did you have a relationship with Richard Markman?"

"Nearly two years."

Tucker and JT exchanged glances. Tara stopped to take another sip of water.

"Richard wasn't concerned that you were underage?" Tucker asked.

Tara shook her head. "No, if anything, it turned him on even more."

"And you fell in love with him."

"Oh, yes." A look of yearning washed over the young woman's face. "Richard is the most amazing man I've ever met. He's handsome, brilliant. He made my career. I was just another starlet when he put me in *Dangerous Curves Ahead.*

JT placed another full glass of water in front of her.

"Was Richard in love with you?" Tucker asked.

"Was Richard in love with me?" Tara repeated, as if the man was joking.

She tossed her head back, and stared up as if a video of their life together was flashing on the ceiling. Then she turned and looked at Tucker with eyes years older than her age. "Richard was absolutely, positively, and desperately in love with me. We were going to be married."

"But he was already married. He didn't file for divorce, isn't that right?"

"That's only because Dixie was going to bleed him dry of every penny he had," Tara burst out.

"So, no divorce?"

"Yes, he was going to divorce her," Tara insisted, annoyed. "I'm sure he was planning on telling her while we were here. He told me not to worry." She pinched her forehead, trying to remember. "He said to give him a week and he'd be rid of her."

Tucker and JT exchanged glances again. "What did he mean, 'be rid of her,' Miss Linley?"

Tara shrugged and stared off again. "I don't know. I guess he meant he was finally going to tell her he wanted a divorce. Maybe he figured out a way to pay her off. He just said, 'Trust me.'"

"So you think when he asked Dixie for a divorce, she killed him."

"Well, isn't it obvious?" Tara said with a look of distain. "Of course, she killed him. She was insanely jealous. Everyone knows that."

"And the last time you talked to Richard was when?"

"That day we were in the car and you came by."

"What about the western party at the hotel?"

"I saw Richard, but that stupid little phony was hanging all over him. We didn't speak." She looked away. "Oh, we did film a sequence. But there were lots of other people around and we never spoke to each other on a personal level. He just told me what he wanted from the movie."

"So the last time you actually spoke to Richard about anything personal was when he talked about gettin' rid of her, when you were in his car, is that right?"

"Yes." Tara looked from Tucker to JT and back again. "You know their marriage was really over years ago," she said matter-of-factly. "She slept around with younger men. He told me that." She appeared to be hoping for a nod or some kind of gesture that indicated agreement.

Instead Tucker looked over at JT and stood up. "I really appreciate your time, Miss Linley," he said, turning back to her. "And I'm really sorry for your loss. I will need to get an official statement from you tomorrow, so I hope you can stick around."

"No problem with that, Sheriff," she said with an edge to her voice. "I'll be more than happy to see the little witch rot behind bars for the rest of her life." Tara got up and began to walk toward the door.

"Would you like me to walk you back to your suite?" JT asked.

"Oh, no. I'll be fine. I think I'll join the others by the pool." Tara said, "But thank you."

JT closed the door behind Tara and turned to Tucker. "What do you think? She wouldn't have known Markman was coming home today, and she certainly had motive enough to try to kill Dixie."

"She had that all right," the deputy said, already headed toward the phone. "She could have done it." He turned and gave JT a funny look. "Except for one thing. She's so stupid I reckon she couldn't figure out how to swat a fly."

Tucker picked up the phone and punched in two buttons. He was rewarded by a familiar voice. "Hey, Dolly," he said, "you still got them ribs?"

Chapter 11

Old Town Mesquite originally sprang up where two rivers intersected. The lay of the land was flat and the edges of the river were often punctuated with leafy cottonwoods and the gray-green of tamarisk trees. The ground, itself, a clay-sand mixture deposited by centuries of flooding, gradually inclined from the water's edge until it reached the wall of a mesa where it dramatically shot up a hundred feet.

As the settlement of Mesquite grew, some folks decided not to endure the occasional flood from the river and opted to live on the mesa instead. The area sprouted like sagebrush, only slowing down in the early sixties when the interstate by-passed the town. Snowbirds, along with their RV's, still flocked to the area each winter, all wanting to escape the snow in the north and bask in the warmth of sunny skies.

Old Town radiated a certain charm, and the businesses located there still flourished. A few of the original adobe houses from the early 1900's still stood, all recycled into quaint little shops and art galleries. The oldest bank in town, a renovated relic of the 1930s, sat above an eighteen-inch raised curb designed to allow the occasional flood waters to roll by. That problem ceased to be a worry when the dam was built, but the curb stayed, adding itself to the old west ambience of the area.

Rachel looked up at the art deco clock that hung from the black arm on the front of the bank. It was five past one and she was late. She quickened her pace and passed the old hotel, which was an apartment complex in its present incarnation, and finally arrived at the First Street Pharmacy.

When Rachel stepped inside, she felt like she'd stepped back in time. At the rear of the room, a strong wire cage contained a raised platform where a gray-haired pharmacist, dressed in a white lab coat, was filling prescriptions. Oiled wooden floors creaked under her heels, and the smells of years gone by intermingled with those that came from the lunch counter to her left.

Several of the chrome stools were filled. She was grateful none of the customers looked familiar. Finally Rachel noticed her lunch date waving to her from the little alcove that only allowed room for two small tables.

"Hi, Dewey," Rachel said, sitting down opposite him. "I got here as fast as I could. I'm not that familiar with this area and afraid I got a little confused."

Tucker decided there was no sense pointing out that Rachel was often confused, especially now that he needed her help. "No problem, Rachel. I appreciate your comin' down here to meet me in between my appointments. This private enough for you?" He glanced out at the pharmacy floor.

"It's fine. I doubt Dixie or anyone that knows her would find their way here. I feel a little guilty talking about this." She took a quick look behind her. "Even so, I decided to tuck my hair up under a hat and wear sun glasses."

"Yeah, great disguise."

A man with a stained apron appeared at their table with two hamburger plates, two milk shakes, and set them down.

"I ordered for you. Hope you don't mind. I got a meetin' at the bank in thirty minutes.

"Thanks," Rachel said and sipped a little of her drink. "Wow. This is a real milk shake. It's delicious."

"Yup, and these are the best burgers in town."

"I'll have to bring Heather here. This is such a quaint place. She'd love it."

"And speaking of Heather," Tucker said, looking down at his plate. "I need to know abo—"

"Yeah," Rachel said, interrupting him. "Heather already told me she blabbed to JT what I told her and he blabbed to you." She picked up her burger, the bottom half of which was wrapped in baking parchment, and looked at it.

"Don't take the paper off," Tucker said.

"Okay," Rachel said and bit into her burger. Juice leaked out of the bottom and some shredded lettuce fell out of the top.

"Well, I understand you overheard the conversation between Dixie Markman and Lars Ekberg. The part I want to know about is where Ekberg warns her about someone tryin' to kill her."

"Mmm," Rachel mumbled, her mouth still full. She took a sip of her drink and swallowed. "Actually, the first night we went to the meeting Lars said someone with the initial D had a cheating husband and D needed to protect herself."

"There coulda been other ladies with the initial D."

"True, but rumors had been floating around about Richard and Tara for a while. So when Dixie got back to her suite, she confronted Richard about it. He denied having anything to do with Tara at first."

Tucker pulled out a little spiral notebook and scribbled in it. He looked up. "Then what happened?"

"Dixie told me she looked in the trash and found the empty wine bottles."

"Hmm." Tucker scribbled in a little spiral notebook. "That's when the fight started, right?"

"Not so fast." Rachel started to feel a little uncomfortable talking about her friend. "Since Richard drinks Wild Turkey and Tara drinks Rhine wine, Dixie did accuse Richard of lying and they kind of got into it. That's about the time I got home. At first I heard voices. Then they got louder. I put on my robe and went out on the patio. I heard Dixie scream, then a crash. That's when I almost called nine-one-one"

"And Dixie came to see you the next day, is that right?"

"Yes, in my office."

"Did Dixie look like she was hurt physically?" Tucker looked at her without expression.

Rachel hated that. She couldn't read his face. "No," she said. "I think she fared a little better than Richard."

"Yeah, I saw the scratch marks on his face." Tucker chomped into his burger and chewed a bit. "Did she say anything about wantin' to kill him?"

Rachel stiffened. *Where was he going with this?* She took another bite out of her hamburger and began to chew, giving herself a few seconds to consider her reply.

"Don't think ahead of me, Rachel, just answer the question."

Rachel chewed vigorously and took another sip of her milkshake, determined to keep from implicating Dixie in Richard's death. "Okay. During their argument, Dixie threw a lamp at Richard and missed. She told me that next time she would aim better. But she was *joking,* Dewey! We *laughed* over it!"

Tucker wrote some more in his notebook then bit into his burger and thought about it a while. "So what about this White Eagle prophecy? Did you hear Ekberg say anythin' about that?" His mouth was full of food, and a bit of juice leaked down his chin.

Rachel turned her head to the side to keep from looking at him. She studied the round, chrome clock on the wall. It was right out of the fifties with a fluorescent light around the edge that turned colors from pink to blue. She poked at her french fries and ate one of them before she looked up at Tucker. His mouth was finally closed and he had wiped his face.

"Yes, I heard him talk about it," Rachel said. "Dixie said she wanted me to be close by, so I really couldn't help overhearing."

"I don't care about that. Just tell me what the guy said."

"I heard him tell her to beware of high places and the tree of death. Then he said, 'A gift can be your poison.' So afterwards, when Dixie wanted me to go up the mountain where they were filming, I did. That's when I saw Richard try to make Dixie fall off the overlook."

Tucker stopped writing and squinted at her. "What do you mean? Did he physically push her?"

Rachel was tempted to embellish what she saw, but stuck to the truth. "No, but if I hadn't screamed, and if Ferdie hadn't grabbed her and pulled her off that rock, she would have sailed right off the cliff. You can talk to any of the guys that were up there filming. They all saw it."

"Hmm. I may just do that," Tucker said, making more notes in his little book. "Tell me about the poison marshmallows."

Rachel swallowed the bite of burger she'd nibbled on. "When I realized Richard had threaded the marshmallows on an oleander stick instead of the toasting forks, I grabbed them and threw them in the fire. Most men would be grateful if I saved his wife. But not Markman. He was furious."

"And you're sure the stick was from an oleander bush?"

"Yes, absolutely, and Toro verified it. We both know what an oleander branch looks like." She stared at Tucker to make her point. "I even saved the thing and gave it to Buddy, so you can check it out yourself, if you don't believe me."

"I might do that."

"Well, I think it's obvious Markman picked the twig ahead of time and put it by the hay bale. Maintenance put out the bales first thing in the morning, so he had plenty of opportunity. I placed the two buckets of toasting forks by the pit before noon. Everyone could see them, and Richard could have easily grabbed one of those to toast the marshmallows. That is, unless he wanted to use an oleander branch just so he could kill his wife."

Tucker made more notes and refused to comment. "You were the first one to reach Dixie after she and Markman drank the poisoned wine. Did she tell you she switched the glasses?"

Rachel felt her face flush and pretended to be interested in her fries. "Well, I guess she forgot to mention that to me at the time. I mean, she was pretty hysterical when I first saw her."

"She was that, all right."

"Later, when she talked to you, she said she remembered Ekberg's warning, about how a gift could be poison. I'm sure that's why she did it."

"But she barely touched the glass to her lips. So maybe she knew poison was in both of the glasses."

Rachel narrowed her eyes, realizing where the deputy was headed. "You can't mean that, Dewey."

"Hey, you got a jealous wife who knows her husband is cheatin'. She suspects he's tryin' to kill her. You told me yourself you stopped two attempts. She finally decides to kill him first. But the poison doesn't kill him. So bein' an actress an' all, she cries up a big storm when he gets injured—and she makes sure she hurts herself a little bit, too."

Rachel clapped her hand over her mouth. *What have I done?*

"Then on the very night she brings her husband home from the clinic, there's a nest of bark scorpions in their bed," Tucker continued. "Only she ain't in the bed with him."

"No! It wasn't her," Rachel cried.

"And why is that?"

"Because I just know she didn't kill him."

Tucker rubbed a bit of stubble on his chin that he missed with the razor. "Yep, that'll stand up in court, all right."

"Like your evidence will?" Rachel snapped. "It's all circumstantial. Anybody could have put that tray on the bell desk."

"I know."

"You know?"

"Yeah, I know. I didn't say I was going to arrest Dixie, so you can git off your high horse."

"But she's a suspect?"

"Yeah. Right along with a few other people who hated Richard's guts."

Rachel squinted at the deputy. "And would I happen to know any of those particular people?"

"Maybe." His voice as cold as the frosted glass in his hand. "I could be lookin' at one right now."

"What? You can't mean *me*." Rachel almost knocked the remains of her drink over. "Tell me you're joking."

The deputy wasn't smiling. "I'm afraid a couple of people at that western party reported hearing you say somethin' about killing Markman."

"What? I—I don't believe this."

Tucker flipped back through his notepad a few pages and recited from his notes: "I'd like to kill him. I'd like to make that rotten scumbag suffer in such a way, he'd wish for an eternity in Hell instead."

Rachel fell back in her chair like a ball of risen dough punched down in the bowl.

"Do you deny saying that?" Tucker asked calmly.

"No, I don't deny saying that." Her voice was flat, subdued.

"Did ya kill him?"

"Of course, I didn't kill him."

"Okay. I needed to hear you say that. I never really thought ya did."

"Dewey Tucker!"

"Don't 'Dewey Tucker' *me,* Rachel Ryan," the deputy said, jabbing his finger toward her. "And while you're at it, you might try keepin' that ol' temper of yours under control."

Rachel was about to speak, but Tucker held up his hand to silence her. He pulled out his cell phone which was vibrating like a rattler's tail.

"Yeah, JT. What'd ya need? What?" Tucker shook his head in disbelief. "Well, I'll be. Just stay put and don't touch nothin' in the room. We're headin' out that way right now."

"What happened?" Rachel asked.

Tucker pulled out his wallet and dropped a couple bills on the table, more than enough for the lunch and tip. "Let's go," he said, and looked at his watch. "Guess I'll be missin' my meetin' after all."

"Tell me what happened," Rachel demanded, holding her ground.

"They just found Lars Ekberg on the floor, unconscious. Looks like he overdosed."

Chapter 12

JT was sitting on edge of the sofa in Lars Ekberg's suite with his head buried in his hands. He didn't see Deputy Tucker clump through the open door, but heard his steps and felt his presence. JT slowly lifted his head.

Rachel burst into the room. "What happened?"

JT's eyes were red. "I think he overdosed. That's what it looks like, anyway."

"Is he alive?" Rachel asked.

JT just shook his head.

"How long have Evan and Frank been here?" Dewey asked him.

"A couple minutes."

"I already called the ME. She's on her way. Watch for her, will you?"

The deputy plodded toward the bedroom. Rachel looked around the living room, not sure what to do, and finally eased onto the sofa next to JT. She started to speak, but everything she thought of saying sounded stupid or trite, so she sat quietly with her hands in her lap.

JT leaned back against the cushions but didn't look at her. "He left a note," he said quietly. "It's still on the computer."

"I better tell Dewey," Rachel said, springing up from the sofa. Evan and Frank were coming out of the bedroom. "Hey, guys," she said, sympathy in her voice. "You must be getting tired of coming up here."

"Heck no, Rachel," Evan quipped. "Without this hotel, we could be out of a job."

Rachel affectionately patted his shoulder and edged into the bedroom. Ekberg was lying on his side on the carpet, his arms extended out gracefully, as if he'd simply fallen asleep and slipped off his chair. She glanced over at the computer. The monitor's screen saver was flicking on pictures of natural wonders. Next to the keyboard sat an orange colored prescription bottle with the lid off.

"JT told me he left a note on the computer," Rachel said. "You want me to pull it up?"

"Can you print it out and save the e-mail and not touch the keyboard or anything?"

"Give me a second."

Rachel left the room and came back with a hat pin. "I knew I carried this thing around in my purse for some reason," she said, holding it up.

The printer whined and spit out two copies.

"Rachel."

"You never saw that," Rachel said, giving him one copy and walking out with the other. She sat down on the sofa next to JT and read the note:

Dear Cee-Cee,

Please forgive me for what I've done. I can't bear to face the mess I've made of everything. The thing with Dixie Markman blew up way out of proportion and I'm sick over it. I was stupid and should have listened to you.

Even worse, as you will soon hear, Anthony betrayed me. The anguish I am feeling is so unbearable, I cannot even think clearly anymore. That he stabbed me in the back is bad enough, but to steal money from people who trusted me—well, there are just no words.

The final blow is that White Eagle has gone. Yes, my precious sister, he left me, just like Anthony did. I have nothing left. Absolutely nothing.

Forgive me, dear one, and don't be dis

Rachel looked up and stared into the room, imagining the betrayal, the pain Ekberg must have felt. Then, as if her feelings were like an open book, she snapped it shut. She read the letter a second time, analyzing every word. The reference to Dixie Markman puzzled her. *What did it mean?*

"JT? Did you notice what Ekberg said about Dixie Markman? About the thing that was blown up out of proportion? JT?" Rachel looked up.

JT was gone.

☙☙☙

Rachel drifted through the lobby, her heels clicking against the tile. Except for that, the large room was oddly quiet, with few guests in view during the brief interlude between the check-outs and the check-ins. She glanced at her office, with its french doors tightly closed, and casually slipped in behind the registration desk.

"Did JT come in?" Rachel asked the clerk who was busy accessing information on the computer.

"Yes," Amalia answered, "but he doesn't want to be disturbed," she added with an apologetic look.

"Tough cookies," Rachel said. She knocked on JT's office door and entered before she heard a response.

JT was sitting at his desk in with his head bent over and his hands in front of him. He slowly turned his head and said quietly, "Did it occur to you, Miss Ryan, that I might wish to be alone right now?

"Of course, Mr. Carpenter. Why do you think I barged in?"

JT gave her a sour look and resolutely crossed his arms over his chest. "What do you want?"

"We need to talk about Lars' suicide."

"Why? I'm sure there'll be thousands of people doing that for us. We may even get photographers here from the National Scoop or whatever Heather reads."

"Yeah, and that's kind of what I wanted to talk to you about." Rachel eased into one of the chairs in front of JT's desk. "When are Heather and Buddy bringing my nephews back?"

"Tomorrow morning, sometime. Is that all you wanted?"

"Not exactly. Look, you know how sensitive Heather is. She has such a soft heart for everyone."

JT snapped to attention. "You aren't thinking of *not* telling her, are you? It will be all over the stupid papers."

"I hate it when you do that! Don't anticipate what I'm going to say."

"Then get to the bottom line," JT said, meeting her eye-to-eye.

Rachel looked up at the ceiling and let out a huff of air. "Look, JT, you need to get used to the fact that suicides are a fact of life at hotels. People check in to do the job so they won't leave a mess at home. Why do you think high-rise hotels have their windows sealed shut? They've gotten tired of cleaning up after jumpers. Not to mention the old farts, who are popping ED pills like candy and manage to drop dead on top of their illicit protégés—"

"Okay, okay," JT said. "And your point is?"

Rachel's eyes went soft. "The point is, I'd like to offer you a little advice, if you're willing to listen. I promise I won't even repeat the "you're our hero" speech I gave you that last time you got depressed."

A weary smile tugged at JT's lips. "Go ahead. I'm listening."

"I'd like to recommend what a former boss of mine did when three people killed themselves at our hotel in two months."

"Which was?"

"He simply did *not* overreact."

JT looked at her steadily. "You think I should play it cool."

"Very cool." Rachel nodded in agreement. "Everyone will follow your lead. Acknowledge what happened, yes, but don't let it be the end of the world."

"And the bad publicity?"

Rachel stood up to leave. "Think of the old Hollywood adage: The only bad publicity is no publicity." She turned in time to see Amalia come to the door, about to knock.

"Oh, Rachel, excuse me," she said. "There's someone at the front desk waiting to see you. He says it's of great importance."

Wondering who that could be, Rachel walked out and turned the corner. "I don't believe it," she exclaimed, setting eyes on the rugged-looking man standing in the lobby.

She ran out to greet him, and flung her arms around his neck. "Alex Tucker! Why didn't you tell me you were coming?"

Alex hugged her tightly and kissed her in front of every pair of eyes in the room. "I didn't know myself until just a few hours ago. I have to go to Phoenix and pick up a prisoner. On the way over I decided to take a little detour."

Rachel pulled back and looked at him. "You look great," she said. "How *are* you?"

"I'm good—and you look beautiful." He smiled his crooked smile at her and his eyes drifted around the room at their audience. Two men were now within hearing distance. "Is there some place we can go that's a little more private?"

"Of course." She grabbed his hand. "Follow me."

Rachel led him to the Plantation Dining Room, and Alex slid into one of the booths against the front wall.

"You hungry?" she asked, sitting down beside him.

"No, but I wouldn't mind some coffee and maybe a piece of pie. I've still got a few miles to go."

"You could stay over. We have room."

In the dim light, the color of the beads around her neck tinted her eyes a pale jade. Alex stared into them. "Do you really think that's a good idea? You might find me knocking at your door at one o'clock."

Rachel felt heat rush to her face and she dropped her eyes. She hadn't meant to make it sound like a sexual invitation. Yet, she was melting and could feel her body pull toward him, toward whatever masculine thing he was emitting. She gave him a penetrating look. "Life does get complicated, doesn't it?" Sanity prevailed and she moved away. "Let me get a waitress. Is coconut cream pie okay?" she asked, remembering one of his favorites.

He smiled, a bit of amusement dancing in his eyes. "Sounds great to me."

Rachel darted off to the kitchen and flustered around getting coffee for them. She was back in a minute, toting a tray with two mugs of coffee, and slid into the booth close to Alex. She could feel the heat from his leg next to hers. "It'll be quiet in here for another hour. We don't open for dinner until five."

"Good. It might take you the whole hour to fill me in, according to what Uncle Dewey tells me," he teased.

"Oh, really? What did our dear deputy sheriff have to say?"

"Only that you were up to your neck in dead bodies again."

Before Rachel could reply, a young waitress appeared at their table and set their order down. Leaving them with a quick smile and a fresh carafe of coffee, she headed back to the kitchen.

After a small bite of pie and sip of coffee, Rachel relayed the events that led up to Ekberg's suicide.

Alex reached out for Rachel's hand. "Are you okay? This has to be tremendously hard on you." The tone of his voice, the softness that filled his eyes, betrayed his feelings for her.

"Actually, I am okay—for now, anyway. I may fall apart next week, but right now, I'm holding it together." Rachel looked away and poked at her pie absentmindedly. "I'm just frustrated that all these pieces of a puzzle are out there floating around and nothing fits. What do the Markmans have to do with Ekberg? Who is Anthony Pander, really? Did Ekberg make up all that stuff he told Dixie? There's nothing solid to grab on to, if you know what I mean."

"I certainly do know what you mean. That's the story of my life. That's what I do." He rested his hand on top of Rachel's. "And I hate to tell you this, but I found some information that will probably confuse things even more."

"More information? About what?"

"You remember you asked me about Benny Ammato?"

"Yes, of course. He delivered the cheese plate to the Markman's room. He's also on JT's list for a couple offenses."

"Really? For what?"

"Harassing a couple of the female employees." Rachel dropped her eyes. "We also suspect him of being a peeping tom, but don't have any proof. As soon as the movie people leave, Benny will be out the door."

"Huh. Well, that's interesting." Alex took a bite of his pie and drank some coffee while he digested the information he just learned. "You remember I told you I couldn't find zip on him."

"Yes. So did you find something after all?"

"Yeah. He had a juvenile record which had been expunged three years ago."

Rachel's eyes widened. "Really? How did you manage to find that out?"

"Oh, I have my ways," he said, his eyes teasing.

"I'm sure you do." She cast a sly glance at him. "So what did he do?"

"Accessory to robbery. He was fourteen."

"Fourteen? Oh, boy." Rachel leaned back against the back of the booth. "I bet he was with some older guys."

"Right. It was a gang initiation. They hit up a Circle-K."

"Anything else?"

"Possession of drugs."

"That's quite a record for a teenager." Rachel leaned forward and took another stab at her pie. "But Benny hasn't been in any real trouble since then, right? Other than being a jerk, I mean."

"Not in this country."

"Then, I don't really know where he'd fit in the Markman's case, unless we could prove he had a motive to kill him. That's what it takes, right? Motive, means, and opportunity?" She began to twirl a strand of hair around her finger. "I did a little snooping, too. Benny knew the Markmans. He used to live in LA, and he had a personal recommendation from Dixie Markman. He worked for her at one time, according to his personnel file."

Alex raised his eyebrows and grunted.

"I—um, looked through all the files of the recent hires and he's the only one that would fit. There was one other guy I considered, but if you talked to him, you'd know it couldn't be him."

Alex looked thoughtful and took another sip of coffee. "Anything else?"

Rachel nodded. "What about the idea that Ammato planted the scorpions in Markman's bed? Dixie could have been the motive. As a bellman, he certainly had the opportunity and the means. But..." Rachel's voice faded off as she traced the rim of her cup with her finger, thinking. "Benny could probably catch a few scorpions, but I'm not sure he'd be bright enough to figure out the poisoning part."

She paused and looked down at her hand. It had drifted over to Alex's forearm where she was stroking the soft hair on it. Embarrassed, she jerked her hand away.

"On the other hand," she said, feeling her face turning pink, "I think everyone in the world knows that scorpions are poisonous."

Alex brought his hand up to his face, trying to hide a smile. "I know Uncle Dewey talked to him once and I think he pretty much wrote Ammato off as an idiot. But even if he wasn't that stupid and thought of the scorpion angle, given his history—and being a male—he'd be more apt to try to kill someone with a gun or a knife."

"That's a scary thought." Rachel shuddered, recalling her confrontation with him at the pool. "Do you mind if I share that information with JT? And the stuff about his juvenile record? I think he'd fire Ammato quickly if he knew."

"I really can't let you do that, Rachel. I'm not supposed to know myself."

"Okay, fair enough," she agreed. "But at least we know about him. Other than him and Becky—AKA, Rebecca Callahan—we don't know of anyone else who had been in the room. I mean, except for Tara and the maid."

"Were you satisfied with Becky's explanation?"

"Well, it's obvious she passed out that day in her office. And her story about her ex-husband makes sense. She did change her name a while back. I know Dewey called her doctor and the prescription is legit. She also appeared to be genuinely horrified when she found out about the poisoned champagne."

"So then what?"

"Exactly." Rachel stared off, deep in though. "The trouble is, there are ways someone could have access to a key card, if he really wanted one. Stealing one from an employee, using a bribe, a threat. Even getting a card from someone who normally wouldn't have access to the room. So where does that leave us? I'm fresh out of ideas as to what to do next."

"Hmm. Maybe I can help with that." Alex opened the file folder at his side and handed her a sheet of paper. "A little information about Ekberg and his sister, Cecilia."

"Cee-Cee." Rachel nodded, "Of course. We need to bring Ekberg's stuff over to her," she said, her mind already planning her next move. "I could ask Buddy to fly us over."

"Ah, Buddy." Alex tried to keep his voice nonchalant. "How is he?"

Rachel blushed. "He's fine. We've gotten to be good friends, ever since that night—"

"It's okay, Rachel." Alex covered her hand with his. "He's good for you. He's good *to*—" There was a long pause. "He's ready to settle down. He'd make you a good husband."

Rachel locked on his eyes, searching them. "Maybe. What about you?" she asked, and immediately wanted to slap her own mouth, take it back, for she really had no desire for marriage, not now, not with anyone.

"I'm lousy husband material." His crooked smile turned up one side of his mouth. "You can ask my two ex-wives."

"I remember you said you've been married twice, but I thought you were joking." She looked at him from underneath her lashes. "Were you faithful?"

Shocked at herself for asking so intimate a question, she mentally bonked her forehead on the table. *What in the world am I doing? Why can't I keep my mouth zipped?*

Alex smiled his half-smile again, obviously nonplused. "For as long as I was married."

"Which was?"

"The first time, a year. The second time, ten months."

"So you're pretty good for a short time, huh? A few weeks of fireworks and then back to business?"

"I'm afraid so." Alex's expression became serious. "The job's a marriage killer. You get a tough case and it's long hours and a lot of exposure to what's ugly in life. A woman gets tired of it—the loneliness, the crazy hours, the bad moods."

Rachel locked eyes with him. "I can imagine most women wouldn't appreciate that." *But I'm not like most women,* she almost added, but kept her tongue for once.

They sat quietly for a few more moments, savoring the time they had. Alex glanced down at his watch and looked back at Rachel with a question in his eyes. Rachel smiled and slid out of the booth.

Alex stood up next to her and pulled her tightly to him, confidently. She yielded to his kiss, a deep and sensual one, feeling him up against her, and then pulled away.

He spoke softly, his voice inviting. "If you're ever in the mood for fireworks, let me know."

She felt herself moisten—not so much because of what he said and how he said it, but from the silent, invisible, voluminous broadcasting of his male pheromones on her frequency. She didn't doubt for a moment there'd be fireworks, didn't doubt she could convince him to stay, even overnight, with just a word. But she stepped away, her hand sliding down the length of his arm to his fingertips.

"I'll think about the fireworks," she said, deeply conflicted, and led him out of the room.

ℰ⁓ℰ⁓

Deputy Dewey Tucker and Dolly May Roundtree stepped through the double doors of Domino's restaurant at precisely five-fifty-nine. The owner, Anna Venkman, positioned herself near the bar where she was able to survey her little empire, and she frowned when the deputy and his garishly dressed date passed through the portals of her fine French restaurant.

Tucker, himself, was hardly more stylishly dressed. He wore an out-dated polyester-and-wool blend jacket that was slightly too small and a short-sleeved white shirt that had yellowed with age.

Anna Venkman noticed with dismay he was wearing a tie. A ridiculously old one, that was true, but it was a tie none-the-less, and the reason she could not refuse him entrance to her beautiful establishment. As the couple looked around, Anna quickly stepped up to the hostess, whispered a few words, and then stepped back into the shadows.

Dewey Tucker, for his part, immediately set his eyes on the refrigerated glass case on his right and was mesmerized by it contents. It was filled with every type of confection known to man, all of which seemed to be covered either in chocolate or whipped cream.

Dolly was awed by Domino, the larger-than-life mannequin on her left, which was dressed in a black and white harlequin costume complete with jester's cap. Every few seconds, the white-faced Domino blinked and seemed to come alive with the jerky movements of a robot.

Before the couple could look any father, the hostess called out a welcoming greeting and asked if they had a reservation. Tucker was quickly beside her, looking down at the list, and pointed to his name. Disappointed he was listed, the hostess led them to a table in the back of the room near the kitchen door.

A black-suited waiter rushed up to them, held out a chair for Dolly, and seated her graciously, following that with a bow of his head. He then whipped the white cloth napkin from the table and unfolded it on her lap, centering it carefully over her red taffeta dress.

Moving quickly to the deputy's side, he reached for Tucker's napkin, only to have his hand grabbed. "I can spread my own dang napkin on my lap, thank you," the deputy said.

A second waiter appeared with menus. "Allow me to recommend the escargot as an appetizer, Madam," he said, turning to Dolly.

Dolly looked up, beaming, then recognized the young man. "Why Roberto, what are you doing here?"

Roberto stiffened, then his eyes shifted to the far left and right before he leaned over and pretended to point out something on the menu. "She offered me a lot more money plus benefits," he whispered. "But she's a nightmare to work for."

Dolly murmured a word of sympathy before Roberto straightened and resumed his former demeanor. "I'd like the escargot," she said then asked if Dewey wanted to share.

"Sure," Tucker said, looking over the menu. He couldn't even figure out what half of the appetizers were and was already feeling out of his element. "And bring the lady your best margarita and me a bourbon and water, pronto."

Dolly took over the ordering and, knowing JT had given them five hundred dollars to spend on whatever they wanted, selected items she'd read about, heard about, but never went to a place that actually served such fancy food. After she finished ordering, the couple settled in and surveyed their surroundings. Dolly was loving it, having seen beautiful interiors in magazines before. Tucker was plainly uncomfortable, both from wearing a shirt and jacket he'd outgrown a couple of inches ago and also from the array of the eight pieces of silver-plated flatware set precisely in front of him.

Before the couple even had a chance to scope the whole place out, their drinks arrived. Dolly looked lovingly across the table at Tucker. "Shall we toast?"

Tucker turned pink. "Sure. You say it."

"To a beautiful evening," Dolly cooed, beaming.

"Right." The deputy practically swigged down his whole drink.

Before Dolly's second sip, the escargot arrived. She sat up excitedly as the plate was placed between them.

"What the hell? Those are snails," Tucker said, a mite too loudly. People at the next table turned their heads to look at him. "I ain't eatin' them."

Clearly chagrinned, Dolly gave Roberto an apologetic look. "Don't worry, I love them. Why don't you bring the deputy the fruit mélange?"

"Yes, madam," he said formally, with the emphasis on the second syllable, and turned on his heel.

A creamy crab bisque was served next along with bread and mixed grain crackers baked in restaurant's own kitchen.

Dolly lifted her soup spoon. "When I eat in a place with so many pieces of silverware, I always start at the outside and work in," she said, hoping to help her date avoid a faux pas, like the one he made when he used his seafood fork to spear and eat his fruit cup. She smiled with relief when he picked up the correct piece, happy she took time to read the book on manners she borrowed from the public library.

They got through the salad course with no problem and handled the lobster dish with aplomb. Things began to fall apart when the Roberto brought the finger bowls, and Tucker proceeded to sip his with the remaining spoon beside his plate.

"That's a finger bowl," Anna Venkman hissed, walking up and handing him the warm towel in her hand. "You dip your fingers in it to clean them."

Tucker flushed with embarrassment, but Dolly was too inebriated after drinking the whole bottle of wine by herself to care. She said, "Well, without the towels it looked like a cheap broth to me, too. I thought you were using it like an intermezzo."

Anna sniffed, insulted and amazed Dolly knew what an intermezzo was, turned away sharply and left. Tucker wanted to reach out and hi-five his date.

They were both stuffed by then, but decided to order dessert and after dinner drinks. After all, JT wanted them to try everything so they could give him a complete report. Roberto brought the desert tray, Dolly picked a napoleon and Tucker decided on a slice of chocolate torte. When he served Dolly, he slipped her a card with his phone number. "Call me," he whispered.

They lingered as long as they could over their after-dinner brandies watching the other patrons before they finally called it a night. They left Roberto an extra-large tip.

When they arrived at the foyer, a large crowd— obviously having left a local bar— suddenly came flood-

ing in and pressed their way around the glass case displaying the fancy desserts. Dolly found herself being
pushed backwards, against Tucker. The deputy, himself,
was pushed back, and then he suddenly felt a hand reach
for the gun at his side. In one swift motion, he spun
around, grabbed the arm of the offender, pulled him forward and off-center and the larger-than-life mannequin
tumbled off his stand into the crowd and onto the floor.

Anna Venkman surged into the foyer and witnessed
her beloved Domino facedown and lifeless. She spun into
such a rage she frightened the boisterous crowd with her
screams of "Get out! Get out!" and the foyer full of people, including Dolly May Roundtree and Deputy Dewey
Tucker, quickly fled out the tall double doors.

☙❧

After Detective Alex Tucker kissed Rachel good-by
and left the hotel, Rachel mindlessly finished her day,
took a book to bed, and didn't fall asleep until well after
midnight. Even then, it was a fitful, restless sleep. She
couldn't keep thoughts of Alex from going through her
mind. She wondered why she had let him go again, wondered if she should have given in and asked him to stay
the night, wondered if she should have packed up and left
with him.

No. It was his move. He was the one who had left.
Yet the soft-edged images of his face flooded over her,
crowding out everything else. She lay there feeling drawn
into the deep darkness of his eyes, felt the warmth of his
lips on hers—

"Stop it!" she shouted into the darkness, and pounded her pillow in hopes of pushing it into a position more amiable to a restful sleep. It didn't work.

She finally got up, massaged her neck, and made her way to the kitchenette in the semi-darkness. She opened the refrigerator, hoping to find some non-expired milk. She did. She poured herself a glass and then scrounged for a cookie. Success. She sauntered over to the sliding glass door with milk and cookie in hand and popped open the door. The air on the patio was cool and refreshing without a hint of a breeze. At three in the morning it usually was.

She leaned against the railing and surveyed the grounds, her gaze falling on part of the courtyard nearest her. Colored spotlights tinted the tall, knobby clumps of monstros cacti a purple color and the odd-looking boojum tree a fiery red, turning the desert garden into something from another world. Nothing stirred. Rachel's eyes shifted west, over to the parking lot where a small pickup caught her attention. She straightened up, suddenly alert. It was Rosario's truck. There was no doubt about it. Rosario had bought the Ford slightly used and slightly dented, and had it repaired and painted at Tom's. It was shiny and beautiful and painted a lovely shade of rose.

What is she doing here this time of night? Rachel's eye flicked over to the guest rooms in front of the truck, puzzled. *A date? No. It's against the rules, and besides, she would never do that. Not Rosie. She'd never leave her son unless it was some kind of emergency, and she would have called me if there had been one.*

Rachel cried out, slapping her forehead as the realization hit her. *Man, I hope I'm not too late.* She dashed back into her suite, and threw on some clothes, and was out the door.

❧❧❧

Just an hour earlier Rosario had counted the money, locked up the lounge, and stopped by the front desk to turn in the night's take.

"Was it a good night?" Kory asked.

"Not bad," she answered, handing him the bag of receipts. "You?"

"It was busy earlier, but nobody's been in since eleven-thirty." The night clerk pulled back the lid of the safe and dropped in the envelope. "Drive carefully. Lots of nuts of there."

"Yeah, I know. I served a few of them earlier. I almost eighty-sixed them."

"Then be extra careful."

"Thanks, I will. *Buenas noches.*"

❧❧❧

Rosario pulled her truck out of the employees' parking lot, but instead of pulling into the driveway to go home, she drove around to the west side block of guest rooms and parked in the last space. She hurried down the sidewalk and around the main building, lugging her heavy tote bag. She entered the cavernous lobby though the front door. The entrance to the lounge was only a few feet to her right. She paused at it, took a deep breath, and made the sign of the cross. Then she quietly unlocked the door and slipped through it unnoticed, appreciating the cover that the piped-in elevator music afforded her.

The darkened lounge offered only the minimal blue lights off the electronics, not enough for Rosario to navigate through the bar safely. She dug for the small flashlight in her purse, pulled it out, and pointed its light at the floor. In a matter of seconds she arrived at the store room at the end of the bar and squatted in front of the door. The black hair she had planted between the frame and the door was still in place.

Rosario entered the small room, pulled the door shut, making sure it was secure with a quick jiggle of the knob. She flashed the light around the area. At the back of room, a tall rack held over seventy bottles of specialty wine, five of which were Dom Perignon. The less expensive house wines were packed in cartons to the left of the rack. Rosario visually inventoried the strong wooden shelves to the right. She had placed several top shelf bottles of liquor in full view and placed a few empty cartons below them. The stage was set.

Her gaze traveled to the towers of beer directly on her right. The assorted beverages had been brought in the day before and she had asked the delivery man to stack them to her specifications. The beer towers formed a backwards "L". This made for a small, partially enclosed area right near the entrance. Rosario stepped inside it, sat down on a small stack of beer cases, and was hidden from view. Then she waited.

It wasn't long before Benny Ammato and Candy Kartcher pulled up in front of the hotel entrance in Benny's Firebird. Candy ran ahead of him through the lobby where she immediately rushed behind the front desk and jumped into Kory's arms. By the time Benny strolled up to it, the couple was in the midst of a passionate kiss.

"Okay, okay, I'm here," Benny said, straightening his uniform and feeling annoyed by the couple's public display of affection.

Candy broke away from Kory's embrace. "Thank you for doing this, Benny," she said, her eyes filled with gratitude. "We haven't been able to get together for three days because of our schedules."

"I know," Benny said, joining his friends behind the marble counter, "and I don't mind doing this, really. Kory's done me favors, too, and besides, nobody ever comes in this time of night. Only this time, try to be a little more quiet, will you? If someone does happen to show up, and he hears you guys, that will be the end of your fun and *both* your jobs."

"You're right," Kory admitted, "but if someone wants to check in, knock on the door first, then go back and tell him—"

"Okay, okay, I know the drill. Just get out of here." Benny dismissed them with a wave of his hand.

"Thanks again," Candy called out as Kory led her toward JT's office.

Benny stood quietly and waited until he heard the click of the office door before he stepped into the lobby. He made a complete sweep of the room with his eyes. He knew the only other employee on duty was driving around the property in the security cart and never came into the main building unless he was called. He listened to make sure there was no sound coming from the boss's office and, satisfied, made his way to the lounge.

Benny glanced around before he tried the key in the door. It was a key he had someone make from a wax imprint of the master key he had borrowed from Kory. It still worked.

Once inside the lounge, Benny turned on the miniflashlight that hung from his keychain. As usual, it was enough for him to see his way behind the bar, and he was careful to stay centered on the rubber mats that lined the floor and not touch anything on either side. When he entered the storeroom, he pulled the door closed and flicked on the light. He stood at the entrance, momentarily blinded.

His eyes barely adjusted, he headed straight toward the hard liquor. He pulled his choice of bottles off the shelves, and filled two of the boxes quickly, knowing he might not get another chance. He never heard Rosario slip out behind the cartons of beer.

"Hands up!" she shouted, anger and authority overriding her normally sweet-sounding voice. "I have a gun pointed right at your back so you better do exactly as I say or you're one dead gringo." She carefully opened the door with one hand and slowly backed out of the room. When she was clear of the door, she barked at Benny, "Get up and turn around."

When he did as commanded, she told him to move out of the room. Rosario slowly backed up and told her captive to follow.

He did so silently, appraising her and her choice of weapon with cold, calculating eyes. It was a .22 pistol, deadly at close range, but what about fifteen feet? Could the dumb broad shoot straight? He stalled, trying to create a distance between him and the gun.

"Hurry up," Rosario demanded, finally reaching the door to the lobby. She opened it, one hand still holding the gun, Benny now ten feet away. "Kory!" She called through the open doorway, "I need help! Call 911!" Her voice bounced off the stuccoed walls.

Benny realized his mistake. Had he been closer, he might have been able to overpower her and take the gun away. He began moving toward her.

"Stop!" she commanded, both hands on the gun. He stopped. Rosario reached for the door again, this time holding it open by propping her foot against it. "Kory! Kory! Did you hear me! I need help!" she screamed. This time her voice had a slight quaver to it.

Benny's eyes suddenly showed a hint of amusement as he realized Kory would never hear her. He watched her face carefully as touches of fear appeared on it, and he waited to make his move. She turned her face slightly toward the door to call again. Her eyes strayed from his face for a split second and he lunged at her legs.

Rosario shot, but the bullet missed its mark. Benny knocked her to the floor and they rolled towards the bar, Rosario kicking and screaming with every ounce of strength she had.

꿍꿍꿍

Rachel had run down the sidewalk while trying to zip her jeans and work her pager at the same time. No luck there. Going with the priority, she called security and shouted at Jeremy to meet her at the lounge. She pocketed the pager, zipped her pants, and yanked open the back door to the lobby. She sprinted across the floor, then stopped. No one was stationed behind the front desk. *Where is everyone? What the heck happened?*

Then she heard the shot. She raced for the lounge, yanked open the door and flipped on the lights. She saw the two people rolling and fighting on the floor, the gun a few feet away. Rushing to the bar, she grabbed the first bottle she found and when she turned she saw Benny flip on top of Rosario and reach for the gun. Rachel cracked the bottle over his head and Benny Ammato collapsed.

Rachel kicked the gun away and rolled Benny off the bruised woman. She helped Rosario up just as Kory and Candy burst in the door, followed by a wide-eyed Jeremy.

"Jeremy, call 911," Rachel ordered, and then pointed to Kory and Candy. "You two get back to the front desk and wait. Make sure the deputy and the ambulance get back here."

While she notified JT she noticed Benny twitch. She picked up the gun and held it on him while Rosario found her way to the closest chair and collapsed into it.

"You okay?"

"I'm okay." The pale-faced bar manager then leaned over and hung her head and arms down in an attempt to keep from fainting.

Rachel pulled over a chair and sat in it, waiting for Benny to regain consciousness so she could have an excuse to whack him again, or for Deputy Tucker to arrive, whichever came first.

But it was JT who burst into the room and took sight of his bar manager sitting with her head between her legs, Benny Ammato laid out on the floor like a dead man, and Rachel with a gun in her hand.

"What happened!" he demanded.

Rosario raised her head, speechless, and turned toward Rachel.

Rachel looked down at the unconscious man on the floor. "Well, for starters, I just wasted one really fine bottle of tequila."

∽∾∽

It was nearly noon before Rachel showed up for work. The events that had occurred earlier that morning were still fresh in her mind.

By the time Deputy Tucker left with Benny Ammato in handcuffs, Kory and Candy had been fired, and Rosario was on her way to the medical clinic in Mesquite by ambulance. Heather had arrived shortly after JT and took over the front desk. She told Rachel to go home and sleep in. "I'll cover for you until you get here," her sister assured her. "I went to bed early and already had a full night's sleep."

Rachel left reluctantly, but the adrenalin seeped out of her body on the walk home and she fell asleep immediately when she dropped into the bed.

By the time she arrived in the lobby the next morning, Buddy had already delivered his handsome twin passengers. "Justin! Joseph!" Rachel cried as she ran to her nephews, laughing, arms open. "Or is it Joseph and Justin?"

"Oh, Auntie Rachel, it's so good to see you again," Justin said, hugging her tightly.

"We've really missed you," Joseph said, taking his turn.

"Let me look at you," Rachel said, stepping back. "I can't believe you've grown another inch since winter break." She looked from one twin to another.

"We actually have," Justin said. "We're six-four now."

"And we have so much to tell you," Justin added. "Do you think we could take the Hummer and go down to Mexico and hit the beach like we did at Christmas?"

"Er—ahem," Rachel muttered, glancing from side to side. She lowered her head. "See guys, it's like this," she whispered. "Your dad was not too happy with me after he found out about our little adventure. I'm just recently back in his good graces."

The twins nodded solemnly but their blue eyes looked disappointed.

Rachel added, "We can go over to Alixta for the day, but with the drug wars going on in Mexico now, it's best if we stay within the city limits."

Justin nodded. "That's okay, there's plenty to do around here."

"Good. When we get a chance, I've got a bunch of juicy stuff to tell you about the movie Richard Markman was making on Blood Mountain."

"Richard Markman? Isn't he the old guy going out with Tara Linley?" Justin asked.

"Well, actually," Rachel whispered, her eyes darting back and forth, "he's not really going out with *anyone* right now. But I'll tell you all about that as soon as we get some time alone."

JT walked over and slung his long arms around both of his twins. "So are you guys hungry, or what?"

"Dad, we're eighteen," Joseph said. "We're always hungry."

"Wonderful. The pool's heated and snacks are on the way. After a swim, we'll have Chef Henri whip us up a few of his special mesquite-grilled T-bones."

"Sounds great," Joseph said. "We've eaten frozen pizza for breakfast, lunch, and dinner the last three days. Steak and potatoes would be a welcome change."

"Come on then. Let's grab our suits."

After a couple hours in the pool and a shower and change, the Carpenter family walked along the portico toward the main building. The twins were dressed in jeans and T-shirts, but JT wore pressed slacks and a Hawaiian shirt with a muted flower print. The stylized flowers, printed in three shades of red, were on a beige background the exact same shade as his pants.

Buddy trotted up beside Rachel. "Sorry I'm late gang, I had a quick meeting with the front desk manager." In a much lower voice, he added, "And I hear there's been a bit of activity at the hotel since I've been gone."

"Oh, you got that right," Rachel said. "I'm not sure *activity* is the correct word, but we've certainly had our share of excitement." She smiled coyly and whispered, "Buy me a margarita later and I'll give you all the juicy details."

A private dinner was set up in the Ocotillo room for them. Their table for six looked a little lost in the large meeting room, but it was soon filled with lots of laughter and the wonderful mixture of aromas emanating from the kitchen.

Heather was so excited to be surrounded by her whole family, including her "adopted" brother, Buddy, she literally glowed with happiness. She looked lovely dressed in her red flowered dress, one that almost matched JT's shirt. JT looked very much the part of the proud papa, and even Rachel was on her best behavior.

Within minutes, Manuel brought in large platters of mesquite grilled steaks, baked potatoes, and steamed vegetables and served them to the group. After everyone dug into their steaks, conversation started back up.

"Hey Dad," Justin said, "I heard a fancy new restaurant opened up in town."

Everyone stopped talking and turned to watch JT. "That's right, son, it did. It's a pretty nice place, too."

"Are you going to send some spies over to check it out?" Joseph asked.

JT smiled. "I already did. Deputy Tucker took a lady friend to dinner there last night, right after it opened."

"So how was it?"

"Unfortunately, it was very nice. The food was excellent and the place is beautiful."

"Uh, oh," Justin chimed in. "Bad news for us. Could it hurt business in the Plantation Room?

"It already has, but we don't know if it will affect us in the long run." JT said looked over at Buddy for backup.

Buddy didn't look too concerned. "It will cut into our dinner sales, but we have the rest of our operation to carry us. Domino's has a couple small alcoves for parties, but no real private meeting rooms. We have the café and the hotel to carry us through the summer months."

"But will the Plantation room be able to stand on its own?" Justin asked. "Will you have to close it down on weekdays?"

JT looked uncomfortable. "It's a little too soon to tell. We'll just have to wait and see what happens. The novelty of a new restaurant may wear off."

An awkward silence settled over the room, and Rachel was eager to restore the original joyous mood of the group. "Tell us all about college life," she said to the twins.

"It's great," Justin said, having just speared a juicy chunk of steak. "We've found a few other kids our age to hang out with. They've skipped grades like us."

"Yeah, they're sophomores, too, but from the east coast," Joseph added. "It works out great. Three of them are girls, so we have our own social life, more or less. We have a lot of our classes together."

"That's wonderful," Buddy said. "Have you guys thought about picking a major yet?"

"Well, I'm seriously considering microbiology, medical research, something along those lines," Justin said.

Rachel dropped her fork in her plate and held her breath. She and Heather looked at each other.

"I think that's wonderful, guys," Heather said, softly. "You know your grandfather and grandmother Ryan were both research microbiologists. They were brilliant, just like you."

"But you got your good looks from the Carpenter side of the family," JT said, with a wink and a nod.

"Phew!" Buddy exclaimed, waving a hand in front of his face. "It's getting a little thick in here. I may have to go out for air."

Everyone laughed.

The subject of her parents' deaths skirted, Rachel began eating again, and the jokes and good times continued.

After pushing his empty plate aside, JT looked up to see Chef Henri coming into the room wheeling in an old-fashioned baked Alaska on a cart. "Now I know why I wanted in on this hotel deal," he said.

Manuel picked up the empty platters as Chef Henri carved up the beautiful desert and served it. After each person managed to down a small slice, Buddy touched Rachel's hand. "About that margarita…"

Rachel was finishing her cappuccino. "Let's go now," Rachel suggested. "That way the Carpenters can have some private time together. I bought a new blender, so let's go to my place instead." She lowered her voice so only Buddy could hear. "I need to have a quiet conversation with you."

Buddy's eyes lit up.

"No, not *that* kind of conversation."

"Ah, me love," Buddy said in his Irish brogue. "Aye can see the luck of the Irish is not with me tonight."

"No, not tonight." Rachel laughed, and slipped her arm through his as they walked out of the room.

⌁⌁⌁

Buddy walked over to the sliding glass door in Rachel's suite. "Shall we sit outdoors?"

"No, I don't want to take the chance of being overheard," Rachel answered.

She placed a towel on the marble counter under the blender, but the appliance still made a ghastly grinding noise when she turned it on to mix the drinks.

By the time the margaritas were the consistency of snow-cones, Rachel had finished salting the thick, hand-blown glasses.

She took the drinks to the sofa, handed one to Buddy, and took a long sip from her glass.

"How are you doing, Rachel? I mean, really." Buddy brought his drink to his lips.

"What do you mean? I'm fine."

"That's exactly my point. You're fine."

"What's that supposed to mean?" She frowned.

Buddy took a sip of his margarita, squeezed the lime and dropped it in his drink, giving her time to think. "You're fine for someone that has seen two dead bodies in as many days."

"It's been more than two days. You're exaggerating."

"And you're side-stepping the point."

Rachel slipped off her shoes and tucked a leg under her. She stared off to the side, mute.

"I would think that seeing Ekberg after he committed suicide would have really affected you."

"Stop." Rachel held up her hand in protest. "Don't go there."

"Rachel, Heather told me about your parents a long time ago. I saw how you were when you discovered the Donovan woman's body last year."

"Stop, Buddy. I mean it."

Buddy took her hand and gently brought it down.

"It's okay. I'm not going to hurt you. I know what's going on with you, even if you don't know yourself."

"Oh? Now you want to psychoanalyze me, *too*?" Rachel pulled away and picked her drink back up. "Is this Heather's doing?"

"No. Heather has nothing to do with this. I just noticed a big discrepancy in your behavior between then and now, that's all."

Rachel leaned against the back of the sofa and glared at him.

Buddy reached for her hand again. "Look, I know we always kid around, but you must know by now that I really care about you. I don't want you to be hurt."

Rachel dropped her eyes and stared at her drink. "What did Heather tell you?"

"About your parents?"

Rachel replied with a slight nod.

"She said they were murdered when you were thirteen and that you found them."

Anger was in her eyes now. "Did she also tell you the police decided it was a murder-suicide? That they said my father killed my mother and they never bothered to investigate anything else?"

"She told me that, too. I can understand how that could be the worst..." Buddy's voice trailed off when he couldn't find the right word.

"It was. It nearly killed me." She downed the rest of her drink in one swig. "Now you know why I'm so messed up." She stood, walked over to the blender, and poured the rest of its contents into her glass. "Shall I make another batch?"

"I'm good. I figure you'll want to kick me out now, anyway."

"Only if you continue to bring up my past." She walked back to the sofa with a little swing to her body and slipped into the seat.

"Okay. I'll change the subject. How about if we fly over to Las Vegas tomorrow and get married?"

"Ha!" Rachel exclaimed, spilling a bit of her drink on her top. "I don't like Vegas." She picked up a napkin and brushed the spill off her blouse.

"So, how about Hawaii?"

"No. I'm just not ready to get married yet. Not to you, not to anyone. I think it's pretty obvious I've got a few things to work out. Plus, I have a murder to solve."

"I didn't realize solving murders was part of your job description."

"I've been told that, more than once. But it's something I feel compelled to do." She looked thoughtful. "Maybe if I can find out who killed Markman, it would fix something. Something inside me. I know it sounds totally wacko."

"Actually, it doesn't. I don't agree with it, but I can understand it. Really." Buddy ran his hands through his hair and thought about that a while. "Okay," he finally said. "What can I do to help?"

Rachel looked puzzled. "Really? You'd really help me?"

"Why not? The sooner the killer is behind bars, the sooner we can get back to normal. So bring me up to speed on what's going on."

For the next few minutes Rachel gave Buddy the latest information on Dixie Markman and the Church of Inner Light. She pulled the copy of the suicide note out of her purse and let Buddy read it.

He shook his head. "Unbelievable. It's almost incomprehensible that all this has happened in one place."

"I know, and what's even more amazing is that Dixie Markman is tied up with Lars Ekberg. Somehow, somewhere, there's a connection. If we could just figure out what it is, we might know the identity of the killer."

Buddy looked down at the suicide note and read it again. "Does Heather know about this?"

"Only what JT has told her. I advised him to play things down and not make too big a deal about it with her or the staff."

"Well, that was smart." Buddy's eyes glanced around the room and settled back on Rachel. "What about Dixie? What does she have to say?"

"Not a whole lot, I'm afraid. Dewey told her not to leave town so she's been staying in her room and ordering room service." Rachel's eyes dropped. "I'm afraid she's been drinking quite a bit, too. She won't even answer her phone."

"As in she's staying drunk all the time?"

"I suspect so."

"And what about Tara Linley? Is she still here?"

"She hasn't checked out, as far as I know, and I don't know a whole lot more. Dewey's been pretty closed mouthed since we've disagreed on some issues." Rachel took a long sip of her margarita and licked her lips. "You may have noticed we've got quite a few empty spaces at the hotel. Dixie sent everyone home except her own personal assistant. I think Tara is staying on her own money, just hoping to see Dixie get arrested for Markman's murder."

"It's quite a mess, isn't it?" Buddy shook his head, still amazed at the whole situation. "So what's going to happen with the movie?"

Rachel shrugged. "Your guess is as good as mine. But as of right now, it's scrapped."

"Huh. I can see the dollar signs floating down the drain. Probably millions of them."

Rachel laughed, then reached up and mussed Buddy's hair. "You're still the consummate CPA, Mr. McCain."

"Ain't that the truth," he said, laughing with her. "So what do you want to do now?"

Rachel handed Buddy another sheet of paper. "Alex Tucker gave me this. It's information about Ekberg and his sister, Cee-Cee."

His smile was gone. "I heard he came by."

Rachel was caught off-guard. "He did drop by yesterday, but just for a short time on the way to Phoenix. We had coffee together, that's all," she added, not wanting Buddy to feel jealous."

Buddy drew back. "Hey, it's okay. No problem. It's not my business anyway."

"Buddy, it was no big deal," Rachel said, thinking maybe it *was* a big deal to Buddy. "We just had coffee and I told him what was going on with the Markmans and the Inner Light group. It wasn't personal."

"Okay, let's drop it." He seemed satisfied and looked down at the paper. "So what about this? He located some background on Cee-Cee?"

"Yes, and guess what? Cee-Cee used to be an actress."

"No kidding?"

"Scout's Honor," she said, holding up her hand. "And not only that, but I found her house on the satellite map. It's in a lovely older neighborhood, only about seven miles from your office."

Buddy looked up at Rachel's guilty smile.

"Let me guess," he said. "You want us to fly back to LA and pay Cee-Cee a little visit."

"Well, I know you have to fly back to LA tomorrow, and I thought if I went along, we could take over all Lars' personal effects and find out how she's doing, but I know this is the busiest time of year for CPA's so if you couldn't take time off, I could rent a car and drive over and—"

"Rachel?" Buddy asked, interrupting her. "It's not a problem." He placed his hand on top of hers. "Give Cee-Cee a call and ask her if we can come by about nine o' clock. I told JT I'd bring his parents over Saturday afternoon, so that will work out perfectly."

She looked at him quizzically. "We'd need all that time?"

Buddy tapped the arm of the sofa nervously. "Not really. But I'd like you to meet a friend of mine."

Rachel watched his fingers. "A friend?"

"Yes, a good friend. He's a doctor."

Rachel's mouth dropped. "Aw, geez, Buddy!"

"Hey. You don't have to commit to anything. I just want you to meet him, that's all."

Rachel eyed him suspiciously.

"As a favor to me. Just meet him. That's all I'm asking you to do."

Rachel sighed deeply. Her eyes flicked around the room while she considered his request.

Heather had put him up to this, she was sure. Was there no end to her meddling?

"Okay," she reluctantly agreed. "But only to meet him. That's all. I'm not doing anymore therapy."

He reached for her hand again. "Whatever you want, Rachel. I mean it."

Chapter 13

The sky was a shell of azure blue, except for a strip of cloud two fingers up from the horizon. JT strode outdoors for his morning check of the property and looked up. It would be hot by afternoon, he guessed, might even hit the nineties.

He crossed the parking lot to the courtyard and strolled along the path that led to the pools. He inspected the landscaping. The Jacaranda trees were starting to bloom: tips of lilac-tinted blossoms were poking out from the bare branches. A few steps farther and JT picked up the scent of a sweet acacia tree. It was dropping heady balls of fluff, layering the ground with a yellow carpet.

Toro was supervising the morning clean-up crew and JT stopped to watch them. One man was sweeping down the sides of the pool with a long handled brush and another was hosing off the flagstone patio that encompassed the area. In one quick move, Toro hoisted one of the patio tables over his head, moving it aside like a child's toy.

JT thought about the day he had met the huge Native American man with the scar running down the length of his face. Toro had come by to ask for a job. JT hired him, even after learning the muscular man had served hard time for killing a man in a bar fight. No one else thought much of his decision at the time, especially Deputy Tucker, but Toro turned out to be one of the best employees they had.

The men on the pool detail were finishing up, and JT headed toward the main building, ready for his morning jolt of Joe. Everything around him looked good and smelled good. Sometimes, he thought, that alone made it worth leaving LA.

"Hey, JT!" Dewey Tucker called to him as he came out the back door of the lobby.

"Good morning, Deputy. Want to join me for breakfast?"

Maybe later," Tucker said. "I need to go see Ms. Markman. She didn't answer her phone all day yesterday."

JT squinted at him. "You aren't planning to arrest her, are you?"

Tucker squinted back at JT and tugged on his white mustache. "Now, why'd you be thinkin' somethin' like that?"

"Are you?"

"Why?"

"Well, we can go on all day not answering each other's questions, Dewey. But if you're planning on talking to Dixie Markman, I'd suggest waiting until later in the day.

"Why is that?"

"She hasn't been doing too well. She's been drinking, sleeping late, ordering room service, and won't allow visitors—not even Rachel."

"Humph," Tucker muttered. He clutched his arms over his chest and gazed down at the sidewalk as if some bit of insight would pop up at him.

"If it's any help, Buddy and Rachel are flying over to LA this morning and expect to meet with Ekberg's sister, Cecilia. They're hoping to find some connection between the Markmans and Ekberg."

Tucker looked up. "Don't say?"

"Well, you know Rachel. She thinks Dixie didn't do it and she'll leave no stone unturned trying to prove it."

"Yeah, I'm afraid of that. You know what happened last time."

"But this time, Buddy is with her."

Tucker looked down again and twiddled his mustache a bit more. "Yep, I think that's prob'ly a good idea. That girl does have a good feelin' about things every once in a while." He squinted up at JT. "But you won't go mentionin' that to Rachel, now will ya?"

"Oh, no, never," JT said, grinning. He pulled on the door to the lobby and held it open for the deputy. "Let's go get some breakfast, shall we?"

e⁄ɔe⁄ɔ

The sun had burned off the southern California smog by the time Buddy and Rachel tied down the plane and drove to Cecilia Stevenson's home.

They parked under the shade of a eucalyptus tree, one of several that grew on the edge of Cee-Cee's proper-

ty. Green waxy shrubbery lined the house along the foun-
dation, and white potted chrysanthemums dotted the
stairs at exact intervals, which led to a freshly painted
porch. The house, a good example of the early 20th cen-
tury bungalow, sat behind a manicured front lawn. The
only things out of place were a few stray eucalyptus
leaves scattered on the yard.

Buddy and Rachel unloaded Ekberg's computer and
personal effects. Nearly everything fit on a rolling cart
except for the two large suitcases Buddy toted.

As they approached the house, Rachel noted it
looked anemic with its light gray shingles and white
wood trim. Even the wicker set that decorated the porch
was painted white, and its pastel blue cushions did little
to brighten the area. Rachel imagined Heather wanting to
use a heavy dose of color to redecorate the whole place.

When Cee-Cee opened the door, Rachel caught a
look of surprise on Buddy's face, guessing he expected
Cee-Cee to be carbon copy of her brother. Rachel remembered seeing photos of Cee-Cee in the book Lars had
signed for her, but in real life she appeared much darker,
much shorter, and wore her hair in a short, masculine
style.

Cee-Cee welcomed them into the living room where
white walls and slip-covered furniture showed little con-
trast to the bleached wood floors. "Can I get you some
iced tea? Water?" she asked.

"Iced tea would be fine," Buddy answered for both
of them.

Rachel looked around the room. Except for a couple
of green plants and a piece of modern art on the wall, the
room was devoid of color.

Cee-Cee brought in the tea on a bamboo tray and set it down on the coffee table in front of her visitors. "I really appreciate your bringing my brother's things," she said with deep sincerity. "Also for making sure my arrangements for his body were followed. I can't tell you what it meant to me." She started to choke up and paused.

"We were more than happy to help," Buddy insisted and took a sip of his tea.

"Your brother was a kind and caring man, and I'm sure you miss him terribly," Rachel added.

"I do. We were very close." Cee-Cee gazed down at her hands resting in her lap. She had the same long, elegant fingers as her brother. "I suppose you're going to ask me about Richard Markman."

Buddy and Rachel exchanged a quick glance.

"Well, we did find his letter," Rachel said, "the one I forwarded to you. We thought, perhaps, you might want to eliminate any speculation between his death and Richard's death."

"Yes, I believe I would," Cee-Cee said, looking up, her brown eyes rimmed with red. "I told Lars to drop the whole thing, to forget about it, but he wouldn't, he just couldn't let go."

"Let go of what, Cecilia?"

"Hatred. Pain. Revenge." She looked out the window, let out a deep breath and leaned back into her chair. "He wanted to get back at Richard for something that happened a long, long time ago."

"You were an actress," Rachel said.

Cee-Cee turned to her, alert. "How did you know?"

"I didn't, but you have a bearing, an air about you." Rachel lied without a shred of guilt. She certainly didn't want Cee-Cee to know Alex had investigated her.

"An Actress," Cee-Cee scoffed, shaking her head. "Yes, I *was* an actress, and it seems a lifetime ago."

Rachel took a sip of her tea, but her eyes couldn't leave Cee-Cee's face. Although her skin was darker, Cee-Cee's face was carved with the same length and angularity of her brother's.

"I was working in a movie that Richard Markman was directing," Cee-Cee continued. "There was a young girl, well, she was sixteen actually, and she played a supporting role in the movie, like me."

She got up and paced back and forth. "After a while, I began to see that something wasn't quite right. The way Richard was with her. There were little clues, some intuition on my part. Long story short, I suspected he was molesting her. Then one day, I stumbled upon them together, in a very awkward position. I worked up my courage and approached Richard about it, suggesting that the two of them in his office behind closed doors might raise suspicions." She stopped by the window and touched the plants.

"What did he say?" Buddy asked.

Cee-Cee turned to him. "He was furious. He denied anything was going on, and told me to mind my own business." She began to pace again. "So I did something that I suppose was very foolish. I called the girl's parents." She gazed around the room and her eyes settled at a point beyond the wall. "It got ugly. Very ugly. The police were called in, and then the press got a hold of it."

"That must have been hard on you," Rachel said.

"Not at first. The girl's family took the brunt of it. But in the end the daughter rescinded her testimony, and the father disappeared with a large chunk of cash, courtesy of Richard Markman."

Rachel gasped and shared a look with Buddy. She turned back to Cee-Cee. "Then what happened?"

"Richard blacklisted me."

Rachel blinked. "That means you couldn't get work as an actress anymore."

"That means I couldn't get work as an *anything* anymore."

"Oh, how awful," Rachel murmured.

"Yes, it was awful. Lars was furious. He was my protector, you know." Cee-Cee's eyes turned soft and a hint of smile came to her lips.

"Then what happened?" Rachel encouraged.

"Nothing for a long time. I got divorced, went back to school, finished my education, and established myself as a statistician. I've lived a comfortable life."

"Until?"

Cee-Cee sat down, opened a packet of sweetener, and poured it in the extra glass of tea on the tray. "Until Lars saw Dixie Markman in the audience at your hotel. He'd heard the Markman group was at the hotel but never expected Dixie would show up at his lecture. He e-mailed me about it, upset all over again. I told him to get over it. I did, years ago."

"But he couldn't."

"Lars was so sensitive; the slightest wound to him was like a big gaping sore." She took a long sip from her glass. "When he saw Dixie at the lecture, he decided it was payback time and let her have it with both barrels."

"You mean he made all that up? All the stuff he told Dixie?"

"Oh, heavens, no. Lars would never do that. But sometimes he'd hold back hurtful things."

"But with Dixie he didn't."

"Right. And if it caused a problem between her and her husband, so be it."

"But why punish her for what her husband did?"

Cee-Cee's eyes flashed wide open with anger. "Because she lied! She covered for Richard. She told the police she was in the office area at the times in question and that Richard's door was always open. That was absolutely not true. The day I walked in on them together, Richard and the girl, his door was closed and Dixie was nowhere around."

Rachel clapped her hand over her mouth, closed her eyes, and shook her head back and forth in distress. If this were true, Dixie was more than co-dependant. She was guilty of covering up a crime.

"I told you it got very ugly."

Rachel felt the sick feeling in her stomach spread to her bones. "How awful for you, how awful for that family."

"And you know what makes it even worse?" Cee-Cee asked. "I really don't think that young girl was the first. Or the last."

"You may be right about that," Buddy said. "I think Richard Markman had a problem with young girls."

"And a co-dependant wife," Rachel added, remembering how desperate Dixie was in protecting Richard.

"But now he's dead and he won't hurt anyone again," Cee-Cee said, with an air of triumph. "And I know Lars didn't have a thing to do with it."

"But who did?" Rachel asked. "Did Lars know who the killer was?"

Cee-Cee shook her head. "No, but he thought the killer was a woman. I think that may narrow it down to about four thousand suspects. Some little girl may have grown up and sought revenge."

"That's quite possible," Rachel said. "Do you remember the name of the girl or her parents in the case you were involved with?"

Cee-Cee shook her head slowly. "No. I worked very hard at forgetting all of this the last ten years. I suppose some night at three in the morning their names will pop back in my head."

"Will you call me if they do? It would save me a lot of research. The girl would be around twenty-six years old now, wouldn't she?"

Again, Cee-Cee shook her head. Her eyes began to tear and she looked away. "I'm afraid not, Rachel. I heard she died a year or so later. They said it was a suicide." She looked up at Rachel. The tenderness in her eyes was replaced with resignation. "But no matter what anyone says, I know it was Richard who destroyed that girl."

ᘓᘓᘓ

Buddy could sense something wrong while he drove through the late morning traffic back to his office. Rachel remained oddly silent.

"You okay?"

"Yeah, fine."

"You sure? I'm not used to your being this quiet. I'm kind of getting a bad feeling—"

"I'm fine," Rachel snapped. "I'm just thinking."

Buddy looked over at her. Rachel appeared to be oddly rigid. "You're not upset, are you? I mean about meeting Larry Pinkerton?"

"Dr. Pinkerton? Why should I be upset about that? Just because my sister and you conspire to get me to see your shrink friend, why should I be upset?" Rachel stared straight ahead with her arms crossed tightly against her chest.

"Rachel, we *care* about you. We want to make sure you're okay. You've been through a lot in the last week."

"So? Just because people die I'm supposed to freak out? I'm stronger than that."

"Of course you're strong. It's just that Ekberg…he was a nice, gentle man. A good man. I know you liked him. I know it had to be hard on you, seeing him lying on the floor like that, the pill bottle just inches from his fingers."

Rachel refused to look at him and just sat staring straight ahead, mute. Her lips were pressed tightly together in a thin line.

"He was a little different," Buddy continued, "but it was obvious he cared about people. He loved his sister, and you could sure tell his sister loved him. You can see she misses him terribly."

Rachel's lips began to twitch, but she didn't utter a word.

"He was so devastated about what Pander did to him, and I can't blame him. He sincerely wanted to help everyone, and yet in the end, his partner and his spirit guide abandoned him. If there was only some way we could have helped him. Maybe we could have—"

"Stop!" Rachel cried out. Tears welled up in her eyes, but she continued to sit still, staring out the windshield as if she were mesmerized by something off in the distance.

Buddy turned sharply into a strip mall and parked. He popped open Rachel's seat belt and raised it gently over her head. She offered no resistance, but merely looked blankly out the windshield, the tears now seeping over her lower lids. Buddy took her by the shoulders and pulled her to him, wrapping his arms tightly around her. Only then did Rachel break down and allow herself to cry.

ᏣᏔᏣ

By the time Buddy's plane hit the tarmac at the Mesquite airport, the temperature hovered at ninety-one. But the humidity was so low—a mere twelve per cent—the heat index registered a pleasant eighty-six degrees, much to the delight of the deplaning passengers.

It wasn't long before Buddy and Rachel led Tom and Vi Carpenter into the hotel lobby. They were greeted by JT, Heather, and the twins in a reunion that was both loud and happy. It took a few minutes before Rachel was able to pull JT off to the side.

"Anything new about Dixie?"

"Only that Dewey's planning on arresting her today if she doesn't talk to him."

"Oh, no," Rachel groaned. "I better go see what I can do. I'll catch up with you guys later." She rushed off.

Justin ran after her. "Hey, Auntie Rachel, wait up."

Rachel stopped. "What's going on, Jus?"

"Joseph and I met Tara Linley today." He had a wide grin on his face and was already showing signs of a tan from being out in the sun so much.

"Really? How'd that happen?"

"We were out by the pool and she came over and just started talking to us."

Rachel glanced ahead at the casitas and figured Dixie wouldn't be leaving her suite any time soon. "Come on, walk with me," she said.

"Um, Rachel, did Dixie really kill Richard Markman?"

Rachel stopped and her heart nearly did, too. "Did Tara tell you that?"

"Yeah. Did she kill him?"

Rachel shook her head and started walking again. "I can't believe Tara would say that to you. Someone she just met. What an idiot!" She turned to her nephew. "Justin, I really don't know what to say, but I honestly don't know for sure who killed Richard Markman. Nobody does. But Deputy Tucker thinks Dixie might have done it. There's a list of a half-dozen people who *could* have done it—and a lot more who would have liked to.

"So I guess he wasn't that nice of a guy."

"I'd say that's an understatement. Actually, Richard was a creep, a low-life on the level of an amoeba. I suspected *him* of trying to kill *Dixie.*"

"No kidding?" Justin looked surprised.

They had reached the stairs to Rachel's casita. She sat down and patted the spot next to her. "Here, sit. I was going to save this for later, but I might as well tell you now."

"Awesome." Justin said, joining her. "I knew you'd be the one with the real dirt."

Rachel laughed. "I hope that's a compliment."

A few minutes later, after mulling over Rachel's story, Justin looked up at the row of casitas. "So Dixie's still hiding inside, huh?

"I'm not sure "hiding" is the correct term for what she's doing, but yes, she won't open the door. I was on my way to try to talk to her."

Justin absent-mindedly picked up a pebble off the sidewalk and threw it into the parking lot. "I wonder if she knew Richard was going to marry Tara as soon as they got divorced."

"I doubt Dixie knew she was even *getting* divorced. What she tells me—and what the truth is—are two different species of animal."

"Yeah, that makes it hard. When people are liars, I mean. You never know when they're telling the truth. It's hard to be friends with them because you never know where you stand."

Rachel pulled back and looked at him. "You're pretty smart for a man, you know that?"

"Sexist," Justin accused, and laughed. "But that's why I had to ask you about Tara. I didn't think it could be true, all that stuff she was saying. She told us she started having sex with Richard when she was sixteen."

"What?" Rachel gaped at him. "Sixteen? She actually told you that? That's statutory rape."

"I know. But that's what she told us. Joseph and I kind of looked at each other and didn't say anything."

"I'm glad you told me. It confirms two things: First, Tara is a total idiot. Second, she either told you the truth and lied to Deputy Tucker, or she lied to you and told the deputy the truth."

"Aye, there's the rub."

"William Shakespeare, Hamlet," Rachel said off-handedly.

Justin grinned, remembering their little game. "'To-morrow and tomorrow and tomorrow...'"

"'Creeps in this petty pace from day to day.' Also Shakespeare, Macbeth," Rachel shot back.

"A cheerful heart is good medicine, but a crushed spirit dries up the bones."

"Proverbs, the *Holy Bible*. Give it up, Justin." Rachel hugged her knees and rocked back and forth on the step. "Did Tara say anything else?"

"Not really. But she said she'd be out by the pool later. Do you want me to pump her for more infor-mation?"

"Ah, a man after my own heart." She stood up. *What a perfect opportunity to have a spy in the enemy's camp.* "But, Jus, I think it's best if you stay out of it. This could get very complicated, and your dad would tar and feather me if he found out you were feeding me information."

Justin stood up to his full height and towered over her. "So who's gonna tell him?"

❡❡❡

It didn't take Rachel long before she stood at Dixie's door, pounding the life out of it. "Open up, Dixie! It's me, Rachel," she yelled.

"Go away," a voice sniveled from inside.

"Dixie, either you open the door *now,* or the deputy sheriff will be here to arrest you within the hour." Rachel wasn't sure of the time frame on that, but an hour sounded good. "If you want me to help you, you better open up. I've seen the jail, Dixie, and it's not pretty."

An unidentifiable wailing came from the room.

"And there's no booze in jail. No cigarettes, either! I'd hate to see you stuck in there for the weekend before your lawyer can get here and post bail."

The door opened a crack and a pale-faced, red-eyed Dixie Markman peered out. "What can you do to help me?"

Rachel held up a cup of black coffee so Dixie could see it through the gap in the doorway. "First you can drink this."

Dixie unlatched the chain and reached for the cup with a shaky hand.

Rachel slipped inside and sniffed the air. It smelled of cigarettes and body odor. "Phew. It stinks in here." She walked over to the sliding glass door and opened it. Two doves sitting on the iron railing flew off with a loud fluttering and Rachel took a breath. "It's pretty warm out, but it smells a lot better."

Dixie had removed the lid of the coffee cup and was gingerly sipping at the caffeine-laden brew in silence.

Rachel walked back to the sofa and sat down, patting the cushion on the other end. "Sit down, Dixie. We need to talk."

Dixie slipped down on the sofa and averted her eyes. "What do you want to talk about?"

"Well, for starters, if you don't want to end up being charged with the murder of your husband, I suggest you tell me the truth about a few things."

"Like what?" Dixie asked, still refusing to look Rachel in the eye.

"I need to know about the case of the sixteen year old actress who was molested by your husband about ten years ago."

Dixie jerked her head up. "He didn't molest her! He didn't touch her. She made that up."

"What?" Rachel's jaw fell open. She rose from the sofa. After all the effort she'd extended on Dixie's behalf—defending her, saving her life twice, and putting up with the resulting embarrassment—this woman just lied to her, lied right to her face.

"Bye, Dixie," Rachel said. "I'll come visit you in jail." She walked away.

"No, wait! Rachel, don't go."

Rachel turned her head when she reached the door. "I said the truth, Dixie. I already know what went on but I want to hear it from your very own lips."

Dixie opened her mouth to speak, but before a sound emerged, a large fist banged on the door.

Rachel jumped. "Who is it?" she asked, forgetting it wasn't even her suite.

"Deputy Sheriff Tucker, Ms. Markman. I need to talk to you a moment," the voice said.

Rachel looked at Dixie.

Dixie's eyes were wide open now. "No! I don't want to talk to anyone," she called out. "Go away."

"Sorry Ma'am. This is going to be the last time I'm going to ask you to open the door. If you refuse, management will unlock the door and I will arrest you for obstructing justice."

Dixie shot a horrified look at Rachel. "Just a moment," she called out. "I'm not quite dressed."

She motioned to Rachel to come closer and whispered. "Now what do I do?"

"I think you better open the door."

Dixie timidly turned the knob and peeked through the crack. "I'm not really dressed for company," she said timidly.

"I ain't company, Ms. Markman, and I ain't the fashion police. Now open the door."

Resigned, Dixie let out a sigh and let the deputy inside.

Tucker noticed Rachel immediately and gave her an annoyed look. "What are you doing here?" he asked.

"Visiting a friend, obviously."

The deputy's face showed displeasure and he turned away from her to focus on Dixie. "Ms. Markman, I need you to come with me to the station right now to answer some questions."

"Right now?" Dixie asked coyly, batting her eyelashes. "Deputy Tucker, I really need a shower and a change of clothes. Could you give me a couple of hours?"

"You're comin' in to answer questions, Ms. Markman, not to do a fashion show." Tucker wasn't smiling. "And I'm afraid you don't have much choice as to *when*."

Dixie dropped the coy act along with her smile. "Is this about Richard?"

"Yes, ma'am, it is."

Tucker had taken off his Stetson when he entered and he began turning it in his hands. Rachel couldn't decide whether Tucker was nervous or irritated, but she was finding the exchange between the two interesting.

Dixie shot a worried look at Rachel and then turned back to Tucker. "You're not arresting me, are you, Deputy?" She forced her voice to sound strong and fearless.

"No, ma'am. But you have refused to answer your door when I've knocked, and you've refused to return my phone calls." His voice was cold and he stopped twirling his hat. "If you refuse to come with me now, I *will* arrest you."

Rachel heard the sharp intake of Dixie's breath and saw a flash of fear cross her eyes.

"Do I need to call my lawyer?" Her eyes were pleading. She wasn't acting now.

"It's up to you, ma'am. You have the right to have one with you when you're questioned. But you still have to come with me now."

Dixie mentally debated her plight, and then with every bit of energy and arrogance left in her, she finally stepped out the door, chin up, like a queen.

Fascinated by Dixie's chameleon-like behavior and Tucker's no-nonsense approach to America's Sweetheart, Rachel followed the two of them out and pulled the door shut behind her.

∽∾∽

Rachel took a shortcut through the courtyard and spotted Heather crouched down on the sidewalk.

"Hey, sis, what are you doing? Looking for ants?"

Heather stood up and faced her sister. "Honestly, Rachel, you really do have a bug obsession. I was actually looking at this poor display of petunias."

They both gazed down at the few withered plants nestled in between some aloes.

"They *are* pretty sorry looking, aren't they," Rachel said. "I wonder why JT decided petunias should go there instead of something like ice plant or prairie zinnia, if he wanted color. Or even penstemon, if he wanted a little height. That patch could use a little height and they're available in red."

Heather was staring at her sister. "Since when did you know about desert landscaping? You've barely been here six months."

"Oh, you know me, I read all the time. I found a little booklet somewhere about Arizona desert plants. I'll give it to you if you follow me to my office."

"Sure." They turned toward the main building. "So what's the latest with Dixie?"

"Lots of news there," Rachel said as they walked and related the long version of events that had recently transpired with Dixie and Sheriff Tucker, mainly to help clarify the details in her own mind.

By the time they were seated in Rachel's office, she had brought her sister up to date.

Heather frowned at her sister. "So you're saying Dixie outright lied to you when you asked her about that molestation case?"

Rachel mentally backtracked. "Well, yeah, but I think she was going to tell me the truth if Tucker hadn't knocked on the door."

"But she *did* lie to you, sis. She denied everything. She said the girl made up the charges."

"Um, well, I guess, maybe she did." Rachel looked away, embarrassed.

"Maybe? You're not sure? Then what *do* you call what she said? Was it the truth?" Heather was leaning into her now, her eyes penetrating.

"Well, no…it wasn't the truth, but…"

"But what?"

"Geez, Heather! What is the *problem?*" She felt like she was on a witness stand or something and was already regretting telling her sister about Dixie.

"No *problem,*" Heather said quietly. "I was just wondering why, as a person of integrity, you would want to be friends with a liar, especially one that lies to *you* after you went through a great deal of trouble to save that person from losing a million dollars in a scam, not to mention saving that person's very own life."

Rachel lowered her eyes. "I suppose you're right." She let out a deep breath and sadness seemed to envelope her. "I guess I just didn't want to see what was painfully obvious."

Heather grasped her sister's hand in affection and then stood up. "You know, sweetie, you've gotten way too involved with this mess. I think you need a change of scene here. There's some kind of street event and craft fair going on down in Old Town. I'm going to take Vi to see it, maybe eat some junk food while we're there. Why don't you get out of the office for a while and come with us? The front desk can take your calls."

Rachel perked up. "You know, that sounds like a great idea. I love craft fairs, and I happen to know of a place downtown that makes the best milk shakes you ever tasted."

After agreeing to meet in twenty minutes, the sisters parted and headed to their casitas to change into more comfortable clothes. Soon Rachel bounded down the stairs in shorts and tennis shoes and nearly bumped into Becky Beeman who was striding along the sidewalk, jotting down notes on her clipboard.

"Oh! Sorry, Rachel," Becky exclaimed, barely avoiding a nasty collision. "I guess I'm as bad as people who text while driving."

"Not quite," Rachel said, laughing. "You didn't crash into my car and I think my toe will survive. So, what are you up to?"

"Nothing much. We just changed out the Markman's suite—I mean, Dixie's old suite—now that Deputy Tucker is done with it. And I just heard Deputy Tucker took her off to jail."

"Oh, boy. How'd you find that out?"

"Rachel, don't you know? Housekeeping knows *everybody's* secrets," Becky teased.

"I bet you're right about that. What else did you hear?"

"That her attorney, R. J. Greenwood, just booked the end suite for himself."

"No kidding? You know that for sure?"

Becky nodded. "I checked with the front desk and recognized the name. Greenwood's always been the top lawyer to the stars. He's as rich as most of them, too," she added with a laugh.

"Hmm. I hope that doesn't mean she's been arrested," Rachel thought out loud.

"I know what you mean," Becky said. "If she really killed Richard, she deserves a medal." Her eyes popped open and she cupped her hand over her mouth. "Oops. I'm sorry. I take that back. That was terrible."

"Hey, forget it. I've had the same thoughts myself." But Rachel took another look at Becky. "You knew them, before, didn't you?"

"*Everybody* that worked in Hollywood knew the Markmans."

"So what kind of reputation did they have? I mean, *really*."

Becky looked embarrassed. "You don't want to know, Rachel. I know you're kind of friends with Dixie."

"No, I'm *not* friends with Dixie. I just tried to help her, that's all, and yeah, I really do want to know about her. But some other time. Right now I'm meeting Heather and we're taking JT's mom to that craft fair in Old Town."

"Oh, that sounds like fun. I love those things— especially the junk food." She smiled and held up her clipboard. "I gotta get back to work. See you later."

Rachel watched Becky hurry off, wondering what she knew about the Markmans. She'd definitely ask her later, but right now there was a craft fair and a vanilla milk shake calling her name.

Chapter 14

It was nearly dark by the time Rachel reached the steps of her casita, tired from her evening at the street fair. She noticed the lights were on in Dixie's place. *Guess Tucker didn't put her in jail after all. Heck, he might have even paid her to go away.* Acting on impulse, Rachel decided she wasn't too tired to pay Dixie another visit.

This time Dixie let her in quickly, probably happy just to have someone to talk to, Rachel thought. She was cleaned up, but appeared to be depressed.

"I'm not supposed to drink—lawyer's orders—but do you want a Pepsi?"

"Pepsi's fine," Rachel answered, and asked her about her visit with Deputy Tucker.

"It was pretty horrible until my attorney showed up," Dixie answered, absent-mindedly brushing some crumbs off her knit top. "Tucker kept asking me questions and I kept refusing to answer. But once R. J. was on the scene he told me when and what to answer and when to keep my mouth shut. It was a tremendous relief." Dixie sat down and brushed something off her slacks. "You know, that deputy's office is filthy."

"Yeah, I know. I've seen it."

Rachel was glad to see Dixie had cleaned up—and sobered up—and perhaps would be able to hold a decent conversation. She sat down on the sofa opposite her and tucked one of legs under her.

"I'd like to start off where we left off this morning," Rachel said. "Only this time, I don't want to hear any lies. I don't believe you killed Richard, but I know Dewey Tucker does. I've checked out a few things that might be of help to your case, but if you try messing with me, then we're done. Understand?"

Dixie glanced up at her and then looked back down at the hands in her lap. "Yeah, I get it," she grumbled. "What do you want to know?"

"Let's get back to the sixteen-year-old girl."

"Okay." Dixie took a long sip of her Pepsi, set the glass on the table, and sighed. "We were making *Love Unlimited.* I was the lead, but there was a young actress, quite talented, who played a supporting role. She was almost seventeen and it was her first film. She was a pretty blue-eyed blonde, and although she was a great natural talent, she needed some coaching."

Dixie stopped to light a cigarette and Rachel waited quietly. When Dixie exhaled, she turned to Rachel. "Long story short, Richard and I both worked with her."

Dixie leaned back against the sofa and looked Rachel in the eyes. "Sometimes I coached her, sometimes Richard did."

"So what was the problem?"

"The problem was another actress, a bit player, really, who didn't like the idea of Richard spending time alone with this girl. In my opinion, I think she was after Richard herself. She decided, in her mind, something was going on. Then she put that idea in the head of the girl's parents. They shook us down for a large cash settlement so we could get on with our lives." Dixie took a long drag off her cigarette and tapped the ash off in an ashtray. "End of story."

"End of story?" Rachel was incredulous and crossed her arms over her chest. "You make a big cash payout for no reason? Did the girl say Richard touched her?"

"She said Richard had sex with her." Dixie eyes implored Rachel's. "But it wasn't true."

"How do you know that, Dixie? How do you really know it wasn't true?"

"I know Richard wouldn't lie about that," Dixie said, looking down again.

"Oh, really?" Rachel asked. "Now we *are* talking about the same Richard who was romancing Tara Linley and tried to poison you and make you fall off the mountain, right?"

Dixie didn't lift her head.

Rachel bore down on her. "Tell me the truth, Dixie. Is this the one and only time something like this ever happened?"

Dixie stubbed out her cigarette. "No, but it was the last time and the worst time. She looked up with pleading eyes. "You have to understand things like this happen in Hollywood all the time."

Rachel shook her head in disgust. "So the older actress, the one who caused the problem, was her name Cecilia?"

Dixie blinked in surprise. "How did you know?"

I told you I already knew what happened. I just wanted to hear the truth from you, Dixie. Now tell me what happened to Cecilia. Did you blacklist her?"

"No! Who told you that?"

"Well, what happened? Why didn't she work again?"

"Oh, you know how those things are," Dixie said, shrugging. "People hear things. She became damaged goods."

"Damaged goods," Rachel repeated noncommittally. She wanted to reach out and slap her. "And the young girl? What happened to her and her family?"

Dixie sighed and thoughtfully put a fist up against her mouth. "The father took the money and disappeared. About six months later, the girl slit her wrists. She died." Dixie dropped her eyes. "It was horrible."

"Yes, I imagine it was," Rachel said softly. "So where is the mother now?"

Dixie shrugged. "She kind of disappeared afterwards. She might have moved away." She reached for the pack of cigarettes and Rachel put her hands over Dixie's.

"Dixie?" Rachel asked softly, with all the compassion she could muster. "Can you remember her name, and the name of the girl's father?"

∽∾∽

The next morning Rachel sat behind her desk, waited, and watched. When JT left his office to have coffee with Deputy Tucker, Rachel snuck out of her own office and let herself in JT's private sanctuary.

She stood for a moment, as if she were debating something with herself, and finally placed an envelope on JT's desk addressed to Deputy Tucker. She looked back at the doorway and quietly closed the door, ensuring privacy for what she had planned to do.

Over on the far wall, she eyed the painting of a large saguaro cactus executed in blue-greens and purples. It was tall and narrow and framed with a heavy, ebony frame. Giving the frame a gentle yank at the bottom, she pulled it away from the wall like she was opening a book, and revealed a metal box set into the wall. She stared at the rows of silver and gold-colored keys that filled it.

Checking through the little white tags hanging from them, she finally located the key she wanted. Holding it up for a moment, her conscience nagged her one last time. *You could end up in big trouble—maybe even dead,* it cautioned her. Turning a deaf ear to its warning, she closed the frame with a loud snap. The office door behind her opened.

Rachel spun around. Heather stood in the doorway. "Rachel, what are you doing?" she asked softy.

"I—uh," Rachel stammered, feeling heat rush to her face. "I needed a key." She tried to sound nonchalant.

Heather shut the office door. "You needed a key? You have a master key card. What else would you need?"

"I…uh, I needed a…um," Rachel said, her mind grasping at the air, knowing she carried everything she needed.

Heather walked up to within inches of Rachel's face. She held out her hand. "Give it to me, Rachel." Her voice was quiet but firm.

Rachel's face was beet red. Resigned, she finally put the key in Heather's hand.

Heather looked at the key and read the tag. "I was afraid you'd want to try something like this."

"Heather, please!" Rachel begged. "This could solve the whole case, if you'll just let me do it."

"Rachel Ryan," Heather said with more authority. "It's illegal for you to break into someone's trailer."

Rachel pulled back. "That may be so. But if I can find out who murdered Richard Markman, it would be worth it to break the law to find out."

Heather stared at her. "You can't be serious."

"I *am* serious. Just because Dixie turned into a self-serving, self-absorbed, co-dependant idiot is no reason for her to take the rap for a murder she didn't commit." Rachel looked at her sister earnestly. "Heather, I know your sense of fairness wouldn't allow that. Besides," she added, "You have a right to unlock the door. The trailer belongs to you, and who knows? People forget to lock things, even trailers. I just happen to knock, and the door just happens to open and I call out, no one's home, I take a quick look, maybe 15 seconds, and then I leave. No one will ever know.

"Rachel, think about what you're saying. This is crazy talk!"

"Okay. You win." Rachel threw up her hands and began to walk away. "I'll take care of it myself. You don't have to be involved."

Heather stepped in front of her. "Wait. What do you mean?"

"I'll just break in, somehow."

"Rachel, you can't mean that." Heather stared at her sister.

Rachel stared back. "Heather, I'm sorry, but I do mean it. Dewey Tucker is doing absolutely nothing to solve this case and is going to arrest Dixie on circumstantial evidence. Dixie may not be a nice person, but she's not a killer. It's just not right that he's going to arrest her. I can't let that happen."

The two sisters stood and stared at each other. Heather blinked first.

℮ℐℰℐ

It didn't take long for Rachel and Heather to sneak out the back door and head across the parking lot. They climbed the stone and gravel steps that curved their way up the hill and hurried across the cracked surface of the old tennis courts.

Heather looked around as they approached the trailer, her eyes nervously scanning the area for signs of life. She inserted the key in the lock and stared at her sister. "You know we're going straight to Hell."

The steel door unlocked with a pop. Rachel grabbed the handle and pulled. "Guard the door."

"You have thirty seconds, Rachel. I mean it. I'm going to count and then I'm going to leave."

"Okay, okay," Rachel said impatiently. "One," she said as she leaped up the stairs. Only a few seconds passed before she cried out. "Heather! Heather, you've got to see this."

Heather peeped through the doorway and saw her sister standing along side a small table that jutted into the room. Rachel pointed at a pair of photographs at the back of the table. A single rose in a vase stood between them, and a votive candle perched in front of each photo reminded Heather of church.

"It's a memorial," Rachel said.

Heather climbed into the trailer and looked at the two photographs. The one on the right was a stunning teenage girl with long blonde hair and perfect cheekbones.

The photo on the left was of the same girl in the same outfit, most likely from the same photo shoot, but her face was nearly touching that of an older woman who looked very much like her. The older woman looked like she was in her late thirties, and had the same long blonde hair, blue eyes, and perfect cheek bones as the girl.

"Mother and daughter," Heather stated, still staring at the photos.

"Yeah, and dye the hair of the mother, add a few years, a mole on her cheek, brown contacts, ugly glasses, and who do you get?"

"Becky Beeman?"

"Bingo," a soft voice said. Heather and Rachel spun around to see Becky step up into the trailer.

"Too bad there's no prize." Becky added and shut the door behind her. "Have a seat, ladies," she said, gesturing to the sofa behind the table. "Make yourself comfortable."

Heather and Rachel meekly sat down and gave each other a "what-do-we-do-now?" look.

Becky pulled up a chair. "So, here we are," she said. "To what do I owe the pleasure of this unexpected visit?"

"I think you know the answer to that, Becky." Rachel said, deciding to go for it.

"I think I *don't* know, Rachel," Becky said. "Why don't you tell me?"

Rachel locked eyes with her. "It's over, Becky. We know you killed Richard Markman. You went out at night and collected those bark scorpions and put them in Richard's bed."

Becky laughed. "That's ridiculous."

"Oh, is it? It's a pretty horrible way to die." Rachel softened her look and her voice. "And he definitely deserved it for what he did to your daughter." She turned her head toward the photographs on the table. "She was an absolutely beautiful young woman."

Becky's demeanor crumbled and her eyes moistened as she gazed at the photograph of her daughter. "She was beautiful in every way. She meant everything to me."

"That must have just killed you," Heather burst in, pressing her hand to her heart. "I know that if it happened to one of my boys I would have wanted to do the same thing."

A tear leaked down Becky's cheek and she wiped it away with the back of her hand. "When my husband made that deal with Richard, I knew I would never have justice, but at least I figured my daughter would get a good college education and a start in life.

"But...it didn't happen."

"No," Becky said, "It never happened." She lifted her head to look at Heather. "My husband emptied our bank account and disappeared. I mean *really* disappeared.

The day I buried my daughter, something just snapped inside my head. I knew I'd have to kill Richard, no matter what I'd have to do, no matter how long I'd have to wait."

Becky reached over to the counter and grabbed a small bottle of water, and cracked it open. She took a pill container from a drawer, opened it, and popped one in her mouth, swallowing it with a big gulp of water.

"At first, it was all I could think about." She shifted her gaze to a distant point beyond Heather. "I became obsessed. I spent every night, before I went to sleep, planning. I mean *every* night. I kept going through every conceivable way you could kill a person and not get caught. After a while, I got to a point where I didn't care. I started planning how to kill him even if I *did* get caught."

"Then what happened?" Rachel asked. She glanced over at Heather and saw tears on her sister's cheeks.

"I had a nervous breakdown." Becky looked down again. "I think I would have killed myself then, except it would have left *him* alive. I couldn't let that happen."

Becky looked up, and what almost appeared to be a smile crossed her face. "It took a while to recover, but I eventually started working again, in hotels, as a maid, then as head of housekeeping. I became resigned to my new life. Then I heard about Richard's new movie. I knew instantly that would be my one chance to make things right."

"So that's when you came to apply for a job here."

Becky nodded. "Exactly. I found out through friends they'd be filming on location here sometime this spring. The rest is pretty much history."

"So you tried to kill Richard with the wine, and when that didn't work, the scorpions."

"You know, I really didn't think Richard would die from the wine. He wouldn't be able to get enough into his system. But having him suffer that way was a real plus. A real *plus*."

Becky's eyes were glowing and a satisfied smile formed on her lips. Her face looked euphoric.

The two sisters exchanged a quick, worried look. *This woman is clearly insane.*

"But the oleander stick," Rachel prompted. "You didn't do that."

"No. Markman did that. Can you believe it? That goes to show you what kind of person he was. A lot of innocent people at that party could have died from that poison. But frankly, I really didn't care if he killed Dixie. She was as guilty as he was."

Becky got up from the chair and put the pill bottle back on the counter. She opened a kitchen drawer and Rachel and Heather took the moment to look at each other.

Becky caught the look and laughed out loud. She was either high from the moment or the medication she'd just taken. "I'll bet you're sitting there wondering why I confessed so easily to you, aren't you."

Heather and Rachel didn't dare look at each other again and neither one spoke.

Becky pulled a small pistol out of the drawer.

"Oh, boy," Rachel said, and reached for her sister's hand.

※ ❧ ※

When JT came back to his office, he noticed the letter on his desk right away. He picked up the plain white envelope in his hands and flipped it over. It had Sheriff Tucker's name written on it. The handwriting looked familiar. He sniffed the envelope. It smelled faintly of perfume…something familiar. Chanel No. 5?

"Aw, man," he cried aloud.

He stepped around quickly to the front desk. "Marta? You leave this letter on my desk?"

She looked up from the computer, startled. "No, sir."

"Anybody come in my office?"

"I saw Heather and Rachel come out, but that's all."

JT rushed past her, across the lobby, and out the front door. A tan SUV was pulling out of the parking lot. He pulled out his phone and punched in a number.

"Deputy Tucker," the rough voice answered.

☙❧☙

Becky stood behind the chair, waving the gun back and forth, almost giddy with the relief of unburdening herself of her of long-held secret. She looked at Heather. "You're the best boss I ever had. You've been really good to me, Heather." She turned to Rachel. "And you've been a good friend, Rachel."

"Becky, you've been wonderful to us." Heather burst in. "You've made an amazing difference in the housekeeping department and you've saved the hotel a lot of money in just the short time you've been with us. We love having you with us."

"I know," Becky said, holding the gun steady. "I've done my best. And I've really appreciated having the job. My plan wouldn't have succeeded without it."

"Then why..." Rachel asked, her eyes drifting towards the gun.

"Oh, don't worry." A strange smile formed on Becky's face. "I'm not going to kill you. I never intended to kill *you*." She slowly raised the gun.

"No! Stop, don't do it, Becky. Please, not now." Heather begged, realizing what Becky had planned. "We'll help you. We can help you make bail. You could still work for us."

Rachel glanced at Heather like she was loony, but then nodded in agreement, realizing where Heather was headed. "Yes, we know a good lawyer, Becky. He can get you off."

"Oh, you know that's not gonna happen, ladies," Becky said, giving them an incredulous look and shaking her head. "You've been cutting me enough slack lately as it is. And I sincerely doubt they'll let me make bail on murder one." The smile vanished from her face and a deep sadness settled in. She slumped against the counter. "You know I'm sick."

"I guessed as much," Heather said. "What is it? Cancer?"

"Brain tumor," Becky nodded solemnly. "Inoperable. They say I only have four or five months now. It's getting almost unbearable."

Dead silence filled the trailer. Heather and Rachel were at a loss for words.

A loud knock at the door exploded on them. "Becky Beeman, open up!" a loud, gravely voice shouted. "It's Deputy Tucker!"

"Becky, please." Heather held out open hands to her. "I'm begging you."

Becky hesitated, looked at each sister in turn, and put the gun back in the drawer. "I'll let him in."

The trailer shook when Dewey Tucker climbed up the narrow steel steps into the trailer. He took in the room, the two sisters sitting on the banquette, and locked eyes for a moment with Rachel. "I got your note," he said. "Ms. Beeman," he began, turning to Becky. "I need you to come down to the station with me to answer some questions." His voice was firm, but not unpleasant.

Becky looked at him without speaking, and then at Heather and Rachel. She smiled. "It's okay, Deputy. I'm ready."

Epilogue

The April days continued to grow longer and hotter, with one or two minutes of sunlight stretching out each afternoon. Rachel sat quietly at the end of the pool, reading, while the water cascaded over the Jacuzzi, muting out all other sounds. She was so absorbed in a Don G. Porter mystery, she never heard Heather walk up to her and didn't even raise her head until she saw Heather's Birkenstocks.

"So how was Becky?"

"She was okay," Heather replied, nodding. "Amazingly, she's getting good medical care at the prison hospital. She's on a morphine pump right now, but she's still cognizant when she's awake. She seemed content. Actually, she seemed happy."

"Hmm," Rachel said. "I'd be happy, too, if I were hooked up to a morphine pump."

Heather smiled and sat down next to Rachel. "We talked. She still declined our offer of an attorney. I think she knows she doesn't have much time left, so why bother. I suspect she may be right. She was very pale and gray-looking."

"Well, I guess that's the best we can expect. It's a shame about her life, though."

"I agree. It's really sad." Heather turned to stare out at the horizon and frowned. "I noticed Buddy's car was still gone. You didn't happen to hear from the guys, did you?"

"You mean about the lawsuit? No. And don't get your hopes up, sis. Dixie probably slammed the door in their faces, on the advice of her lawyer, of course."

"But she likes JT and Buddy."

"Maybe, but she likes money a lot more. She sees a way to make a quick bundle off our insurance."

"But we weren't responsible for her husband's death," Heather moaned. "We tried to help her."

"So? What does she care?" Rachel continued, not bothering to soft-pedal her views to her tender-hearted sister. "The movie is in the trash can and her husband is dead. She wants somebody to pay, and right now, it's us."

Heather stared down at her shoes and blinked to keep from crying. "It's not right. She shouldn't profit from something like this. She was as guilty as Richard for covering up his crime. She doesn't deserve to make money off it."

"Welcome to the real world, sis." Rachel reached over and squeezed Heather's hand. She glanced over when movement caught her eye.

Buddy pulled up to the curb in his BMW and he and JT climbed out.

"Hey, guys, how did it go?" Rachel called out.

JT walked up to Heather and planted a kiss on her forehead. "It went fantastic." He was grinning from ear to ear. "Dixie decided to drop the lawsuit."

"What? That's great. But why?" Rachel was perplexed. "What happened?"

"Well, first of all, I convinced Dixie that none of us knew Becky Beeman was Rebecca Callahan and we'd be willing to go to court to prove it. But more important to Dixie was the specter of Richard's past raising its ugly head."

"Aye," Buddy said, breaking in with his Irish brogue. "JT managed to persuade the little lass she'd be better off without those nasty tabloids tainting the memory of her dear, departed husband."

Heather gazed up at JT in adoration. "Oh, honey, you're so smart. You could have been a lawyer."

"Yeah, honey, you're *so smart,*" Rachel teased.

"Oh, 'twas nothing," he said, totally ignoring Rachel's comment. "Once I unleashed all my masculine charm on her, she simply fell under my spell and gave up."

"Oh, boy," Rachel said, rolling up her eyes, and Buddy laughed.

"And what about Tara Linley?" Heather asked. "Any news on her?"

"I heard she's already signed up for another movie and is already promoting it in those tabloids," Rachel said. "We had a couple of those reporters come around yesterday, but nobody here talked to them. Since Tara was long gone, they left."

"Hmm," Heather said. "I wonder if the hotel will get some free publicity out of this. I'll go into town later and see if any of the scandal sheets have her story."

JT looked at his wife. "Heather, that stuff is garbage."

"I know, sweetie," she smiled, blinking her eyes at him. "But it's *interesting* garbage." Her eye caught a lone figure standing a polite distance away. "JT, I think Rosario needs to speak with you."

JT turned slightly and waved the young woman over. "What do you need, Rosario?"

Rosario flashed them all a dazzling smile. "I heard some great news, and double checked it to make sure it was true."

"What is it?" JT asked.

"You know that new restaurant, Dominos?"

"Yes."

"You probably heard how difficult that Anna Venkman is to work for…"

"Well, I surmised as much, yes."

"I just found out her chef quit and moved back to Phoenix."

"No kidding."

"It's true. I know the bar manager there. She said the chef and Anna got into a big fight yesterday afternoon and he quit. She packed up and left town today. Not only that, Anna and the restaurant manager aren't getting along well either."

A spirit of euphoria surrounded the group after Rosario left.

"I can't believe how everything worked out, after all," Heather said, reaching for JT's hand. "No more lawsuit, no more Benny Ammato, and no more Domino's."

"Oh, I'm sure Domino's will have another head chef before long," JT countered.

"They will," Rachel said, "but Anna Venkman will always have a hard time keeping good help. That won't make for a stable business. I've heard a few rumors, myself, about the discontentment among the staff members."

"Well, I'm just glad the whole thing is over with so we can go on to other things," Buddy said.

"Amen, brother." JT's eyes twinkled. "But we need some kind of project to keep Rachel out of trouble."

"Thanks a lot, guys." Rachel muttered.

"A project?" Heather asked, slyly looking up at her husband, "You mean the kind of project that might involve a big pile of junk you brought over in the pick-up the other day?"

JT turned his head in the direction of the maintenance building and nudged his wife in that direction. "Everybody just follow me, and *don't* try to spoil my surprise."

"I thought you hated surprises," Buddy said.

"Yeah, but only when they're popped on *me*, not on *you*," JT said.

The maintenance door was opened to an odd assortment of metal equipment stacked in the middle of the floor. Everything else was neatly positioned in its proper location on the walls or shelves and Toro was standing in front of the workbench with a cabinet door in front of him, a screwdriver in his hand, and a happy greeting for everyone.

"Mr. JT? Do you want me to pack all that stuff in the truck for you?"

"I'd appreciate that, but there's no rush. It goes in the Hummer and the truck, along with a few other items. But we won't need it until the weekend."

"Okay. I'll take care of it." Toro put the screwdriver down and picked up the cabinet door. "This goes back to 105," he said, gave the door a little slap, shambled around the pile of equipment, and went out the door.

Rachel gazed down at the large pile of tools and equipment. "So, what exactly is all this stuff?"

"This *equipment,* my dear sister-in-law, is our new project."

"What? We're going in the junk yard business?"

"No, we are going in the *gold* business."

"What?" Heather asked. "The gold business?"

"Yes, the gold business." With that, JT pulled a little coin envelope out of his pocket and poured the contents in the palm of his hand. "Take a look," he said to his wife, displaying a small gold nugget the size of a popcorn kernel.

"Oh, my goodness! Is that real gold?"

"Yes, it certainly is. One hundred per cent pure."

"Next you're going to tell us that you found it on our property," Buddy said.

"Yes, I did that, too." JT grinned. "Over on the north side below the old landing strip and a little to the west."

"Wow." Rachel said. She picked up the nugget and held it to the light. "This is amazing. How did you find it?"

"I was out walking, looking around, and I crossed a wash and looked down. There it was."

Everyone stood quietly, staring at the nugget, while the implications of JT's find sank in. Looking at all of them, JT finally announced, "We're going to go prospecting for gold this weekend. We'll bring some lunch and a couple of coolers of water, hats, gloves, even a tarp for a shade. It'll be a lot of fun."

"Great. We can bring a couple lounge chairs for when we poop out," Heather added.

"Good idea." JT nodded. "So what do you say? How about we meet at the café at six o'clock Saturday morning? After we eat, it will be light enough for us to unload the equipment and set up."

"Sounds like a plan to me," Buddy said. "Six o'clock." He stepped over to the door and opened it. "I'm ready." He held out his hand in an "after you."

"Yeah, me too. We could strike it rich," Rachel exclaimed, heading toward the door. "And the best part is: we won't have to deal with anymore dead bodies."

"Oh, Rachel, please don't say that out loud," Heather said, following her out. The sun had slipped behind a low bank of clouds and a warm spring wind blew over them. "Don't even *think* about dead bodies. Don't even *hold* that thought in your *mind*," she said, holding up both hands with fingers crossed, her voice trailing after her like cookie crumbs.

About the Author

Joanne Taylor Moore was born in Massachusetts and enjoyed life on a small, family farm where she learned to love nature and develop her imagination. She has published some of her poems and written newspaper articles, but mystery novels are her favorite genre. Her Blood Mountain series is about life and murder in the Arizona Desert. Moore lives with her husband, Larry, in Yuma, Arizona, and loves to spend her free time reading, designing jewelry, and visiting her four children and eleven grandchildren.